HIGHBORN JEZEBEL

Dressed only in a shift, Lady Artis lay stretched upon Captain Ironhand's bunk in the torrid afternoon heat, her petticoats and mantilla strewn across the floor.

"What are you going to do with me, Sir?" she asked defiantly.

"If I did what I would like, I'd lash you to the mast and give you the cat-o'-nine-tails."

Her eyes blazed with fury. "You affect tremendous indignation for my sins, Captain Ironhand. But are they sins? What is a woman made for if not for love?"

> *"New heroine as provocative as*
> *the author's famous Kitty."*
> **TULSA WORLD**

Books by Rosamond Marshall

NONE BUT THE BRAVE
KITTY
DUCHESS HOTSPUR
LAIRD'S CHOICE

by

Rosamond Marshall

WILDSIDE PRESS

CAPTAIN IRONHAND

CAPTAIN IRONHAND

1.

Ex-Naval Person

JAMES CHALLONER, RECENTLY OF THE ROYAL NAVY AND now, because of a royal lady scorned, reduced to sleeping under heaven's blue canopy, wakened upon the morning of April 2, 1772 in St. James's Park, London. Loath to move damp-stiffened joints, loath, above all, to let thought unwind from the bandages of sleep, he tried to sink back into oblivion, but here came Memory with a sharp scalpel to reopen and probe the death wound given him a year ago.

His sloop *Somerset* had been making up the Bay of Biscay in fair weather. He'd been reading in his quarters. Laurence Sterne's *Tristram Shandy*. It was after midnight. His door had opened without leave and one of his brace of exalted passengers had entered.

"Do I interrupt your meditations, Captain?"

It was Her Royal Highness, Countess Erminie, wife of Count von und zu Brust-Kleiningen, a deadly-sweet woman in her early thirties, with a clear complexion and a small mouth, painted with scarlet salve. Her porcelain-blue eyes had stripped him to the buff.

"Why are you so . . . so backholding with me, Captain Challoner? I am fond of pleasure and youth and laughter. You know my husband, poor dear. His gout makes it hard for one who has such a passion for life as I."

Her shameless pressing of him, until he'd found himself backed into a corner, stammering like a schoolboy.

"You . . . Your Highness! If Your Highness will allow me to escort her to her cabin."

At this, she'd straightened herself in royal dignity.

"How dare you refuse me the service you give other women who find you to their liking!"

"Service? Is Your Highness referring to the inmates of her stables, or her kennel?"

She'd turned pale with rage, and then she'd set about deliberately, wrathfully, to destroy the elaborate edifice of her coiffure, tear her gown at the bosom, claw her own white arms until the blood flowed—all this, while screaming at the top of her voice.

They had come, his cabin page and a young ensign with cheeks like clabber—witnesses who could do no other than damn him to hell.

Poor, gouty, old Graf von und zu Brust-Kleiningen!

"You vill command your ship, sir, until we drr-rop anchor in Portsmout. Den . . . I vill have you brroke, sir! Brrroke!"

Challoner sprang to his feet. "Forget it!" he muttered under his breath. "What good does it do to remember?"

But how could a man forget an accident of fate that had destroyed a lifetime career in a few seconds? On the heels of the countess' staged rape scene—court martial and dishonorable discharge, then the *Via Crucis* that had led him twice across the map of England and back. What tinker's chance had an ex-naval person of finding work in ordinary walks of life?

"Have you recommendations, Mr. Challoner?" Then that arched eyebrow look. "Sorry. We do not hire without letters from former employers."

Challoner passed a dirty but shapely hand over his lean cheeks and stubborn chin—a two-day beard—but he carried a razor and an inch of soap. And there was Rosamond's Pond, gleaming in the morning sun.

Kneeling pondside, he shooed away the waterfowl that bustled up to him looking for largesse of bread crusts. "Friend ducks, if I had a crust, I'd eat it myself." Wetting his precious soap inch, he lathered his cheeks and, using the mirror of the water, shaved himself with the last of a set of seven precious ivory-handled razors that he'd stropped, honed and coddled for years. The other six had been sold for bread and cheese, along the way.

After finger-combing his hair, Challoner tightened the string that kept his club tidy. Neckcloth pulled taut, buttons in holes (all but one which he'd lost), and belt girded, he was ready. Ready for what, Good Lord?

"Fine day, sir," said a voice at his elbow.

Challoner turned. The speaker was a seaman, from the cut of his jib. On the beach, like himself.

"Fine day, indeed," Challoner agreed, upon which the stranger pulled a piece of paper out of his pocket.

"Sir, if I may be so bold . . . can you read?"

"Why yes, I can read," said Challoner, concealing a smile.

"Well, sir," said his interlocutor, "wot do this 'ere pyper say? The part after WANTED?"

The "pyper" was a throw-poster and its advertisement was short and to the point. Challoner read out loud:

> "Wanted: Master between ages 25-35
> with or without papers.
> See Messrs Whitney and Frost,
> 14 Ferry Road, Lambeth."

"Bad luck!" muttered the man. "I'm no ship's master." He turned and walked away without so much as a thank-ee!

"Nor am I, presently, a ship's master," thought Challoner, but he read the advertisement again. Master, with or without papers. Interpreted by a reader of nautical mind, the item could have only one meaning. We want a man willing and able to do the devil's work at sea! What had he to lose by inquiring? And Ferry Road was near the wharves where, if one were lucky, one might pick up a ha'penny, toting some merchant's bale or box.

At the precise moment Challoner started to cross the winding, tree-shaded bridle path, a lad in jockey's cap and woolens—stable hand or exercise boy—came racing hell-for-leather toward him on a kingly horse of bay color. All this Challoner saw, just in time to leap out of the way, but the effort put him off balance and sent him sprawling in the mud. No less annoyed at the added damage to his shabby attire than by the sense that he must present a ludicrous spectacle to the onlooker, he'd barely recovered his footing when the lad came back, holding his mount under tight rein. What a horse!

Brought up in the world of his sporting Squire father—world that had stepped to the tune of hunting horns and racing trumpets—Challoner had loved horseflesh with all the ardor of his carefree years, then he had come to hate it for the ruin it had wrought upon his family and himself. The Squire, his father, not only bred and trained racers, he bet on them, and his gambler's luck was as lean as the chances he took were fat. In time, and with steady advance in his chosen career, Challoner had overcome his resentment of the equine race and was able to look at a horse with a cool eye. This animal had all the properties a racer should have, to wit:

Of an asse, a bigge chyn, a flatte legge and a good hoof;
Of a haare, a grete eye, a dry hede, and well runnynge;
Of a fox, a fayr taylle, short eeres, with a good trotte;
Of a woman, fayrbrested, fayr of heere, and easy to leape
upon;
Of a man, bolde, prowde, and hardy.

Then Challoner noticed that the snip of a lad was laughing at him with loud ha-has, grimaces, finger-pointings and knee-slappings!

"Ha-ha yourself!" Challoner seized the bay by the bridle rein, the lad by the scruff of his woolens, and separated one from the other with a twist of the wrist, then, slipping the reins over his left arm, so as to have two hands free, he turned the laughing one across his knee.

"Now, Jock, I'm going to teach you a lesson, not to ride down pedestrians!" Bang! Bang! on tender buttocks!

The lad squirmed, kicked, howled for mercy, all in vain!

But as Challoner spanked, he became conscious that this "lad" had unusual forms for one of the male sex. Good heavens! He set his victim on his feet. Boy or girl? Jockey's breeches, boots and gloves said "boy," but what about those shapely globes that had ironed themselves upon his thigh with such electrifying effect?

Challoner gave the cap a tweak. The "boy" had a mop of red-gold curls, cropped short, and a pair of mermaid's eyes, green and amber and algae-tinted, the whites like precious pearls.

"So . . . you *are* a girl!"

"Ye . . . yes!" she sobbed, rubbing the place where it was sorest.

"I wouldn't have paddled you, if you'd told me in time," said Challoner in gentler tones. "What's your name, girl?"

"Kit, sir."

"So . . . now you're sir-ing me!"

She sidled up to him with a coquettish look of her amazing eyes. "I know a gentleman when I see one."

Amused, mollified, Challoner asked, "How, pray tell? I can scarcely look like a gentleman?"

She nodded sagely. "Oh, clothes are no matter! There are better ways of telling. Firstly, you're brave. How few would have dared lift a hand to me . . . up on a racer? Secondly, you have a gentleman's hands. Thirdly, you're handsome the way gentlemen are handsome."

Challoner tried to turn a fatuous smile into a friendly grin. "And just how are *gentlemen* handsome, I'd like to know?"

In answer, she stood on tiptoe and planted a great resounding kiss on his lips, then, snatching away the reins, she tossed them over her bay's head and vaulted into the saddle.

Challoner caught the little heel as it was about to kick.

"Wait, young lady! I'd hear more of your idea of . . . a gentleman."

She sat back on the leather with a resigned look on her tear-smudged face. "Must I let Daemon get the heaves from a chill while you quiz me on the ways of gentlemen? Go look in your mirror, sir!"

"I have no mirror," laughed Challoner, who felt himself unaccountably drawn to the minx he was holding prisoner.

"Well, then . . . come to Great Stanhope tonight, at eight. The mews behind Grantley House. The green door with the horse's head knocker. I'll tell you all about gentlemen."

"Who *are* you?" exclaimed Challoner.

"My name is Kit. I'm the daughter of Lady Grantley's trainer. If you keep me here much longer my father will take the whip to me for bringing Daemon in cool."

"Great Stanhope? The Mews? I may come at that," grinned Challoner, loosening his grip on the tiny booted ankle.

She gathered up the reins with all the ease and grace of a veteran rider. "You'll oblige me, sir. I'll even serve you tea and little cakes and hold my pinky . . . like this . . ."

Her diminutive little finger in the horseman's glove pointing skyward in comical fashion, she touched the bay with
her heel and wheeled away.

For a long moment, Challoner stood gazing after rider
and horse with a bemused expression on his face, then,
slowly, almost reluctantly, he set his long legs in motion.
Daughter of a stable master, eh? That would explain her
perfect horsemanship. But she'd none of the accents of
her father's kind. No cockney twang. No North Country
drawl! No Scottish burr. One could almost surmise that
she'd been raised in a boarding school for young ladies.
"My name is Kit," she'd said. Kit for Catherine, perhaps?
Bold little thing! With her one, big kiss, she'd managed
to convey the idea of spring in a country garden, dawn on
a tropic isle, or, less poetic, but infinitely more nostalgic,
the childhood of one James Challoner! New-mown hay.
The scent of a stumbling foal, milk and baby smell combined. Carefree hours of innocence, so lavishly expended
and so dear, in memory. Trainer for Lady Grantley, eh?
Kit's pa must be damned good, for Lady Artis Grantley's
racing luck was as solid as her million pounds of fortune.

Concerning the lady herself . . . no solidity there! Hot
sauce of club dining rooms and relish of officers' mess,
Lady Grantley's life and loves were the ingredients that
add flavor and piquancy to a leg-o-mutton or a dish of salt
pork with rutabagas.

Challoner's step was lighter and his humor uplifted as
he trudged through Princess Street and down Great Smith.
London Town was now wide awake. Drays moved pon-
derously over the cobblestones. Housewives shook patch
quilts out of their windows. Vendors and barrowmen were
wheeling their stands into their places of business.

The aroma of frying fish made Challoner's mouth water.
He walked on at a faster pace. But here—a bakery! Oh
that fragrance divine of fresh bread! His last meal had
consisted of a cabbage root, dug at the edge of a garnered
field, with a stick.

Passing the door of a tavern, at the sign of the Swinging
Goose, in Marsham, Challoner's belly seemed to shrink
until it made one with his spine. Roast beef! Should he
enter and ask for a chore, any chore, that would buy him

the wherewithal to stretch the wretched, neglected organ back to size? No!

An old woman in a shawl opened a cornucopia of brown paper and took out some stale bread which she crumbled and threw to the pigeons. They swooped down, gluttonous things, devoured the bread, cooed, puffed out their breasts, wheeled and strutted for their ladies.

Challoner pulled his belt a notch tighter and walked on. The Town was giving way to the Docks. All streets ran into the river. He threaded between the drays and wagons taking on or putting off loads. The air was purple with draymen's curses. He jumped a plank, down which the hogsheads were rolling. What was in them? Salt beef? If one should burst, he'd make a grab and run!

Number 14 Ferry Road was a red brick warehouse with barnlike doors and barred windows. A man of middle age with a stocking cap on his bullethead was acting as doorman.

"Walk in," he said, before Challoner could address him.

Behind the door was a vast shed, jam-packed with derelicts like himself. A few wore seaman's dress, but the most part were in rags. Young or old, their hangdog air betrayed their bankrupt state.

"You, there, with the hat!" hailed a man in a pea jacket who was standing guard at the far end of the shed, a musket across his arm.

"Are you addressing me?" said Challoner in his quiet voice, that had been known to make strong men tremble.

"Are you addressin' 'im?" mocked one of the derelicts, a burly man in gray wool breeches and a waistcoat, no shirt or coat. " 'Ear 'im! Are you addressin' 'is lordship?"

"Yus!" bawled the man with the musket. "It's 'im I wants. Step lively, mate!"

At this, a murmur broke out among the waiting men and someone shouted, "Last come, last served!" When the mob began to push toward Challoner with fists raised, it suddenly became important to him not to retreat.

The first one who rushed him got a set of knuckles in his eye, the second, a bloody nose. Then the pack bore down upon him and it was toe to toe and blow for blow. He'd put three men down and was bracing himself for the fourth when he saw a grimacing lout rush at him with a knife. He caught the fellow's wrist before the blade could rip, but in so doing, he tripped and fell in a tangle of bodies.

"Boats away!" bawled a bull-throated voice. Into the melée charged a cannon ball of a man—round head, round, red face, fringe of black hair under his seaman's cap. Arm like a weaver's beam! All this Challoner saw with only one eye—someone's elbow was in his other.

The human cannon ball plucked him clear of the roiling pyramid as a jackstraw player lifts his straw.

"On yer feet, sir!"

"Thanks!"

Challoner hadn't time to wonder why his friend in need had sir'd him. Here came the pack again!

Back to back, they stood off the onslaught while maneuvering until they could make space—a kind of boxing ring. Then the real sport began!

Bullethead no sooner had his big fists on a victim than he spun him around for treatment by Challoner.

" 'Ere, sir!"

"Thanks!" Challoner let fly a left to the chin.

"This one, sir."

"Thanks again!"

Seeing so many of their fellows fall right and left, the weaklings took to their heels, leaving only the hardy souls.

A giant in a torn blue smock charged Challoner head on.

Challoner used Greco-Roman and threw him. Bullethead kicked him unconscious.

A powerful young lad leaped on his back. A second man aimed a blow at his solar plexus that would have knocked the breath out of him had it landed, but Bullethead's big boot stopped the blow in mid-air and his fist finished what his boot had begun.

Challoner wiped the blood from a cut on the forehead out of his eye. "Any more?"

"Looks like there's no more," said Bullethead.

He was right. Men lay around like ninepins when the bowling ball has made the strike, but not a one showed the will to carry on the fight.

Rescued and rescuer faced each other.

"This man hasn't been on the beach long," thought Challoner.

And Bullethead who knew men was thinking, "This one's got Navy writ all over him."

The armed guard had neither lifted a finger nor spoken a word until now. "You two," he called. "Inside!"

Challoner preceded Bullethead into a small office that reeked of stale pipe smoke. Behind a cluttered desk sat a small man in rusty black with a string of white neckcloth.

"Have either of you papers?" he said, eying the pair.

"I 'ave," said Bullethead. He tossed a grimy packet on the desk and stood back.

"Boggs," said the man in black.

"Will Boggs," said Bullethead. "That's my name."

"You?" said the man in black to Challoner.

"I've nothing but the name I was born with," Challoner answered. "Perhaps you've heard of me. Ex-Captain, James Challoner, of the Royal Navy."

"I've heard of you," said the wizened man after a moment's scrutiny of the speaker. Opening a tin moneybox, he drew out a purse. "The two of you, go to the baths, outfit yourselves clean, eat your fill, then report here."

Challoner felt Boggs pressing at his heels as they left the warehouse.

"Sir . . . 'ow much in that purse?"

Challoner turned to the wall, not to be seen by pickpockets, and poured the contents of the purse into his palm.

"Six ruddy Georges!" exclaimed Boggs hoarsely. He held out his hairy wrist. "Pinch me, Capt'n."

"You pinch me," grinned Challoner, returning the sovereigns to the purse, "and leave off the captain."

"Aye, aye, sir." Boggs smacked his lips. "Six quid! It's a cut of rare beef and a tankard of ale for mine."

"And for me."

"Where, Captain, sir?"

"The first tavern we come to."

This proved to be the Lambeth Hawk, snug harbor for two hungry men. They marched to a corner table, sat down and hailed the serving girl. They devoured their rib joint with Yorkshire pudding and sopped the gravy with bread. They ordered a second cut and then called for the cheese board. Satisfied at last, they sat back, tankard in fist, and looked at each other.

"What was your last berth, Mister Boggs?"

"The *Lady Ireland,* out of Hull, sir."

"Beached?"

"No sir. I'd saved a tidy sum . . . was to 'ave married woman I'd been courtin' for four years. Widowed, she was. Had her own little bakery in Knightsbridge. I've allus bin partial to pastries and sweets and suchlike. It were past eight bells. She were wiv 'er sweetie in the downy. Young snip, 'alf 'er age. 'Er oven man! Gor! Wot a 'idin' I giv' 'im. Natcherly, it were the end between the widow and me. I'd gold in me pocket then. I spent it fast. Dice and petticoats. Couldn't find a new berth. Thought I'd try at the advertisement in Ferry Road. It were rare luck took me there. You, sir? Ex-captain did you say?"

"Yes. How I lost my command is a long story I'd rather forget."

"Royal Navy, sir?"

"Yes."

"Gor!" Boggs shook his head. "You're deeper in the slup than me, sir."

"That I am, Mister Boggs," Challoner agreed. He called for the account, paid it and said, "I propose we shop for clothing first and then go to the baths."

The proprietor of a Cannon Road bathhouse welcomed his customers with a questionnaire.

"One bath or two?"

"Two," answered Challoner.

"Lavender soap or yellow? Lavender's one and six, inclusive. Yellow's one bob."

"I'll take the lavender," said Challoner.

"The yellow for me," said Boggs.

"A double cubicle it'll have to be, gents. All me singles is in use, unless you've time to wait."

"A double is agreeable to me if it is to you, Mister Boggs?" said Challoner turning to the ruddy-faced mate.

"Oh, quite agreeable, sir!" said Boggs with the air of one who is honored by his superior's condescension.

Armed with soap and linens, the bathers were shown to a cubicle, wherein were two wooden tubs of satisfactory length, even for a man of Challoner's stature. The bath attendant opened a tap with two mouths and let steaming hot water into the tubs from a wooden trough.

Challoner stripped of his worn and shabby clothing with

eager haste, and, letting himself down into the bath, he experienced a sense of pleasure as distinct as he had ever known. How exhilarating was clean, hot water, laving away the sweat of anxiety, penetrating the joints, restoring man to the intended state which is next to godliness.

"It's comfort, sir!" said Boggs through a mask of suds with which he had covered his face.

"Yes," Challoner agreed.

Boggs rinsed the suds with much puffing and blowing.

"I've allus bin one for a bath now and then, sir."

"And I."

"Used to take to the pond in me young years, sir."

"Yes, indeed."

Challoner lathered himself standing, the thick suds of good-smelling soap like a skintight garment upon him, a scrub brush providing a scraper.

"I knowed you was strong from the way you fought, sir," said Boggs peering over the rim of his tub. "Naked, you're steel and rawhide, but your muscle don't show through the cloth."

"I've done quite a bit of Greco-Roman wrestling," said Challoner and let the matter drop without revealing that he'd been champion of the hold and fall, a King's Letter man and top-ranking midshipman of his class of 1758 at Portsmouth Academy.

Boggs finished his ablutions in silence. Had he sensed that his partner in war and peace was bent on his own thoughts?

"Sir," he said as he handed Challoner a bath towel, "misery has a way o' turning her back on a man when she's done her damnedest to put 'im down. Maybe it's time she turned her back on you and me."

The two men who marched back to Number 14, Ferry Road, were cleansed, barbered and dressed new from head to toe.

Will Boggs' choice was regulation first mate's apparel. Blue pea jacket, trousers, sturdy boots and blue cap.

The breeches and coat Challoner had purchased were cut and colored to navy fashion. Plate buttons and a starched neckcloth gave a brave touch. The boots, though secondhand, were well made. The hat, a tricorn like the old one, sat on his brow with a jaunty air. He'd added a pair of yellow gloves and a dagger belt for elegance.

Always a man of outstandingly fine looks, his appearance had improved during the past terrible year. There was, indeed, a quality of steel or rawhide about him. His cheeks were honed fine by mental suffering and physical deprivation and his eyes burned clearer for knowing that he'd been falsely accused and unfairly punished.

The door of Number 14 was bolted, but a knock brought the same armed guard to the peephole grating. When he saw who was there he let the two in. "Mr. Whitney is waitin' in 'is office, sir," this addressed to Challoner whose mien commanded respect even without trim of gold lace.

The same wizened man in black rose from his desk with a terse "Follow me." The guard lifted a trap door, disclosing steps that descended to a landing where a rowboat was tied. The four climbed aboard. The guard took the oars and rowed bankside along the Thames.

"Where would you say we're bound, sir?" said Boggs in an uneasy whisper.

"I don't know . . . nor do I care," Challoner answered. "This is the first time in many a week that I can't smell myself. I'm grateful for a change of climate."

The rowboat nudged to a landing off Cheyne Walk. The thin man led the way up the steps of a house, Number 16.

It was in good style, as Challoner could see. Windowed, balconied, and with iron gates mounted on strong pillars, topped by sphinxes with bulging breasts, this handsome grille was not without its trim of mud, for at high tide the heavy barges moving upstream sent a fan of silty water spilling over the water-stairs onto the walks, even up to the walls of the houses themselves.

When an elderly house servant answered the bell, the man in rusty black stepped in first. "Wait here, Mister Boggs. Mr. Challoner will come with me."

The library in which James Challoner found himself was the kind he would have furnished for himself. A window behind the great mahogany desk looked out over the river. Bookshelves from floor to ceiling. A world globe on a brass stand. A familiar item on the desk, a ship's compass in an oakwood case.

The door opened and an elderly man in a long silk dressing gown and powdered wig entered.

"Mr. James Challoner?"

"Yes."

"My name is Frawley."

"Admiral Lord Frawley, who won at Sharangar?"

His lordship motioned his visitor to a chair and sat down behind the desk. "It is flattering to a man in retirement that youth should remember—however, I did not have you brought here to talk of my career, but of yours."

"I have no career, your lordship," said Challoner with a wry smile.

"I know," said Lord Frawley. "So it would seem, on the surface. But there are those who know the truth, that your misfortune was a stroke of ill luck, against which a man has no defense. Let me add, Challoner, that I am fully acquainted with the circumstances surrounding the unfortunate incident which cost you your command, but I concur with the Sea Lords. There was nothing they could do but accept the findings of the court."

"I agree with your lordship," said Challoner, who was sitting ramrod-straight in his chair. What was the Old Man leading up to?

Lord Frawley reached for a decanter on a wine table at his elbow and filled two glasses with tawny Oporto, one of which he placed before Challoner.

"I detect no bitterness in you, Challoner. That is admirable."

"A practical means of conserving my sanity, your lordship. It is not true that I do not regret my loss. I loved my career at sea. It was my life. On land, I'm only half a man."

"Tell me, Challoner," said Lord Frawley, "what sentiments made you try your luck in Ferry Road?"

"The desire to go on living the kind of life I like," answered Challoner bluntly. "Master with or without papers could only mean one thing. The applicant would be concerned with sailing a ship."

"There are ships and ships," said Lord Frawley with a faint smile. "I am in a position to offer you a fast frigate of forty guns, twelve of which are a new kind of twenty-four pounder called truck guns. These truck guns are in the testing stage . . . if they pass, we'll have 'em on our ships of the line."

Challoner was suddenly deafened by the loud beating

of his own heart. A frigate of forty guns, when his best to date had been a sloop of twenty guns? Promotion after disgrace? What trap was the Old Man setting?

"The name of the frigate, your lordship?"

"The *Royal Acre.*"

"The *Royal Acre?* She was sunk!"

"Not sunk, Mr. Challoner. Grounded. We took her off. She was convoying two merchantmen, *Gloucester Lady* and *Nora,* up the Portugal coast when a pirate flotilla set upon her and cut her away from her charges, running her aground on Teneriffe."

Lord Frawley rose and went to a cupboard, from which he brought out a nautical chart that Challoner recognized as one of those popularly called "waggoners," after their publisher, the Dutchman Waghenaer. They were now obsolete.

"You may prefer modern charts, Challoner," said his lordship spreading the chart on the desk. "The new ones the East India Company is issuing are certainly superior to these old waggoners. However, little more is known of African waters today than when this chart was drawn, two centuries ago. Note the sea lanes our Indiamen travel. Here, between the Canary Islands and the Bay of Biscay, is the danger point. These new-style pirates do not seize our ships, they shuck 'em like peas and leave 'em to sail another day with fresh cargo for pirating."

"We are not standing idle, your lordship!" exclaimed Challoner. The "we" meaning Navy, had again escaped him. He flushed. "The fleet is always on the lookout for pirates," he amended, lamely.

"Yes," Lord Frawley hastened to say. "The trouble is, these Moors have us outfoxed. Their raids come like lightning and always at the very time when we are in poor position to intercede. We're doubly outfoxed, I'd say, for the seized goods . . . cocoa bean, rum, silks, cochineal, oils, hardwoods, spices, tea . . . are brought to London and here offered to the same merchants who would have been in receipt of them in the first instance!"

"You mean they dare to sell to the original consignee?"

"Yes, and at an advance in price."

"And if the consignee refuses to buy?"

"The penalty is to have the goods dumped on the market

at cut rate, causing the merchants to suffer a double loss of revenue." Lord Frawley let the chart snap back into a roll. "It's a dirty business, Challoner, and it demands harsh countermeasures. Would you like to take the *Royal Acre* to sea against these piratical Africans?"

"Like?" exclaimed Challoner. "It would be my wish devout. But your lordship is forgetting that I'm no longer in service of His Majesty."

Lord Frawley refilled the wineglasses, then continued. "Let us not quibble on meanings, Mr. Challoner. I do not propose that you can hope to be restored to your former status all in a twinkling of an eye. What I propose is something slower and more hazardous . . . that you hoist another kind of flag. The one I refer to is the skull and crossbones."

The joy and hope he had felt ran out of Challoner like blood from a severed vein.

"A pirate's rag?" he muttered. "Never!"

Lord Frawley moved uneasily in his chair. "I realize as well as you that such action would place you in double jeopardy. The Navy on the one side and pirates on the other. Perhaps you have no stomach for it. They say a man, no matter how low he has sunk, can always find a living in the American Colonies."

Challoner rose and walked to the window that overlooked the Thames. There were the ships, captain on bridge, gliding down to the open sea. Brine-scented fog moved upstream to meet them, shrouding their masts and muffling the sound of bells. Could honor be restored by an action of dishonor?

A hand fell on his shoulder. "Sir Francis Drake gives you good precedent, Challoner. There was also one Lord Seymour, Lord High Admiral, who turned pirate. Think it over, Challoner, and, while making up your mind, do me the honor of availing yourself of my guest room for the night?"

Challoner turned. "Sir, you have my answer, now . . . it is *no.*"

"Tut! Tut!" said Lord Frawley quickly. "Think it over, Mr. Challoner."

Before Challoner could utter another word, he went striding away, the folds of his silk robe flying.

Challoner saw in a mirror on the wall, a dreadful ghost

—James Challoner in pirate's garb. "I need fresh air!" he muttered and, slipping down the softly carpeted staircase, he plucked his hat from the hall table and let himself out the front door. Could there be any doubt that Lord Frawley had thrown the bait—an illiterate who asked him to read an advertising paper—the same bait that had landed him in his present uncomfortable position? No! How long had he been under surveillance? How humiliating that a spy should have been following his beggarly progress—seen him dig up a cabbage root and eat it! That intense desire to run . . . run . . . now beset him, again. "Steady on course, James!" he muttered to himself.

"Ride, sir?" said the driver of a hackney coach standing idle at the curb.

Challoner got in. "Take me . . . take me to Great Stanhope."

Why shouldn't he accept an invitation to tea and cakes with a beauty named Kit? There'd be time to ponder Frawley's proposal, later. Or better still, let Conscience decide. For it was first, and foremost, an issue of conscience.

Knowing full well the meaning of the word piracy, and that in order to succeed in the role of pirate, a man must unleash those baser instincts which only years of stern discipline could conquer, he also knew that self-pity, self-justification, self-seeking must be ruled out of mind. Forget all thought of rewards. Forget the risk. Forget the penalty for failure—death! Replace all these with pure, unadulterated love of King and Country. Unless he could do this, a man the likes of himself could not *live* with himself, not even die, to his own satisfaction!

"Great Stan'ope, sir," called the driver, leaning from his box seat. "Shall I drive in?"

"No," answered Challoner. He paid his fare.

The spring night was fallen. A faint breeze blowing through the trees in Hyde Park gave country freshness to the air.

Great Stanhope was a dark, uncanny-looking passage, or so Challoner sized it. The branches of some trees extended out over the wall on the left. Were the gardens of Grantley House behind that wall? A long line of mews to the right, the scent of stables strong on the air.

Advancing with caution not to stub his toe on the uneven cobblestones, Challoner kept a sharp eye out for a green door with a horse's head knocker. There it was! The bells in a nearby steeple were chiming eight o'clock as he lifted the knocker. Rat-tat-tat! The door swung open on well-oiled hinges.

Silhouetted against the light of a lamp at the end of the hall, the girl looked like a dainty doll in her challis frock and white kerchief. The laces of her tiny slippers made her ankles as slim as a thoroughbred filly's. She'd tied a blue ribbon in her red-gold curls. No stable scent about her now! She was perfumed of wood's violet.

"Good evening, Kit," said Challoner.

"A good evening to you, sir," she said, bobbing a curtsy fit for Lady Velvet's drawing room.

He smiled. "When are you going to ask *my* name?"

"I wanted to," she said shyly. "I thought you might tell me."

"James Challoner," he said.

"James Challoner! That's a fine-sounding name. Please follow me, Mr. Challoner. Papa is waiting to meet you. Oh!" she added quickly when Challoner hesitated. "He'll soon fall asleep in his chair. But he never, *never* lets me entertain a young man without a few snores for company."

She led the way along the passage and up a winding stair to what appeared to Challoner to be living quarters over the stables, for the scent of stables was here, in full power.

The room into which he was shown was not large. The ceiling was low and black-beamed. The oak-paneled walls were hung with prize ribbons and copper-plate etchings of horses. Horses! Horses! The very chairs had horses' heads for arm rests.

A man with flame-red hair and axe-hewn features was standing with booted feet spread-eagled in front of a blazing hearth. Hands deep in pockets, shoulders squared under a waistcoat of Irish check, chin tucked into a linen stock pinned with a gold pin fashioned like a whip, he eyed the visitor from under beetling, flame-red brows.

"So . . . ye be the mon me da'ghter near rode down!" North of Ireland brogue! How had Kit escaped her father's heritage?

"No damage, sir. The name is Challoner and I'm much obliged to you for welcoming me into your house."

"The name is Patrick McKenna, Mister Challoner," said the trainer, extending a horny hand. "This ain't *my* house. Kit and me 'ave a cot down Islington Way. But at present, they're holdin' auction at Tat's and her ladyship wants me here in Town. Sit down, sir!" He turned to his daughter. "Kit! The whiskey!"

"What? No tea and cakes?" said Challoner in an aside as the girl brought a dusty bottle of Glenavon and two glasses on a silver tray.

He could not help noticing the tray while his host was doing the honors. It was beaten wafer-thin of fine silver. In the center, the royal arms and a cipher.

"That tray, Mr. McKenna?"

"Me tray? Ah, yes!" His host handed him a ration of the Scottish brew of proportions to make a mere Englishman pale! "My great-grandfather won this King's Plate with Galopin, sir."

"Galopin, out of St. Simon?" said Challoner.

The trainer eyed his guest sharply. "Kit said ye'd the looks of a mon with the know."

"With the know?"

"Know about horses."

Challoner turned to the girl who was sitting demurely on the hearth bench, hands folded across her slim, blue ribbon-tied waist.

"We made no mention of horses, Miss Kit. What gave you the idea I had . . . know?"

"The way you looked at Daemon, Mr. Challoner."

"I was not aware that I had looked at Daemon. Only at Daemon's rider."

At this point in the conversation, Patrick McKenna apparently had decided that he had done his part to entertain his daughter's new friend.

"Well, sir," he said. "Them as knows horses are a different breed from them as do not. If ye'll excuse me, I've my reading to catch up on."

He'd no sooner moved to a great wing chair covered with saddle hide and hid himself behind a newspaper than Challoner moved to the hearth bench.

"Now, Mr. Challoner, shall I make tea? Or do you prefer that poison my father calls nectar of the gods?"

"Tea by all means," said Challoner, handing her the whiskey glass from which he had taken only a swallow, "but tea can wait."

"Wait?" She eyed him from under her long lashes—dark indeed, for a girl with red-gold hair!

"Can't we talk a while?" proposed Challoner.

"Talk? About what?"

"You, of course."

"Me? What is there about me that would interest a gentleman like yourself?"

Challoner was about to answer in the same light vein when a gargantuan snore drowned his opening words. A snort ended Pat McKenna's intake of breath, but oh, the outlet! Challoner grinned at Kit. "Is it like this with all your admirers?"

"Oh, yes!" she smiled.

"Then it's plain to see why some good man hasn't snapped you up for his wife. How could you possibly hear him propose?" This set the girl into peals of laughter.

"Oh, you are funny! Why do you say 'all my admirers,' as if I had dozens?"

"Well, haven't you?"

"Not at all! I had *one,* last winter. He was Lady Grantley's second coachman. Papa called him soft-butt."

"Soft-butt?"

"Papa means . . . those who can't sit a horse."

Challoner took the little hand. "Kit. Is there no place where we can talk without being blown away on your papa's snores?"

"We could go into her ladyship's gardens," the girl answered shyly. "I have the key to the wicket gate."

It seemed to Challoner as he paced moonlit walks with a chit of a girl that he was living a dream as fragile as the cobweb that brushed his cheek. This Kit McKenna—was she flesh and blood or petticoated shade?

One could imagine her—sprite or elf, flying through the air. One could imagine her—fabulous Amazon, riding out of the mountains of ancient Scythia, one breast removed so that the war bow could be sprung! But little Kit was certainly not a-*mazos,* in the Greek sense, not "without breast," and her stature was certainly not amazonian. There was a daintiness about her—a petite-ness that could well arm a man to the teeth in her defense, yet . . . she asked for no defender, for accompanying her delicate air was a sense of equipoise, a strength of eye, of hand and knee that let her control a great bay horse like a child a pet Shetland pony!

"Kit . . . tell me about yourself? Where were you raised? Who taught you to speak the King's English? Who taught you manners? Oh, I'm not forgetting that you tried to ride me down."

"I wouldn't have ridden you down, really!" she murmured.

"Then why did you try?"

"Because I saw you from afar and I wanted to meet you."

"You saw me?"

"Yes. I'd just taken Daemon out and was pacing him when I saw you talking to another vagr—"

"Say vagrant if you like, Kit," laughed Challoner. "The noun and its synonyms fit me like a glove. Wandering, roving, strolling itinerant. Vagabond. Idle and disorderly person. But I do plead innocent to the charge disorderly."

"You talked to the man," said Kit, paying no heed to what he had said. "He showed you a piece of paper."

"He couldn't read," said Challoner. "There was a Help Wanted item from which he hoped much, and was disappointed. Here's the very advertisement." Challoner pulled the shred of newssheet out of his pocket.

"Let me see!" cried Kit. She held the paper up to the light of the moon and when she had read it, she gave it back. "Why did you keep it? Are you a ship's master? Do you hope to find a berth by going to . . . Number 14, Ferry Road?"

He nodded.

"With or without papers?" she said, with a smile that somewhat softened her question.

"Little Miss Busybody!" laughed Challoner. "Shall we carry on? I haven't seen the half of Lady Grantley's enchanted gardens."

"Now I *know* you are a man who goes to sea," she exclaimed. "You said . . . shall we carry on. Only seamen use that expression . . . carry on."

"What a wiseacre we are!" exclaimed Challoner in mock amazement. At the same time he asked himself why he suddenly would rather have cut off a finger than let her know what kind of hot water he was in!

"See here, Mr. Challoner," she said, turning up her adorable face, "if you need work, my father will take you on. I'm sure of it! He wouldn't call *you* . . . soft-butt."

Challoner squared away and placing his hands under her elbows, he lifted her until her eyes were on a level with his.

"Kit! You're kind and fascinating and tantalizing and bewitching."

"Not . . . beautiful?" she murmured, looking him in the white of the eye.

He put her down with a little "thud" of heels on the gravel walk. "Beautiful? I think of 'beautiful' women in terms of grand, full-bosomed things with spreading hips, swanlike necks and marble limbs. Long, shapely arms. Seaweed coils of hair! You? You're the thistledown that blows in a man's eye. You're the mustard seed that roots in his heart and spreads . . . and spreads and spreads . . . till it's one massed field of bloom!"

"Oh!" she cried. "Thistledown. Mustard seed!" and her pretty frown changed to peals of merriment. "Since you have me all sized up, Mr. Challoner, why do we not speak of you for a change? Who are you? How came you to be playing Narcissus in Rosamond's Pond?"

"First tell *me*," said Challoner, "where did you learn about Narcissus?"

She answered with a fresh burst of laughter. "From Miss Pritchet. She was a prime Greek scholar. The *Odyssey* . . . Plato. Myths. I can tell you all about myths."

"Miss Pritchet?"

"Lady Grantley's governess."

"Indeed?" Challoner frowned.

"Why do you say 'indeed' in that tone of voice?"

"I'd scarcely have thought that a girl like you, so lovely, so fresh, so innocent, would have associated with Lady Artis Grantley."

Suddenly, Kit was transformed—purring kitten, into spitting cat!

"Why, Mr. Challoner? Why should I not associate with Lady Artis Grantley?"

"Well . . . firstly, because she's older than you," hedged Challoner.

"She is not!" said Kit flatly. "We're the exact same age. Nineteen."

"Lady Artis Grantley is as old as the Venus myth!"

"Myths! You make me think of Miss Pritchet. Artis is my friend from childhood. My only friend . . . except horses. I could not love her more if she were my own sister. Why, we slept in the same baby cart! We drove the same goat basket! We rode our first ponies, side by side. We sat on the same study bench." Kit's green eyes clouded with tears. "It is true she ran away with Lord Grantley when she was sixteen, and now we seldom see each other. But I know she's never ceased to be fond of me. And I am fond of her."

Challoner could see that he had hurt the girl deeply, but recalling the many salacious anecdotes he had heard about Lady Artis Grantley, he was unwilling to compromise on his dislike of loose ladies—especially loose ladies whom Fortune had endowed with extravagant blessings of wealth and beauty from the very cradle onward. Forgive those frail daughters of the gutter or the hedgerow who rise by making men's beds their stepping-stones. Their lives were symbols of the human struggle for survival, betterment, a place in the sun. But a Lady Artis Grantley? How could one condone *her* follies? Lady Grant-'em-All, they nick-named her. Even the caricaturists of press and pamphlet took their turn at portraying her—Bengal tigress picking her victim's bones. Lady Whip, driving a four-in-hand of lovers!

"What kind of tree is this?" he said, breaking the uneasy silence that had fallen between Kit and himself.

"A tulip tree, and you needn't try to change the subject!" cried Kit, stamping her little foot. "I wish you could *meet* Artis."

"Heaven forbid!" exclaimed Challoner.

Kit plucked at the brass buttons of his coat. "Why? Why? You'd fall in love with her like all the others!"

"No, thank you, Kit."

"You would! You would!"

"And . . . you'll twist off my buttons, young lady!"

"I'd like to! I'd like to twist your neck!"

He gripped her slender wrists. "Listen to me, Kit. Innocence preserves the heart but it also blinds the eye. Shall we forget Lady Artis Grantley and talk about something else?"

She wrenched herself free with the same show of strength that had surprised him at their initial meeting. "If I were a man, I'd challenge you to a duel. And don't think I couldn't put a ball through your heart at ten paces, because I could! I learned pistol shooting with Artis. I learned how to handle both fowling piece and rapier. Would you be surprised to know that I could give you a toss . . . right where you stand?"

"Greco-Roman?" grinned Challoner.

"Yes!"

"Show me!"

She put out a hand, took a brave stance, but he caught her in his arms. "Kit! Kit! I did not come into this enchanted garden to practice Greco-Roman."

She stared at him coldly. "As if I didn't know why you came!"

"Why then?"

"Why, to make love to a girl who kissed you for luck and liking's sake!"

He held her tight. "No. You're wrong. When you kissed me, I was like a man lost in a fog at sea. Strain, gaze, I saw no hope. Then suddenly the fog lifted and there! There you were."

She trembled in his arms, but her tone was still hostile.

"Very pretty, Mr. Challoner. Now, will you let me go!"

He did not grant her request. "Kit! Why quarrel with me over someone who is as distant from you and me . . . as yonder North Star."

"Lady Artis is not far from me," she cried.

Her tone of voice made him sense a steellike hardness of will that provoked him more than mere words.

"Your loyalty to a naughty lady is misplaced, even though she be your father's employer and your childhood companion!" he said sharply. "If I had a sister, I would forbid her to spend even an hour in company of a libertine in petticoats!"

"Let me go!" she cried and, like a vixen, she sank her teeth into his wrist.

Surprise more than pain caused him to loose his hold. By the time he had recovered from the surprise, she was running down the path, full tilt.

"Hell!" cursed Challoner, sucking his blood and taking after her.

But the garden paths were many and the moon had vanished behind a cloud. All of a sudden he found himself gazing up at a row of brilliantly lighted windows. Grantley House itself!

The architecture was in the elegant and simple style of today, the stone not yet patina'd with London smoke and fog. He remembered having received a London gazette whilst his ship was being repaired in Gibraltar from which he had learned that historic Grantley House had been consumed by fire. Presto, a great lady had waved her hand and a new Grantley House had risen out of the ashes.

Were it not perhaps wise to leave before some lackey found him gaping at her ladyship's windows like a love-struck swain? Taking his approximate bearings by the moon that had scudded out from behind a cloud, he retraced his steps, finally found the wicket gate. It was not locked. He slipped out into the alley.

Should he knock on the green door with the horse's head knocker and attempt to salve Kit's wounded feelings? No! "I'll give her time to be sorry," said Challoner to the darkness. For . . . were not women prone to change their minds and kiss the very hand they'd bitten?

2.

The Two Faces of a Female Janus

SIR HENRY FOX, AWAITING THE APPEARANCE OF HIS MOST exalted client, could not put down that sense of nervousness which never failed to beset him when he received pre-emptory summons to the Presence.

"Come at once!" Lady Artis had said in her note that a perspiring footman had run all the way from Grantley House to his chambers in the Temple. And he'd been half undressed—going to bed!

What was it this time? Brawl in Tolliver's cocking rooms? Cat fight at Madame Cornelys? Slapping bee across the dice table? Artis never said "Come at once" unless she was in some kind of a scrape from which *he* must extricate her.

"My indigestion," muttered Sir Henry, patting a "burrp" with his fine white hand.

Why could Artis not settle down with a husband and have children? Augustus "Ozzy" Sutton, staid, sensible, with ample means, good-natured fellow, next in line to the Earl of Stanbrooke, would be just the husband for her. "Poor Ozzy," thought Sir Henry.

No . . . the man hadn't yet appeared who could steady Artis down! Not that she hadn't sampled a huge assortment of men! First, Grantley. He'd been shot in a duel over his wife's vertu (sic)! Then Lord Cantwell. Whatever became of him? Montgomerie (Montie), Lord Crittenden, was her third *grande passion*. She was still holding him in her stud pen! Captain Cunlyp of the Guards? A wild Irish lord named Quine? What deaths had *they* preferred, to abandon by their mistress?

"Ah! There you are, Foxy!" called Lady Grantley from the door which a footman had thrown open. She came

25

skimming across the drawing room in the roll and sway of her Paris hoops. You could hide the dome of St. Paul under 'em!

"Artis!" exclaimed Sir Henry, strutting on lean shanks to meet his patroness. "You're a vision of beauty!"

"Vision of beauty, fiddlesticks!" Lady Artis gave her twenty-inch-high headdress a backward shove. "This monstrosity! Look at it! Feathers, fruits, flowers, jewels! Fanfan is a fool!"

"Fanfan?" said Sir Henry, eying the wig—amazing thing, indeed!

"Fanfan is my new hairdresser," said Lady Artis. She seized her advisor's hand with a little-girl gesture. "Foxy. I have something to ask of you."

"The answer is no," said Sir Henry, adopting a light tone to disguise his dread that she would ask him to unbalance her holdings—sell here, buy there—to satisfy her whim of the moment.

She hitched up her silk-and-lace-hung hoops and backed into a petit-point sofa. "Sit down, Foxy, and tell your stomach to stop growling."

"Er . . . yes," said Sir Henry, seating himself gingerly beside her.

What a beauty she was, the tiny waist reduced to wasplike size and the bosom swelling like bubbles of cream! Patch and powder and rouge paste could mask her natural complexion but they could not destroy the symmetry of her lovely features or dull the aqua-green of her amazing eyes.

"Now, Foxy darling, all I want is the truth."

"The truth . . . about what?"

"About myself."

"O Glory!" thought Sir Henry. "Tell her the truth and she'd have me quartered and dressed by her own game butcher." "Yes, my dear?" he said, clearing his throat. "What is it you want to know?"

"You *will* tell the truth?"

"Of course. Have I ever lied to you?"

"A thousand times. But never mind. What I want to know is . . . am I naughty?"

"Delightfully so!" said Sir Henry with a sudden and gratifying sense of relief.

She regarded him with a chilly eye. "You know what I mean. Bad! Unmoral. Unfit to associate with . . . say . . . an innocent young girl?"

"Artis!" exclaimed Sir Henry with a show of surprise that he was sure his client must see through, as through a well-washed windowpane.

"Foxy!" She gave his hand a squeeze. "It is important that I know."

"Know what?" hedged Sir Henry.

"Well . . . am I . . . bad?"

"Artis! Artis!" said Sir Henry with feeling. "I adore you. I serve you. I see you . . . gallant and capricious! A woman whom Love finds to her liking. Oh, you're naughty all right! You get into scrapes that will cause me to lose the last few hairs of my head . . . but your naughtiness is your charm."

"You're lying," said Lady Artis in a soft voice. "I agree I'm a minx! A hoyden! A spendthrift! A gambler! I pass more time with my trainer and my grooms than I do with my social equals. I like the company of wrestlers and cock-fighters and cardplayers better than I do . . . so-called gentlemen! *But! Am I Bad?*"

Sir Henry felt a dreadful hollowing at the pit of his stomach. Oh, that once, just once, he dared tell Artis the truth! But he knew her too well. Tonight she might accept a truthful verdict. Tomorrow she'd throw it in his face . . . take the management of her vast estates out of his hands.

"No, Artis!" he answered in tones that rang with beautiful courtroom sincerity.

She cocked her little head, burdened with the great wig. "I'm not, eh?"

"Certainly not."

"Can you look me in the eye and affirm that I am not a petticoated libertine?"

"*Artis!*" gasped Sir Henry.

She rose and moved across the room like a ship under full canvas.

"It's no use, Foxy! Because I know the truth about myself. The difficulty is to face it. I remember a line out of Milton that I read with my governess, Miss Pritchet. You remember Miss Pritchet? 'The sun-clad power of Chastity.' There is also a sun-clad power of unchastity! I have it! I

use it! I abuse it! For, in that moment when the power rises
in me . . . I am strong! Strong! I own the world and the
man. Have you ever drunk fine brandy, Foxy . . . drunk to
the point where your very being seems to be made of gut
and gold? But take too much brandy and the gut and the
gold are gone. You're made of rag! You're a Thing to cast
away." She planted herself in front of him, arms akimbo.
"Foxy, what's the matter with me?"

Eminent barrister, silver-tongued orator, able pleader
that he was, for once Sir Henry Fox had no answer ready.
Mumbling, "Well . . . now . . . matter, you say? Is something wrong?" he stalled for time and ideas with which to
cope with his patroness.

Lady Artis stamped her foot. "Yes! Yes! Something *is*
wrong, and you know it. But you're too liverish to tell me.
Your indigestion! Well, *I* am your indigestion, poor Foxy."
She stooped and pressed a light kiss on his cheek. "Foxy
darling. Please! Please! Tell me why I cannot be happy,
living as other women do?"

The barrister took a firm grip on himself, and rising, he
pulled his waistcoat of flowered satin taut.

"Could it be that you have never found true love, my
dear? I know several gentlemen . . . with great names . . .
one in particular, Lord Sutton, who would show you a
world of devotion."

"And why shouldn't he?" retorted Lady Artis. "Add my
fortune to Ozzy's and you could buy the whole of England!
My money! That is what they're all after! Money! Money!"

"Nonsense, Artis," said Sir Henry, who felt himself on
safer ground. "You are reputed . . . and rightly so . . . to
be one of the most beautiful women of the realm. You have
talents such as few women possess. And what is more, you
were born with a brain! Why should a man look only to
your money?"

Lady Artis touched her left breast. "I fear it is here
I am lacking."

"Heart? Have you ever tried letting your heart . . . go?"

Lady Artis stuck out her lower lip in a delightful pout.
"I've let it go so many times that it knows the way back.
That's my trouble, Foxy! My heart never stays where I
send it."

Sir Henry tried to clinch the plea in his client's defense. "It's true love you need, Artis! True love!"

"True love!" she said, mocking his pompous tone. "And where is true love to be bought? Who sells it?"

For an instant Sir Henry's impulse was to say "Love is not a merchandise," but he again resorted to compromise.

"Dear Artis, some lives, like some coats, are cut to a pattern that binds here . . . is too loose, there. Your effort, as I see it, has been to discard the misfit coat. Do not forget that you were an innocent child, just turned sixteen, when you married Percy Grantley."

"Foxy!" cried Lady Artis. "I was playing games with the sons of my father's beaters, gardeners, ostlers, when I was a tiny girl! I was playing . . . not games . . . when I was thirteen. How glad Papa was when I married Percy. 'Infant Jezebel' he called me."

Sir Henry groaned inwardly. What sharp pin had pricked Artis' conceit? He thought with dread of tomorrow. She'd remember every word of her confession and charge it to his account. "You wormed my secrets out of me, Foxy!" In panic he consulted his watch, costly trinket given him by Artis on his last birthday.

"Dear lady, it grows late."

She gave him a quizzical look. "Go, Foxy! And be careful to sleep well."

The barrister bent over his client's little hand. "I am your ladyship's humble servant."

No sooner had the door closed than Artis pulled off her wig, threw it on the floor and trampled it underfoot, crying, "Love be hanged!" The wig, a ludicrous structure built of bent wire and horsehair covered with blanched hair and trimmings, seemed to take the shape and form of a man whose blood she'd tasted only a little while ago. She jumped on the wig with her two feet, hoop skirts and petticoats billowing around her like whorls of whipped egg white. "I'll have you on your knees at my feet, James Challoner! On your knees!" Then she sped out of a french window and through the gardens to the wicket gate that opened into the mews.

Patrick McKenna was at his desk in his office, enjoying a nightcap, when her ladyship burst in.

"McKenna!" she cried. "I want to talk to you."

The shrewd Irishman eyed the beauty who so frequently assumed the role of his "daughter" for her amusement and the bewilderment of others.

"Yes, milady?" She'd her "wild" look, tonight. Red curls in the breeze, a costly gown with mud at the hem.

"McKenna, the man who came here tonight? What is your opinion of him?"

"Strong will. Strong hand. Strong heart," said the trainer, pouring himself another of his favorite Glenavon.

"Pour me some, too," said Lady Artis.

"No," said McKenna.

He was the one person, male *or* female, in Artis' life who dared say yea and nay and she'd never questioned his right to do so, for Pat McKenna was wise with the wisdom of those who lead pure lives and deal with nature.

"Pat . . . I must know who he is? What he does? Where he comes from? Where he is going?"

"Yes, milady," said McKenna phlegmatically. "You know his name, you should be able to go from there."

"Not I," she said sharply. "*You*. Here's the only clue I have. He was on his way to 14 Ferry Road when I met him this morning in the Park. He is a man of the sea and he is poor but he shouldn't be!"

3.

The Devil and the Deep

CHALLONER DID NOT RETURN TO CHEYNE WALK THAT night. The Crown and Mitre gave him shelter. He slept poorly, tossed between the devil and the deep. Two o'clock. Three. Four. "They say a man, no matter how low he has sunk, can always find a living in the American Colonies," Lord Frawley had said. He toyed with an odd idea for a while. Marry Kit McKenna! Take her to the new world. The idea was not without charm. Given time for courtship,

Miss McKenna would certainly say "Yes." Ah, but this was indeed . . . to run! Run, tail between legs!

"You'd have to change your name," he muttered to a shaft of moonlight that cut the wall of the room in two. Well, why not? The name of Challoner was, at present, not worth a cocked hat! "Go . . . pitch hay for Pat McKenna," he soliloquized. "Worm your way into Kit's heart. The big Irishman might even lend you enough money to get a fresh start in Boston."

He fell into deep sleep at dawn—wakened in mid-morning with a change of mind. Go back to Cheyne Walk. Talk to the Old Man again.

He bought a shave at a barber's adjacent to the Inn and, after breakfasting, hacked to Chelsea.

Somewhat to his surprise there were three carriages stationing in front of Number 16. So . . . Lord Frawley had callers!

He decided to wait outside, watch the river traffic, until they had gone, but the Admiral's manservant came running out of the house.

"Sir, his lordship bids you to come in."

So . . . Frawley had been watching at his library window! Challoner gave the servant his hat and was starting up the staircase when the servant called after him.

"Sir, his lordship is waiting in the green room. Here, sir!"

It was a large room, hung with green brocade and handsomely furnished in mahogany and rosewood. A round table occupied the center of the carpet. Seated around the table, Lord Frawley and three gentlemen wearing, of all things, black masks.

Lord Frawley rose. "Mr. Challoner, I presumed you would return, and you have. That is why these gentlemen are here . . . to talk to you. They wish to keep their identity secret for reasons which you may divine. I can only tell you that they are officers of the Royal Navy."

Challoner's quick eye roved around the table. The portly figure at the head, who could he be but Admiral Lord Wilmington? The man on his right—full, pouting lips, a strong chin, Vice Admiral Sir William Benedict! And if Lord Wilmington were here, certainly his flag captain, dapper Ross Elliston, nicknamed "Rosy," was the third masked man.

"Pray be seated, Mr. Challoner," said Lord Frawley, indicating the chair on his left.

A carafe of sherry made the round of the table. The servant passed clay pipes and the tobacco jar. When he had withdrawn, Lord Frawley again broke the silence.

"Mr. Challoner, what have you—"

"Wait, Fred!" said the portly man, and drawing something from his coattail pocket he tossed it into the center of the table, saying tersely, "Here's your new ticket, Captain Ironhand."

The object was a glove forged of gray metal and chased with gold and silver in Cinquecento style—spikes on each knuckle. Its meaning was instantly clear to Challoner. Captain Blackbeard had his trademark. So had Silver-Leg. He slipped the glove on the hand it had been made for. The right hand. It fitted perfectly. The mail gave off a pleasant metallic sound when he flexed his fingers.

"Gentlemen, are there King's papers to go with my new . . . ticket?"

The same man who had tossed out the glove answered.

"No, sir. You sail at your own risk and peril."

"And if His Majesty's ships take me?"

"You'll hang, sir."

Challoner gave the masked company a slow look.

"And if I succeed in my venture . . . bring back the information the gentlemen of the Admiralty need, what then?"

The portly man again made himself spokesman for the others.

"Then, sir, speaking for these gentlemen, I can safely say that you will be reinstated to the rolls from which you were dropped, and with rank of Rear Admiral."

Challoner stared at the mailed glove, flexed the fingers, drew it off, slowly, and placed it in front of the speaker. "How much time have I to decide, gentlemen?"

"Twenty-four hours, sir. You will report to Lord Frawley."

Challoner's little bow served for all four gentlemen. "Sir," he turned to Lord Frawley, "may I inspect the ship you intend placing at my command?"

"You may go to her forthwith, Mr. Challoner," said Lord Frawley, returning the bow, with courtesy.

It was not without a quickened pulse that James Challoner found himself threading his way through Limehouse's Sailor's Town with Will Boggs. The quarter was a crooked maze of streets and alleys that meandered right or left without seeming orientation or purpose. Shipbuilders, chandlers, netmakers and outfitters' shops lined the streets on both sides. A tavern or brothel at every ten paces.

"The *Royal Acre* lies in Shadwell Basin," Lord Frawley had said. "You'll find the Waterman's Arms a convenient center for recruiting, should you undertake this mission."

The Waterman's Arms was a brick-front facing the river. Behind was an abandoned boatbuilding yard, green weeds growing high among the timber stacks.

Pausing on the corner, Challoner gazed upon the slate-colored river, gleaming under a thin veil of rust. Its northern bank wound and bound the horizon with a blackish fringe tinged with red; a few vessels were descending with the graceful slow movement of sea birds, their somber hulls and brown sails balancing upon the shimmering water. To the north and south, ships lying at anchor.

"Lord of the world's great waste, the ocean,
We send whole forests to reign upon the sea,"

quoted Challoner softly.

"Aye, aye, sir," said the uncomprehending Boggs. "She'll be in yon berth . . . carryin' the flag of the East India Company."

The frigate loomed like a strong wall.

"Ahoy there, *Royal Acre!*" hailed mate Boggs.

"Royal Acre ahoy!" answered the Watch, poking his head through a porthole.

"Orders from Lord Frawley. We're to come aboard."

"Then come aboard!"

Challoner ran up the gangplank with Boggs at his heels.

"Sir! She's a beauty!" exclaimed the seaman, as he stepped on deck.

Gripped by an emotion so strong that he actually trembled, Challoner turned his back on the smiling man. Live . . . without this? Never to feel a bounding deck under foot? The vast sky, overhead? A keel, slipping through blue waters? In his heart of hearts, he knew the die was cast. His answer to Frawley and to the gentlemen with masked faces—"Yes."

"Sir," said Boggs at his elbow, "may we go to the gun deck?"

There the new truck guns sat, under lashed tarpaulins, like beasts in their caves.

One tarp removed, Challoner saw that their trucks or wheels were movable, yes, but how much so? In loading position they'd be so close to the bulwark that the rammer handle would have to project through the gunport.

"From the description, I imagined these guns would be more maneuverable than they look," said Challoner to Boggs, who stood, arms akimbo and cap tipped back, gazing at the iron monsters.

"They'll roll at that," said Boggs. "It's more'n you can say of the old kind, but they'll take a heap o' crew."

"Four gunners and a gun captain apiece should do it," said Challoner.

It was then, glancing down at the wharf, that he noticed —or rather renoticed—a man whom he had seen twice before, that morning. He was nondescript of appearance, and for that reason hard to distinguish in a crowd, but Challoner's eye was well trained. Where had he seen him first? Why . . . in Cheyne Walk. Where the second time? Getting out of a hackney right at Shadwell Basin. Admiralty agent? Likely. Well, let him do the job he was paid for.

Challoner liked "his" captain's quarters at first glance. Room and to spare. Cupboards for books and gear. A good desk and chart table. One lockable cabinet for bottles and another for side arms (brass key in lock). And the bunk was wide enough and long enough so that one could sleep without crimping legs.

The fo'c'sle pleased him too. There was room here. Room enough! That old bugaboo, crowding, wouldn't plague the crew.

Forgetting time, he went over the ship from stem to stern and from bridge to hold, until he had seen every foot of her—a fighting man's dream! With her new armament, the truck guns, she'd face the enemy, single, in pairs, or by the half dozen, unafraid.

The sun was setting when Challoner and Boggs, hungry and thirsty, finished the tour of the ship.

"Well," said Challoner, dusting his breeches' knees, "they've offered command of this frigate. If I accept will you sign on as my first mate?"

"I . . . first mate . . . on a forty gunner, sir?" stammered Boggs. "The best I've served was a merchantman, and she was lost in a typhoon in the India Ocean."

"Frightened of a forty gunner, Mister Boggs?"

"What, me? There ain't no ship afloat can scare me."

"Then why do you hem and haw?"

Boggs lowered his voice. "I never held with His Majesty's service, sir. When *they* put the hooks on you, you never get free."

"Did I mention Navy, Boggs? What would you say if I told you she was sailing as a freebooter?"

Boggs' jaw sawed up and down in astonishment. "Sir, a privateer?"

"Something of the kind."

The light dawned slowly on Boggs, but it dawned.

"Freebootin' in a forty gunner! Jehosophat! I'll sign, sir!"

Challoner laughed. "Well, now that we're agreed, go lodge at the Waterman's Arms and keep your mouth shut. I've business in Town."

The "business" that concerned Challoner sometimes wore riding breeches and sometimes a challis gown. She had red-gold curls and sea-green eyes and her name was Kit McKenna.

He would have found it hard to justify the strong desire he felt to see her again. Reason was against it. The hazards of the future forbade it! On the verge of embarking on a . perilous mission, what right had he to seek to engage a young girl's heart? And . . . even succeeding in his mission, were it not folly to engage the heart of a horse trainer's daughter? The practical way for a Navy man without private fortune—marry a young lady with a fat dowry, or at least healthy expectations of inheritance.

The hackney he had engaged seemed to be rolling at snail's pace. "Faster!" he called to the driver.

A Piccadilly flower "girl" with gray locks and wrinkled cheeks sold him a posy through the coach window.

" 'Ere's luck wiv the loidy, guv'nor!"

"Thanks, Maggie!" laughed Challoner. He felt an exhilaration, a pounding of the heart, as the hack turned into Park Lane. "Let me off at the corner of Great Stanhope," he called to the driver.

The vehicle had scarcely pulled in to the curb when a handsome, closed carriage, preceded by runners bearing torches, and harnessed with two dappled grays, rolled out of the great iron gates of Grantley House.

Challoner caught a glimpse of a woman's face, framed in a fanciful powdered headdress. Glitter of diamonds on a mother-of-pearl bosom. Presto! The vision disappeared. So . . . that was Kit's darling, Lady Artis Grantley. Beautiful, yes. But haughty! Cold! Proud!

He quickened his pace through the alley. There was the green door, the horse's head knocker. But no one answered his rat-tat-tat. When he knocked a second time, a voice shouted from down the Mews, "If it's McKenna you want, 'e's gone to Islington."

Challoner tossed the posy over the wall of Grantley gardens and trudged sadly back to Park Lane. The hackney coach was still standing where he'd left it.

"Take me to Number 16, Cheyne Walk, Chelsea," he said to the driver.

"Bad luck, eh, guv'nor?" said that worthy gathering up the reins and clucking to his horse.

Challoner slammed the hackney door in answer. Who would dare say "bad" or "good"? Perhaps chance had saved him from making a second, serious mistake—the first, when he'd said "no" instead of "yes" to a lady with a crest on her handkerchief.

The driver having slowed to a walk at the corner of Piccadilly, Challoner noticed a man on horseback—the same man he'd seen three times before. He turned when the hackney turned, followed at the same pace. Well, Seething Lane could now call off its dog and start the wheels in motion that would change James Challoner into Captain Ironhand.

4.

Lady of the Byways

"THE 'ROYAL ACRE' IS YOUR SHIP," LORD FRAWLEY HAD said. "Do with her what you deem best to attain your goal."

"I'll change her name for one thing," Challoner had said. "She's a lady of the byways, I'll name her the *Paramour.*"

Handed a strongbox packed with bank notes and gold, he had set about manning his ship. His strong right hand in this matter was his first mate.

Mate Boggs scoured every dive where seadogs met. Gunner Captain Jack Scotland was a dried up and dour man from Aberdeen who knew armaments like their makers. Quartermaster Peters, better known as Dutch, was a native of Rotterdam with the phlegmatic and precise mind of a countinghouse clerk. Bosun Pearly had a pair of lungs for outshouting the storm. Scotland, Peters, Pearly; thereafter it was not hard to gather in gunners, jack-tars, hands, cook and cabin boys.

These latter were boys in name only. Captain's lad, "Cricky," was fifty. Mess boy Tom was forty-five, both experts in handling muskets as well as at their chosen tasks: running food trays and keeping captain's clothing and boots bright and clean.

Sailmen and riggers went over the *Paramour's* line and canvas. Gun crews were tested in arduous drills that separated the strong from the weak and sent the latter back to their pothouses.

Challoner procured spare sails and enough powder and ball to arm HMS *Victory* herself. *Paramour's* provisionment included live pigs and laying hens and plenty of limes; salt pork and lard and wheat flour and tea and sugar and salt and raisins and rum. A few medicinals, such as castor bean and sal. A kit of surgeon's tools. Challoner made an all-day tour of Jewry and came aboard with four padlocked sea chests full of sundries, the nature of which he kept to himself.

Browsing through the bookshops of Paternoster Row, he bought a few of his favorites, *not* Laurence Sterne; also a tome by one Thomas Yarborough. *My Captivity and adventure in Africa, including an historical and geographical survey of that country bordering on the Mediterranean, called Morocco.* The book was handsomely bound and lavishly illustrated, the price so modest as to cause Challoner to inquire of the bookseller, "Why does this book cost only sixpence?"

"Because, I've the whole edition! One thousand copies!" came the reply. "The author is my cousin. He was so much in need for a new expedition to the Bosphorus that he sold it to me cheap."

Three weeks had elapsed since the old Sea Lord handed orders and money to Challoner and the Admiralty agent had broken off his spying. The *Paramour* was manned, provisioned and armed.

Challoner sent a message to Cheyne Walk.

Sailing April 21 on the morning tide.

The evening of April 20, he was seized with a sudden irresistible urge to see Kit McKenna before casting off. Folly! But see her he must.

Giving himself a close shave and donning fresh neckwear, he went to Great Stanhope by hackney coach. This time it was McKenna himself who let him in.

"So . . . it's you, Mr. Challoner. We thought you'd gone and forgot us."

"We? Then I take it, sir, your daughter is at home."

"Kit's in the stall with Merry Boy," answered the trainer. "Go along upstairs, Mr. Challoner. I'll fetch her."

The wait was long, too long. Challoner had time to refresh his memory of turfdom's famous names—those excelling equines, sires of present-day English race horses, whose copper-plate effigies adorned the trainer's walls. Arabian, brought from Aleppo in 1704 by a merchant named James Darley. Turk, acquired by Captain Byerly while fighting the Turks in Hungary in 1687. Godolphin, a present to King Louis XV of France from the Emperor of Morocco, later purchased and brought to England by Lord Godolphin. Eclipse, Touchstone, Stockwell, Isonomy,

Vedette. Mohammed's followers—Arabs, Turks, Moors—
might be, certainly were, thorns in the side of Christendom,
but by Jove one must grant that they were masters at breed-
ing horseflesh.

"Good evening, Mr. Challoner."

Challoner turned like a flash. Blue ribbon in her hair.
Blue dimity gown. White stockings and buckled shoes.

"M . . . Miss McKenna." He wanted to tell her how lovely
she was. How springtime fresh! How graceful! How serene
in her young beauty! All he could do was stammer, "M . . .
Miss McKenna."

She tinkled a little laugh. "Well, won't you sit down?"

He hung his hat over the knob of a chair and sat down
gingerly. Why did she make him feel like Gulliver himself?
Was it her dainty size? Or was it that pert, teasing way she
had—you never knew whether she was laughing *at* you or
with you. But you liked it, either way.

"I take it you've found a position that has absorbed a
great deal of your time, Mr. Challoner."

"Er . . . yes."

"Ah! What position? With whom are you located?"

"A shipping concern, Miss McKenna."

"You called me Kit the last time we met," she said with
an adorable frown.

"Kit. Yes. You remind me that you never called me
James, only Mr. Challoner."

"James . . . is such a . . . a solemn name," she said with
a little trill of laughter, "but then you are such a solemn
man."

Challoner transferred himself to the hearth bench.

"Solemn? Not really."

"Oh, yes!" she nodded sagely. "You *do* appear to carry
the weight of the world on your shoulders, Mr. Challoner."

"Are you trying to tell me I'm a prig, a bore?" smiled
Challoner.

Her lovely face softened, brightened. "Oh, no, Mr. Challoner."

The look she gave him strengthened Challoner's courage
to take her little hand. "Kit, I'm going away for a time, but
I'll return and when I do, I'll have something to say to you."

"Say it now!" she cried with a vehemence as sudden as
it was unforeseen by Challoner.

He pressed her hand tightly. "Kit, I wish I dared. But at present I'm a man with no assets except the hopes I entertain for the future. In this condition, it would be unwise for me and unfair to you to bind us with word or token."

She gazed at him with her soul in her eyes. "Why, James?"

He would have swept her into his arms, except that an inner voice said "take care." The playful kiss they'd exchanged earlier in their acquaintance, was one thing. To kiss her now, would be another. For in absence, he'd come to the realization that he loved her, and now he knew that she loved him. Perhaps he'd known it from the start.

> *If then true lovers have been ever cross'd,*
> *It stands as an edict in destiny.*

He dropped her little hand, grown cold under the stress of her emotions. "Kit, listen to me. It is my duty, and it will be my joy, to bring you all that a man must bring his lady . . . not love alone, but also the respect of others. A life free from risk and alarm. A good life. A life of decency and decorum. The way has opened to me. It's of small moment that I must go away. Think what happiness when I return."

"Why go away?" she said in a small voice. "Papa could help you to get a start in some business : . . perhaps a livery stable."

Challoner concealed a smile. "Kit. I've already signed in my new position. There can be no changing of mind."

"I see!" she cried. "You scorn a livery stable."

"No! No!" protested Challoner.

She sprang to her feet. "Oh, yes you do! I can see it in your eyes. You're too proud, Mr. Challoner!"

"Proud?" Challoner had risen. Looking down into the angry, upturned face he shook his head. "You found me shaving in the Park. You called me . . . vagrant . . . and it was true. Why do you say I'm proud?"

"You'd be proud in sackcloth, Mr. Challoner! You'd be proud in a pigpen!"

He reached, caught her close. "Kit! Be sensible! I'm in love with you. But the time is not now to tie us to each other, even in hopes of the future. That time will come when I can hold you in my arms and say without reservation, 'Kit, will you do me the honor of becoming Mrs. James Challoner?' "

A tear of crystal brimmed from her green eyes and coursed slowly down her pale cheeks. "I think you had better go, Mr. Challoner."

Live a thousand years, he'd always remember her like this.

"Yes," said Challoner tersely, "I think so too. Miss McKenna, I am your humble servant." He released her gently and took his hat from the chair knob. "Goodnight, Kit. Not . . . farewell."

Pat McKenna, puffing on his briar pipe at the door of a stable, saw the tall figure of Challoner go through the mews. He smoked in silence. This which had come to pass, the Lady Artis grieving over a man, was what he had feared would come to pass when he'd started inquiry into the life of a gentleman named Challoner.

All his findings and the conclusions drawn therefrom had led him to the certainty that the ex-naval officer was above and beyond the grasp of a Lady Grantley masquerading as Kit. Still less could Lady Grantley win Challoner in his present situation—cashiered Navy captain. The informer—a clerk who had attended the Challoner hearing at the Admiralty (and a race-track enthusiast in need of thirty guineas to cover a gambling debt) had said, "Challoner could have escaped with a reprimand if he'd only opened his mouth. But he would not speak or try to justify his conduct in the affair with the Countess." Such a man would first wish to rebuild his castle of honor before he'd succumb to a woman's blandishments.

But Lady Artis wouldn't accept the report.

"If he's poor . . . without influential friends, why would he not accept help?"

She'd been full of her little scheme to offer him a livery stable! Captain Challoner, ex of the Royal Navy and a Portsmouth man!

"You'll see, Pat! He'll snap at the chance to earn a good living. And, when he's settled, then I'll woo him. But I'll never let him know who *I* am until we're Mr. and Mrs. Mistress Challoner."

The Irishman eyed his beloved lady whose sobs were beginning to subside.

"You never met one like him, did you, milady?"

"No!" she answered with a gusty sigh.

"This . . . feelin' you say you have for him . . . couldn't it be no more than a . . . paper chase after the new?"

"Oh, Pat! You're impossible!" cried Artis, sitting up in her chair and plucking off the blue ribbon that tied her red-gold curls.

"Well, I've seen ye take the bit so many times," said McKenna testily.

"Go on! Tell me I'm a mad, wanton thing! Well, you'd be right. But what I feel for Challoner is different."

"I seem to recall you've also felt 'different' before," said McKenna dryly. He was testing her. In one of her former moods, she'd have given him the tobacco jar in the face for daring to make such a remark.

"I know," she said dolefully. "Where is he off to, in that big ship, Pat?"

"Where? My man couldn't discover. But Mr. Challoner did some strange buyin' in Jewry . . . cutlasses . . . worn nips. Maybe he will trade with savages in some far-off isle."

Artis saw a vision of Challoner's frigate at anchor on a tropic shore. Cannibals surrounding him!

"Pat! Pat! I can't bear it! I love him, do you hear? I love him. I'd lay down my life for him."

"Tut tut!" said McKenna. "What good would ye do 'im dead? Go to bed, Kit. Go to bed."

He'd nicknamed her Kit when she was a baby. Sometimes, even now, he used the name. Why could he not help her in her present dilemma? But she'd forget Challoner as she'd forgotten all the others. Surely she'd forget.

The excitement and exhilaration of sailing was in the air as Challoner climbed to the bridge that morning. His ship presented a lovely picture—the men brisk at their appointed tasks. And what a grand first mate Boggs had turned out to be. Steady, firm, fair.

Challoner watched a closed carriage approaching the *Paramour's* berth. Lord Frawley alighted and started up the gangplank, followed by a footman carrying an oaken sea chest.

Challoner met him at the head of the plank. "Good morning, your lordship."

"Good morning, Captain."

They shook hands and Challoner led the way to his quarters, the footman following with the sea chest.

Lord Frawley threw off his cape and hung his hat on a hook. "Put it on the table, and go," he said to the footman.

"How do you find us, sir?" said Challoner, pouring a glass of sherry for his caller.

"So far, so good," said Frawley. "I see you kept the truck guns under wraps."

"So they'll stay, until I'm well away, sir," said Challoner. "I also waited to paint out *Royal Acre* and paint in the *Paramour*."

"*Paramour,* eh?" smiled the Admiral. "Well . . . open the chest. Its contents are yours."

Challoner could not hide his delight when he saw what the chest contained. "A sextant! Sir, how I've wished to own my own sextant."

"You . . . and every other ship's captain," Frawley agreed. "They're hard to get. This example was constructed by John Bird. I received it only a year before my retirement."

Challoner lifted the instrument out of its oaken case. The arc and index were of brass, the frame, mahogany, the vernier subdivided into minutes. "How many magnifications has the telescope, your lordship?"

"Four and the inversion," answered Lord Frawley. "I also wanted you to have my box chronometer."

"Your lordship is very generous," said Challoner accepting the second gift with alacrity.

"Not generous, practical," said the old Sea Lord. "You'll need better than what those Moors possess, and it is said they are master mariners . . . which I can well believe after observing the results of their navigational skill. You'll find a compass and my old spyglass, very accurate and powerful, in that old compartment. There's also a complete set of East India Company charts in the lower tray, and I threw in my old waggoners for good measure. Oh, I almost forgot. The chest is carpeted with ensigns of every nation. And there's your iron hand, in that tea chest. I packed it in metal so the spikes wouldn't mar the instrument cases."

Challoner grinned. "Does your lordship wish me to keep log?"

"No. A log can be a guidebook in enemy hands. Sail as

pirates sail . . . without records. I'm not forgetting the breeze that will drive your ship. Money."

"I've nearly a thousand left of the sum you gave me," said Challoner. "It should suffice until I take my first prize."

Lord Frawley pulled a fat wallet out of his inner pocket. "Here is five thousand more. Money is no object in an undertaking like this. Remember, once you leave our coasts, you break contact, completely." Lord Frawley delved into the tail pocket of his coat and drew out a small leather pouch. "Here, sir. This is your passport to a new world. We . . . those concerned in your undertaking feel obliged to make one point clear. If you fail and are brought to the bar of justice, we shall not intercede on your behalf."

The pouch contained a black flag with skull and crossbones in white and a small brass button with the initials G. F.

"Your lordship makes it very clear," said Challoner. The black rag seemed to burn his fingers. He folded it and put it back in the pouch—drew the string tighter than need be. "May I ask the significance of the button?"

"It is a token to be used if worst comes to worst. Show it to any of His Majesty's consular agents. It will identify you and give me some clue as to the whereabouts of the *Paramour*." Lord Frawley then reached for his glass. "May I offer a toast, Captain Ironhand? The *Paramour!* Your good fortune! Your future!"

Challoner stood. *"The Paramour!"*

Glasses clicked. Lord Frawley reached for his hat.

"I'll not keep you, Challoner."

Challoner saw him to the plank, watched him get into his carriage and drive off. Then he went to the bridge. No standing at the yards, or breaking of colors, today. No cheers. Let his ship (Oh, the sound of the words "his ship"!) steal from her berth like a sinning woman from her lover's bed.

He gave the orders to cast off and turned to where lay London under her canopy of mist. "No goodbye, Kit," he said under his breath. "Until we meet again. And meet we shall, if I live!"

Gravesend passed, Sheerness Light sighted, the ship's sails caught a bit of breeze blowing down from the North

Sea as she rounded the nose at Broadstairs. Challoner was busy with pen and ink when first mate Boggs announced himself.

"We've a stowaway, sir. A wee lad, but he's able. Says he wants to go to sea. Cook could use him. The potboy he signed never turned up."

"Well, put him to work," said Challoner.

He'd a plan maturing—train a "flying" force of fifty fighting seamen after the model of the boarding and assault crews of hand-to-hand battles at sea, a century ago. These fifty must be drilled in unorthodox procedure. They'd enjoy extra pay and privileges.

The man he picked to head the force was named Maunday (foundling, named for the day of his appearance on this earth?). Needing a title for Maunday, Challoner coined one. "Flymaster." The specially trained men, "Flyers."

The idea pleased and volunteers were quick to offer themselves. Any hour of the day or night they could be seen in hand-to-hand or practicing boarding by net or wielding saber and cutlass in mass duels that made a great din.

As for the *Paramour's* course (her new name shone in brave gold on her bows), he'd a pattern in mind. Clear the Channel quickly and down Biscay in pursuit of a nagging memory of a tale as told by one green lieutenant to another green lieutenant, some eight years ago.

"We put into a little port called San Carlos, north of Cadiz, for repairs to our mizzen. Damme, if it wasn't an authentic pirate hide-out. There was a woman ruled the place. Mamma Jolie they called her. She was a French-woman from Marseilles. Brothel and all the rest. I suspect she was a receiver and dealer in contraband and stolen goods as well as petticoats."

Challoner was pacing the quarter-deck one evening when he sighted a small boy lugging a pail of galley leavings to the rail. The stowaway? He cut a rather pathetic figure.

The *Paramour* cleared Land's End the fifth day out and beat south toward the misty-blue mountains of Spain. Her landfall, Cabo Ortegal. A strong nor'easter rushed at her from the mountains as she rolled down the Spanish coast and swept past the squat, black shape of the Torre de Her-cules, the oldest light tower on Spanish soil—past Cabo

Villano (what a villain of a cape with its dragon spines arching down to the surf), past sun-scorched hills—a church on a rock, a monastery like an eagle's nest, a toothy coastline that came to a snout at Cabo Finisterra.

Her run finished, she plowed past Vigo and Coimbra and, giving Lisbon a wide berth, she rounded Cabo San Vicente and dropped anchor off a small fishing village named San Carlos on the chart.

This seemingly peaceful bay had been his first goal ever since the start of the voyage.

Could the green lieutenant have been right? Could this fishing settlement be a pirates' nest? Using his spyglass, Challoner searched the scene.

A church with a squat tower loomed over a half-moon of sea-front houses with arcaded façades, colored sepia, rose and white. A range of hills sloping to twin promontories at the horns of the bay formed a natural harbor. North and south were sheer cliffs and the village was backed up against a sugar-loaf mountain, crowned with a lighthouse. All this, and the Spanish-Portuguese frontier, marked by the turbulent Guadiana River at their back door. What greater safety for outlaws, smugglers, pirates?

Challoner's glass picked up the masts of three ships lying inshore to the north. The hulls were hid behind the curve of an inlet.

"Send two men in the dinghy to look at those ships," he said to his first mate. "Let them proceed with extreme caution." He watched the two men drop into the jolly boat and pull away.

The scouts' report corroborated Challoner's suspicions that the three ships were pirates. The names painted on their bows, *Nina, Jewal* and *Coira.* They were well armed, the scouts said. Their crews had gone ashore leaving only a skeleton watch aboard. Where would one look for the men of three jackals of the sea if not at some tavern of San Carlos?

Challoner decided that the moment had come to reveal the true nature and mission of their ship to the *Paramour's* crew.

Stacked in his cupboard was the fruit of many weary hours with quill in hand—a contract each, for the signature or mark of every man aboard. The document (odd, indeed, for the year 1772) was the kind in common use in earlier times. He'd taken the "Rules of Agreement" drawn up in 1695 between the Irish Earl of Belloment (for His Majesty William III) and a prominent New Yorker named Colonel Livingstone, the now legendary Captain Kidd, for his model.

KNOW YE BY THESE PRESENTS

That Captain James Challoner, hereinafter to be known as Captain Ironhand, does swear to keep the articles of this agreement, and does require that the signee do likewise . . .

The agreement promised five shares, treasure, money or merchandise, to each common seaman of the ship's company. Petty officers and flymen to receive eight shares, and the officers, ten. The rest went to the captain, "upon whom rest the duties of victualing, arming and maintaining said ship."

There were other clauses which bound the men to rigid discipline, whether at sea or in port, also a clause that guaranteed them fifty guineas in case of loss of eye, leg or arm.

Challoner had added a last clause, devised to prohibit holding females aboard should any be taken prisoner.

Decorated with a scarlet ribbon and seal each, the documents made a brave showing.

The crew of the *Paramour,* going about their duties, could not but observe the strange performance of captain's lad, Cricky. First, he carried a table on deck and spread it with a cloth of red velvet, fringed with gold. Then he placed two silver candlesticks and lighted the candles. Then he placed the Book between the candles. At last, he brought up a stack of papers that measured from his waist to his chin and set them on the red velvet.

Solemn moment for the *Paramour's* captain—this was to be the crossing over, from the side of law to that of outlawry.

He waited on the bridge until all hands had been mustered as ordered. "Ready, Mister Boggs?"

"Aye, aye, sir." The first mate fingered the rag of black with its piracy symbol. What his thoughts were, Challoner did not hazard to guess.

"All hands on deck. When mustered, drummer will give

the roll and bosun will haul down the Jack. Then to a slow roll, bosun will raise the Jolly Roger. Give 'em time for the facts to sink in. Keep the drum rolling. At my signal . . . iron glove to chest . . . this way . . . the drum will cease." Challoner's throat tightened with an emotion somewhere between regret and determination. "I'll speak the piece that will change 'em . . . seamen to pirates."

Challoner set his hat tight and joined the rest on deck, placing himself behind the velvet-draped table to watch the muster.

The crew came at the double. They knew their captain was a stickler for promptness. Soon all were present and well-aligned faces turned expectantly to the velvet-draped table.

Drummer boy (who doubled as mess hand) had hung on his drum. He stood with the sticks poised. At a signal from bosun he let roll, and immediately the Jack was hauled down.

A thousand words could not have told the *Paramour's* company as much as the square of black muslin with its gruesome seal that fluttered up the spanker gaff.

Challoner waited until the mutterings had died away, then, placing the flat of his hand upon the stack of contract papers, he spoke in a clear voice.

"Men. I was obliged to keep you in the dark until such time as I could reveal the true nature of the ship you sail. She is, as you have already guessed, a privateer. Now I shall read the articles of agreement which you may sign, or not sign, according to your lights. Those who do not wish to serve, step to the gun deck. The others shall come forward, one at a time and put his name to his paper, which I will then countersign."

A deep voice spoke from the ranks. "Wot if we don't sign, sir?"

Challoner's eye found the speaker. "You must see that it would be impossible, now, for me to set you ashore."

The meaning of his words sank in. All ears were stretched and every eye was riveted upon him as he began to read the contract. Would not that satanic blood which runs in every man's veins, stir at the idea of loot? Quick gains? When he came to the end of the paper, the silence was so deep that he could hear his own heart beating.

"Who'll step up and be the first to sign?"

"I, sir," said Will Boggs.

Challoner dipped the quill and placed it in his first mate's hand.

And thereafter, it was one man after another, right down to Cook, who put a straggly cross where the name should be. There remained one contract.

"You must have wrote it for the galley boy, sir," said Boggs. "The one who never turned up."

"Yes," grinned Challoner. "That stowaway—Tim?—who took his place. Bring him!"

The lad had to be dragged by the scruff of his pea jacket. A snicker went through the crew at the sorry spectacle he made—one elbow up to ward off blows, cap tilted down almost to the bridge of his nose.

"I'm sorry, sir," said the *Paramour's* cook, "I can't put no starch into *this* one."

Challoner held out the quill pen and pointed to the contract. "Make your sign, Tim. Then you'll be one of us in sharing."

The lad cringed in terror and tried to twist free of the cook's horny hand.

"Make your mark first, boy," said Challoner more sternly than he intended.

The boy took the quill in his dirty little fist and drew an X, then he pivoted on a bare heel and ran like a hare.

Challoner, preparing to go ashore at last, broke out the contents of the chests that he had filled in Jewry.

5.

A Fat Man, Bones, and the Dandy

A STRANGE TWOSOME BOARDED THE "PARAMOUR'S" JOLLY boat. Challoner in a jewel-buttoned suit of black, the breeches so tightly fitted that he looked like a marble Apollo dipped in tar. Dagger and pistols and cutlass at the wide gem-studded belt. His own tumbling curls, sans powder or club, for a head covering. And, the iron glove! He'd contrived a way to hook it into a gold-lace-and-cord bandolier on his left shoulder. What eye so blind that it would not see Captain Ironhand's hallmark? He'd only a thrusting move to make and presto, his right hand could slip into the glove as easy as finger into ring.

Captain Ironhand's companion, Will Boggs, was glorious in baggy breeches and floppy boots and a shirt with torn sleeves that floated like slack sails from his great arms. Dagger and pistols in double and a Turkish scimitar at his belt. A leather waistcoat trimmed with silver studdings. His hat? Surely a relic of Blackbeard!

How quickly the histrion in man could step to the fore! And how quick the actor was to feel his role. Truculence, bombast, and strut replaced self-discipline and restraint. Why, even the temper of the blood was changed.

"Well, Mister Boggs?" grinned Challoner.

"Aye, aye, sir," answered the first mate with a grimace —mirth or ferocity? It would be hard to say.

The quarter boat with its load of flymen, Flymaster Maunday at the tiller, slipped along in the jolly boat's wake. Soot-blackened hands and stocking hoods, black jerkins and hose. Devils! They had their orders—reconnoiter San Carlos from end to end. Signal for rendezvous, the hoot of an owl.

50

The blue dusk had turned to night as the jolly boat nudged up to the wharf where two curly-headed boys were tossing an orange for a ball.

"You young ones!" called Challoner in Spanish, handing each one a coin, "where is Mamma Jolie's tavern?"

The boys became willing guides, leading the way through a maze of streets to the south end of the village. "Mamma Jolie's! Mamma Jolie's!" they said, smiling and pointing.

The tavern looked more like a fortress than a place where wine and food might be sold. Its blocklike buildings climbed the hillside in a series of steps. Its lower wall flanked a harbor, wide and apparently deep enough to float the largest vessel. The entrance was by way of a vine-shaded court. The shrill laughter of women and raucous voices of men could be heard, inside.

"Wait here," said Challoner. "If I need you . . . I'll give the word 'Boats away.' "

He placed the flat of his boot against the tavern door and kicked it open, gesture made for effect, the door was not on the latch. The result was as he'd hoped. Every eye ogled him and the din ceased.

The room was well lighted by ships' lanterns that hung from the arches by anchor chain. Every foot of floor space was filled with tables, each with its full complement of customers. The stamp of piracy was upon the men and that of harlotry upon the women. Bawds of the ports and poachers of the sea.

At the far end of the room, four steps led up to an arch, draped with gaudy, striped curtains, now tied back. Behind the arch, a separate alcove for privileged guests. Here, a round table was spread with a wine-stained lace cloth and lighted by a pair of branched candlesticks of silver. Four high-backed chairs of carved and gilded wood and scarlet velvet cushions were set around the table. On these sat three men and a woman.

The woman drew the eye like a bright color on a neutral field. Plump and white-skinned with large liquid eyes and a quantity of black ringleted hair, soft bare arms and soft bare bosom, she was not young, neither was she old. She sported a Moorish turban on her ringlets, the front decorated with a star of brilliants and a spray of red cock feathers.

Her companions were, the first, a bony African, patch over one eye, dressed in a gold-braided coat hung with medals. The second was fat, with a round face and three double chins. Vast girth cinched with a sash of red and gold. A Spaniard from the looks of him.

Challoner's gaze was drawn to the third man, seated at the woman's right. Of less than medium height and delicate build, he'd a fine Caucasian cast of feature—swarthy skin and jet-black hair. Was he perhaps a Turk? Immaculately dressed in a plain uniform of "regulation" cut and trim, he sported no medals or sashes and his manners were in complete contrast with those of his two male companions. Reserved to the point of primness, he gave no hint that he'd seen the intruder, but seen him he had; that darting eye would miss very little.

Challoner swaggered up the step and addressed the woman in French. "Are you the renowned Mamma Jolie?"

She gave him a long, slow look. "I am Mamma Jolie. Who are you?"

Challoner touched the iron glove. "I take my name from this. *Main-de-Fer. Manos di hierro* in the Spanish. Captain Ironhand in my native tongue, English."

"Come here, handsome," said Mamma Jolie with a beckoning gesture. She examined the iron glove, tested the points of the spikes with her soft forefinger. "Your native tongue is . . . English?"

"Yes," Challoner replied.

"I never saw you in San Carlos before."

"I've never been in San Carlos before."

"Who told you about Mamma Jolie? San Carlos?"

Challoner beckoned to a tavern maid. "Set another of those fine velvet chairs, girl!"

Nothing he could have said would have produced more effect on the three listening men.

Cursing roundly, the fat man pushed back his chair and lumbered to his feet. "This table is private!"

"Wait, Rodriguez!" said the woman putting up a restraining hand. "Let us first see who our guest is. What news he brings. Where he comes from." She beckoned to the servant who brought the chair Challoner had asked for. "Sit down, handsome." It was clear that her word was law. The fat man she'd called Rodriguez resumed his seat, muttering in his throat.

"Lovely lady," said Challoner, "I'll tell you all you want to know after I've wet my throat with a bottle of your best amontillado."

Mamma Jolie clapped her hands. "Bring what my guest desires."

While enjoying the wine of a rich amber color, Challoner kept both eyes open wide and listened with both ears. The woman and her three male companions spoke a monosyllabic patois which they amplified with gestures in the manner of Sicilians, Arabs and the peoples of southern Spain. Even knowing more Spanish than he did, it would have been impossible to understand what they were saying.

The woman turned to him and spoke again in French.

"Where do you come from, handsome?"

"The Caribe Sea," said Challoner.

"What was your business in the Caribe Sea?"

"The same as yours and these fellows' business in these waters."

Her dark eyes seemed to cast off sparks. "Your ship?"

"The *Paramour*."

"Anchored where?"

"At the rim of your bay."

"Why did you come here?"

Challoner filled his glass again and settled back in his chair. "It's a long story, Mamma Jolie. Why do they call you Mamma? You haven't the look of a mother, as I remember mine! I came here because the air is too hot to breathe in the Caribbean, nowadays. The new Governor has no understanding of men like myself. Having received notice to leave or hang, I made a pact with His Excellency. He paid me five thousand pounds to disappear. Now . . . next to Captain Ironhand, who is the most renowned person in our business? You, Mamma Jolie!"

"You heard of me . . . as far away as the Caribe Sea?" the woman exclaimed, and turning to her companions, she repeated, "Think of it! As far away as the Caribe Sea!"

Challoner felt three pair of hostile eyes upon him.

"What do you use that iron hand for?" said the fat man. "To scratch your fleas?"

The quip caused all but the dapper man in navy blue to laugh uproariously. He half rose in his chair and extended his hand across the table.

"I am Captain Hassan, the sloop *Jewal*. This gentleman is El Negrito who commands the *Coira*. Captain Rodriguez, better known as El Terror, sails the *Nina*. Sir, we bid you welcome."

"Not I!" growled the obese El Terror. And his partner on the left, the be-medaled African, echoed his sentiments with a throaty growl.

"Silence!" cried Mamma Jolie. "Let us hear what Captain Ironhand proposes."

Challoner reached for her hand, kissed it, patted it. "Thank you, my lovely. Here's what I propose. Action! My men are rusty from many months at sea. I purposely avoided attacking ships I crossed on the way, because I was told I'd find an ideal partnership with certain Moroccans who rule the Mediterranean. I was also told that to operate in these waters alone was dangerous because the French and my own countrymen's ships of war are everywhere, but my informers said that the Moors know how to outwit both the French and the English, also where to dispose of seized cargo."

His words inspired a fresh exchange of whispers between Captain Hassan and the woman. She turned again to him.

"I think your informer must be a very clever man to have known so much. What was his name?"

Challoner smiled. "Madam, a wise man never tells the source of his information."

"Ah! But you can tell me, Captain Ironhand," she said in a purring voice, and leaning closer she said, "Whisper the name in my ear."

"You are very lovely," whispered Challoner, "may I see you later, alone?"

Her nostrils dilated. She nodded.

"Well? Well?" said Captain Rodriguez. "What did he say?"

"Yes!" echoed El Negrito. "What did he say?"

Only the captain of the *Jewal* remained silent.

Mamma Jolie rose. "You'll be told, when I choose to tell you. Come, Captain Ironhand. Captain Hassan? Would you care to join us?" She led the way, paying no heed to the protests of the African and the fat man.

The room where Challoner found himself was furnished à la Turque. Rich carpets on the floor, a vast couch hung with silks, scent of musk and amber on the air.

No sooner had the curtains fallen over the door than the woman clapped her hands and two giants with black skins appeared. She spoke. They pinioned Challoner's arms behind him with a brutal suddenness that rendered him powerless to resist. The woman and Captain Hassan then went through his clothing, pocket, seam and lining. They even explored the inside of the mailed glove.

Challoner knew what they were after—some paper, seal or cipher that would tell them who he was. These two weren't fools. He also knew that the woman was not invulnerable to a man's good looks and fine physique. How often her eye lingered upon him!

"Rien!" she said, and she added a word in a strange tongue that caused the two black-skinned men to release their prisoner and disappear.

"You will pardon our curiosity," said the dapper little man in navy blue. "I know the English. The pirates of your country are cutthroats and ruffians . . . dregs of the ports! You are not their kind."

"Allons mon beau!" broke in the woman impatiently. "Tell us who you really are?"

Challoner gave her a little bow. *"Très Jolie!* The name I was born with went down with my first ship when I was sixteen."

"That name you affect? That mailed glove? Bah! Rodriguez calls himself El Terror." She laughed in disdain. "Names mean nothing. It is the man and what he has done that counts."

"They call you Mamma Jolie," said Challoner with an impertinent grin. "Have you borne a brood of children?"

The woman turned to her companion. "Leave us, Hassan Bey."

Hassan Bey? So the dapper gentleman *was* a Turk.

No sooner had he left the room than the woman came to Challoner and placed her hands upon his shoulders caressingly. *"Main-de-Fer,* you say you wish to join with

the Moroccans. You are not of those who follow Mohammed. How do you know they would trust you?"

"Mohammed or the devil," said Challoner. "I am not a
religious man."

She regarded him with doubt in her dark eyes. "Fearless
you are to have come to San Carlos without letter or password. Give me ten days. I'll give you your answer . . . either
the Moroccans will welcome you or they will run you out of
the Mediterranean." Moving close, she tempered the sever-
ity of her words with a soft touch at the nape of his neck
. . . a kiss that brushed his cheek like the flame of a taper.

"You said you wanted to see me . . . in private, Ironhand."

"Not unless I am welcome!" Challoner retorted. "I'll
pick up no crumbs from the Moor's table."

Her bright eyes veiled. "You are not only daring . . . you
are impertinent."

"Are not the English noted for their impertinence? We
call it . . . to be blunt . . . honest." He gently removed her
hand from his shoulder and stepped away. *"À tout à
l'heure,* Mamma Jolie."

Returning to the place where he had left Boggs on watch,
Challoner suddenly decided upon a course of action intended to hasten events and bring him closer to his goal.

"Now, Boggs," he said to his first mate, "let us join with
our flymen. I intend to assault Mamma Jolie's fortress at
once."

The woman, Captain Hassan, fat Captain Rodriguez and
the lanky African were again gathered around their private
table to talk over the coming of the man who called himself
Captain Ironhand. The crews of the three pirate ships, *Nina,
Jewal* and *Coira,* were still carousing when a company of
black devils burst in upon them. Hardly an even contest.
On one side, sober fighting men—on the other, sots and
screaming females. But the noise and confusion helped to
cover the real action which was directed against the store-
house in the rear of the tavern.

Challoner led the raid with a ruthlessness that surprised
even himself. A new Challoner—nay, Captain Ironhand
himself—climbed walls, crept along eaves, dropped into
dark courtyards. His first need was to smoke out the pirate

band, provoke them and prove that he was worthy of their respect. Mere words and threats wouldn't do it.

"Come on, Maunday!" he whispered, beckoning the fly-master down from his perch on a roof. *Crrrack* went a lock under leverage of a crowbar.

Challoner's lanthorn cast a pinpoint beam upon a rich store of merchandise. Rolls of brocades and silks. Bales of tobacco, wool, hemp and cotton. Precious hardwoods from far Eastern Isles. Demijohns marked "Attar of Roses." Barrels of rum and wines and spirits. The product of modern times was also represented. A machine marked "London." What was it, a printing press? Ships' masts and ships' sails and coil upon coil of rope of all thicknesses. Anchors. Chain. Here a bale of precious Persian rugs wrapped in canvas. Furniture and chinaware. Clocks, dishes and glassware. A wooden crate labeled "Church Window." Paintings and statuary. A thousand curiosities—from the jawbone of a whale to several giant tortoise shells, packed inside each other like teacup saucers. Cowhides and alligator hides and snakeskins. Tea and coffee, herbs, spices and cacao beans in lead containers for preservation from the damp.

Maunday having broken open a second padlocked room, a treasure trove of Ali Baba was discovered, consisting of chests of gold and jewels and precious plate.

"We'll take all this," said Challoner to Maunday, "the rest will have to burn."

Certain of the flymen moved quickly to lay charges and fuse, while others formed a bucket line and removed the treasure. The raiders broke off the engagement as suddenly as they had begun it, and the boats put away to the *Paramour* with the loot piled high in the bows.

The blast went off with a dull *ker-thunk*. No loud explosion, but the havoc was immense. Sections of wall and roof tiles flew into the air and flames broke out in a dozen places. Soon, the whole mass of buildings was turned into an inferno.

Observing the scene through a night glass he'd had the luck to find in the warehouse, Challoner was well pleased.

"Get under sail," he said to Boggs. "Hold her sou-sou-west. If that scum comes out in pursuit I want to meet 'em without interference from Gilbraltar-based men-of-war."

The moment had come to reward the crew of the *Paramour*. Challoner had the loot carried to the wardroom, and with the aid of scales divided jewels and precious metals, according to contract. A line formed at the wardroom door. Each man received his share.

"Potboy won't come out o' 'is 'ole, sir," Cook volunteered. "Once 'e's in, 'e's like a ruddy weasel!"

"Well, pull him out," laughed Challoner. "Every man gets his fair share and this share belongs rightfully to the lad."

Challoner was changing into fresh clothing when he heard a knock. The door of his cabin opened and in catapulted a small bundle of humanity—propelled, no doubt, by Cook's boot. The potboy.

"Well, lad?" said Challoner as he stooped to pull on clean stockings. "Don't you want your share of the loot?"

"Naw!" said the boy.

"Why not?"

"Cause."

"Because . . . what?"

"Lemme go!" The boy flung himself against the door, but someone was pushing on the other side!

Challoner shuffled into his slippers. "See here, lad, if you want to make the sea your career, you'll have to learn seaman's manners. Come when your Captain commands. Stand at attention. Say aye, aye, sir. No sir."

The lad cowered against the door, face hid behind the dirty sleeve of his coat—spectacle of poltroonery that ceased to move Challoner's sympathies.

"Look here, boy!" He took him by the arm and dragged him over to his desk chair. "Straighten up! Doff that rag of a cap!"

The boy twisted out of his grasp, ran to the other side of the cabin, hid under the bunk.

Losing his patience, Challoner got down and hauled him out by the leg. A mother would use the paddle on him!

The boy never let out a cry but he made himself limp, slid to the floor as promptly as Challoner stood him up. Finally, losing the last shred of patience, Challoner sat him on the desk hard. The shock lifted the boy's cap off his head, uncovering a crop of red-gold curls . . . a pair of aqua-green eyes—

"Kit!" gasped Challoner. Could it be she, or a trick of the senses?

"I tried so hard . . ." she sobbed in a small voice. Suddenly she was in his arms—so close that his heart seemed to stop beating.

"Kit! My darling! Why?"

"Hush!" she said, putting a small, grubby hand over his lips. "Just . . . hold me."

The memory of an evening in a Mayfair garden—the song of night insects, the scent of roses came to Challoner's mind as he clasped her to his heart. He was holding—not a raggedy lad—but a lovely young girl in a challis gown whose fair skin was perfumed with lavender and whose cool lips tasted of honey. He saw, again, a gallant little jockey riding a grand bay down the St. James's Park lane—saw her spur her mount upon a vagabond . . . heard her laughter purl in the gray morning like the trill of a lark.

"Kit! Kit! How could you?" he groaned. "This is madness! Sheer madness!"

She nestled closer. "Don't be angry. I wanted to be with you and I could think of no other way. Oh! James! Can't you understand? I fell in love with you, head over heels! There's no other man on earth for me. I'd rather scour pots near you than dine on strawberries and cream anywhere else on earth!"

Challoner could not keep his lips from seeking hers. "Kit! I shall have to put you ashore. This ship is no place for a lady."

She pressed herself to him with a kind of desperate strength. "I'll go on being potboy! Who'll know the difference? James! Please! Please! Don't put me ashore!"

He gazed into the green-blue eyes that stared into his. "How long do you think you could go unobserved, unsuspected? My crew is made up of rough and ready men. Why . . . they might even manhandle Tim the potboy! No! No! You'll have to go ashore. I'll arrange for your safe return to England."

She squared off, hands clenched. "I won't go! I won't go! I won't. How can I? Father would lock me up in a boarding school! Or he might even disown me! No, James! You'll just have to keep me on your ship. I'll hide . . . never let myself be seen! I'll endure anything rather than leave you."

Challoner gnawed his lip. "My contract with my men says . . . no women aboard."

"What is a contract?" she cried. "A mere piece of paper!"

Challoner felt his ire rise. Why could she not understand and be docile?

"Look here, Miss Kit McKenna, you may have me cornered but I'm not beat. I'll lock you in here . . . until such time as I see a chance to send you back home where you belong."

She gave him a dazzling smile. "Lock me in. Put me in irons. Do anything you please . . . but let me stay."

Slipping the bolt on his door, Challoner summoned his first mate.

"I'm in a fix, Boggs. Our potboy turns out to be girl."

"Eeee," chortled Boggs. "Joined up to be near her love-light. Who is the lucky man?"

"She won't say," said Challoner evasively. "I don't intend that anybody shall find out. I'll keep her under lock and key in my inside quarters until it is convenient to put her ashore."

"Aye aye, sir," said Boggs with a wry grin. He added a question that made Challoner flush. "Wouldn't it be wise to spread the news . . . the lad is ailing from some mysterious, catching fever, sir?"

"Good idea," said Challoner lamely, and coining a word, "we'll call it . . . pitonitus," he added.

"Pitonitus it is," Boggs agreed. "That'll keep 'em at a respectful distance."

Challoner could not but feel that his first mate was aware of some part of the truth. Boggs was no man's fool. Well . . . so be it! But the *Paramour* was awaiting contact with the enemy, instanter. How could a man do battle fore and aft? Kit must be placed out of jeopardy.

Challoner had been right when he had surmised that his daring act against the warehouse in San Carlos would bring swift retaliation.

The *Paramour* was cruising off the coast, south of San Carlos at dawn. Challoner was on the bridge, fingering a key in his breeches' pocket when the Watch sang out from the crow's nest. "Sails ho!"

"Where away?" bellowed Boggs.

"Two dead astern and one to starboard," answered the Watch.

Challoner swept the sea with his glass. The trio of pirates were bearing upon the *Paramour*.

"Have sail trimmed," he said to his first mate. "This is as good a position as any to give them a fight."

He quickly outlined his strategy in conference with his officers. "You, Mister Boggs, Flymaster Maunday, saw the captains of those three ships, last night. Rodriguez, El Negrito and Hassan. One Spaniard, one African and one Turk. It is your task to match captain to ship, for I want the Spaniard and the African sunk with all hands. The Turk to be spared. And hear this. If any of the crew of either of the two ships to be sunk take to boats or jump, pick 'em off with musket fire. Not a man must live."

"Why spare the Turk, sir?" Boggs asked in tones of polite inquiry.

"Because I say so," grinned Challoner.

The three ships were gaining on the *Paramour* as Challoner intended they should. He looked aft through his glass. "Put about, Mister Boggs. Reef canvas for action. Guns will fire when we're in range of the two, starboard side."

Gun captains and crews waited upon six of the truck guns—a sufficient number for the business at hand.

It was the *Coira* who first opened up on the *Paramour*, but her shot fell short.

Challoner, watching the gun crews with a technician's eye, scarcely gave heed. What admirable precision his gun captain had attained! Gun inboard for loading. Gun captain sticks wire into touchhole; the cartridge (a woolen bag of powder) and a wad are rammed back into the barrel until captain feels the cartridge touch his wire. While the shot is being rammed in, gunner pokes a hole in the cartridge with his wire, pulls the wire out and pours a little loose powder into the touchhole. At gun captain's signal, the train tackle is released and the outhaul tackle is used to roll the gun forward until the muzzle projects about two feet from the gunport. The gun captain touches the burning match to the touchhole. A smoky flash! Fire flies up through the touchhole and an iron ball is thrown from the muzzle, twelve hundred yards seaward. Bang!

As the shot goes out, the gun ramps back and takes up short against the breeching. The train tackle is hauled taut to keep the gun back, one man does it, thanks to the leverage he gets from the pulleys; the gunner puts his thumb on the touchhole to kill sparks. The barrel is swabbed out with a wet sheepskin "sponge" to clear it and make sure all sparks are dead in the bore. The gun is ready to load again. Time? A fraction less than a minute. Bang! Bang! Six bangs! The *Coira* is in trouble.

Challoner trained his glass on the *Nina*. She was bearing at the *Paramour*.

And now the trucks were letting loose in earnest. Bang! Bang! Oh, the good smell of powder and burning timbers! The *Nina's* spars splintered and her foreshrouds split to ribbons. Another salvo and her hull received a wound at the waterline. She shivered from stem to stern. Boom! Boom! Boom! Her mizzen got it, dead to center.

"Hard to larboard!" Challoner ordered bosun. "Musketeers stand by to pick 'em off." He watched with a cold eye as his trained marksmen carried out his order, now and then turning his glass on the *Jewal* which was being gunned incessantly and held at such a distance that her shot could not reach the *Paramour*.

The drift was bringing the damaged vessels closer and closer. Panic reigned on their decks. Some of the crews were making frantic efforts to put out the fires that raged through the cordage. Others sought to lower the boats. But the greater number jumped into the sea, there to die by a marksman's bullet. Among these the *Nina's* captain.

"That fat man with the scarlet sash," called Challoner to the musketeer at the for'rd firing position. "Don't miss!"

Captain Rodriguez's vast hulk lurched as the lead found its mark. He sank like lead.

"Quarter boat away," said Challoner to his first mate. "Let 'em do for every last wretch in the water."

He turned the glass on the *Coira* just in time to see a flash of light. The sound of an explosion followed. The *Coira* had split amidships. The halves went up in flame.

He swung his glass to the *Jewal*. Her crew lined the rails as though drawn to the spectacle of death in horrid fascination.

"Bosun, signal the *Jewal*. Captain Hassan to come aboard the *Paramour* or we'll sink her with all hands!"

"Aye, aye, sir."

The answer was given without delay. "Captain Hassan coming aboard the *Paramour*."

Challoner was waiting behind his desk when the pirate captain stepped into the cabin.

Deadly proud, this Turk. There lurked a pallor at the sides of his mouth as he said, "Peace, Ironhand effendi," and gave the greeting of Islam, hand to breast and to lip.

In the brief silence that followed, Challoner saw his gaze shifting from wall to wall, in his dark eyes, envy of a master of ships for a better craft than he has ever sailed.

"Am I your prisoner?" said the Turk. "The Prophet writes, 'Allah's wisdom is inscrutable and his judgment sure.' Your ship has guns such as I have never seen. Why did you not blast me as you blasted the *Nina* and the *Coira?*"

Challoner relaxed his rigid manner. "Sit down, Captain Hassan. I am not King's justice, I am a man who sails for gain. *My* gain. Come to these waters from halfway around the world—rumor was, I'd find friends in San Carlos. What a pity you and your fellow captains had to take the stand I was not welcome. Rest assured, I seized the Madam's treasure before the bonfire was lit. About the *Paramour's* guns, you are right. Our Navy has none such. And now to answer your question as to why I spared you and destroyed the *Nina* and the *Coira*. It was because of you. Sir, I need a friend to throw me some lines. Where do I unload my cargo? Where can I exchange diamonds for coin? Where can I take on supplies in safety? Where can I recruit new men in case of loss? Don't you see . . . I need a friend."

The Turk gave a little bow. "Seek no further, effendi. I am that friend."

Challoner cocked an eyebrow. "Damn me if I don't believe you. It's a wise man who meets luck halfway. Sir, my hand, and we'll drink a toast on it."

The Turk, though a follower of Islam, was not a teetotaler. He answered toast after toast in Vin-de-Cognac.

"What is to be our method of operation, sir?" said Challoner when his guest had somewhat dropped his guard. "Do we sail a twosome or do we rendezvous at given positions?"

"We vary our method as the situation arises," said the Turk. "Take yesterday, when you appeared in Porto San Carlos, I and my defunct friends, Captain Rodriguez and El Negrito, were waiting to rendezvous with a vessel out of Antofagasto, bound for Lisbon with a cargo of gold from the mines of Bolivia."

"You had notice in advance?" asked Challoner with a show of surprise.

"Of course!"

"Then rumor was right. You Morocco-based freebooters are better organized than those of the Spanish Main ever were. Progress! Progress! Avail yourself of every advantage of modern times! That's the thing. Shall we go against this Bolivian as our first joint endeavor?"

"We might, Ironhand effendi," said the Turk after a moment's hesitation.

"Good!" exclaimed Challoner. "Now . . . my next question! What arrangement would you propose for the sharing of spoils? How much for me? How much for you? How much for your superiors?"

"Superiors?" The Turk's brows shot up. "I see you are a practical man as well as a brave one. It is true, all spoils are split two ways. One half is divided between as many ships as have engaged in the action. The other half goes to the Lion."

"The Lion? Who is the Lion?"

"His person is secret."

"I see! Lion takes lion's share. What about prisoners' ransom?"

"The Lion takes all prisoners."

"Damn the Lion. It's too much!"

"Sir! You know not what you are saying!"

"I repeat . . . damn the Lion! I'll sail alone."

"Not for long, Captain Ironhand!"

"And why not?"

"The Lion has long claws."

"Not so long that I was not able to clip a couple this morning."

"Luck, sir!"

"Luck likes genius and daring, and I have both."

"Sir, I beg you, listen. You who freebooted in the Caribe

Sea were used to disposing of your plunder in a haphazard way. Here it is an operation of the utmost delicacy. We have channels by which any amount or kind of cargo can be forwarded to the highest paying markets. There's another consideration. How long could you survive the vigilance of the English Navy without forewarning as to the positions of the men-of-war? Not for long! Protection, markets and sure booty, are these not worth while?"

Challoner assumed a thoughtful air. "You speak the language of reason, Captain Hassan, but I never gave Reason much credit. Let me ponder the matter."

"While I remain here as your prisoner?"

"Not at all. Go back to your ship."

"Free to continue my action?"

"Action against the Bolivian?"

"Yes."

"You'd go against her alone?"

"Why not?"

Challoner slapped his thigh. "By Jove, you whet my appetite! Let *me* take the Bolivian on the Lion's terms." He had thrown the offer like dice, hardly hoping to win.

"Very well," said the Turk with surprising suddenness. "Prove it wasn't luck this morning. I'll lead you to the rendezvous. Take the Bolivian, any way you please. She'll cross us some time within the next thirty-six hours."

Challoner would long have cause to remember those thirty-six hours of waiting. He had thought to have Kit McKenna under control. He hadn't plumbed the depths of a woman's imagination.

With only a thin mahogany panel between himself and a lovely girl, he could not fail to hear her slightest movement . . . almost her breathing! A low sob pierced the wood like an arrow. "James!"

Pulling on his breeches, Challoner unlocked the door. "Are you ill?"

"Yes," she groaned. "It is here . . . that I hurt!" She clapped a tiny hand to her heart—darling, ludicrous figure in one of his linen shirts.

"The stew was greasy," said Challoner. "I'll give you some sal."

"Ugh! No! I'm not ill . . . I'm lonesome!"

Suddenly it came to Challoner that he must place Miss Kit on the defensive . . . or else he'd succumb.

"Lonesome eh? Well, m' dear . . . life at sea *is* lonesome. Back to your quarters, now. Let's have some quiet." He spun her about, pushed her into the inner cabin and hooked the door.

His pulses were beating so wildly that he could not bring himself to try sleep. What were women made of, that they could tease themselves and their victims . . . and suffer only a setback to their female pride? He went on deck and kept a lonely vigil with his thoughts.

All was quiet as he went below at daybreak. He was shaving when his lad Cricky brought a tray.

The click of utensils wakened his fair neighbor in the inner cabin. "James! I'm hungry!" This through the door panel.

When he opened the door, she stumbled toward him over the folds of his nightshirt. Her red curls were wildly tousled. There was sleep in her glaucous eyes.

He controlled the desire to take her in his arms and kiss her awake. "Here's a cup of milk and some bread, Miss Prisoner, and . . . back to your cell!" said Challoner firmly. He choked on his toast. Jove! What a pass for a red-blooded man to be in . . . and him . . . in love!

It was nearly noon. Except for the silhouette of the *Jewal,* Challoner's glass showed only sea and sky, the tinny brightness of it burning the eyeballs.

At last, the Watch hailed from the masthead. "Sail ho!"

What eyes the lad had. If it were the Bolivian ship, the *Lerida,* she was a mere speck in the glass. Yes, the *Jewal* was luffing about. Her signal came. *"Lerida* sighted."

She came up like a duck crossing a pond. Then, presumably, her captain having seen the two lurking vessels, she veered off and broke out more sail. Was she going to run for it? The *Paramour* had nothing to lose in a race— not so the *Jewal.* Her canvas was smaller. She'd lag in the rear.

"Make all sail!" said Challoner to his first mate.

The order sped along the deck. The men went to matching speed. The topmen, having reached the yards, were letting out tops'l . . . with the increase of canvas, the *Paramour* surged forward like a running horse.

Soon the distance between her and the *Lerida* was halved—then quartered. And the *Lerida* came about with a great flapping of sails. Her signals fluttered in the breeze.

"The *Lerida*. Captain Ortego-Patrick. What do you want of us?"

"Heave to. We're boarding," Challoner dictated to his signal man.

"With what authority, sir?" asked the *Lerida's* captain.

"Go to the devil with your authority! You are our prize, sir!"

There was evidence that Captain Ortego-Patrick was ready to give battle, for a puff of gunsmoke burst from the *Lerida's* forward deck. The shot fell vastly short of the *Paramour*.

"Slacken all sail, Boggs. Haul up the Jolly," said Challoner to his first mate. "Put a shot across her bow."

A geyser of water gave the gunner gauge of his good aim, and Captain Ortego-Patrick, proof of the pirate ship's intentions. A white flag climbed the mast.

"We surrender!" bawled the *Lerida's* captain through the horn.

The quarter boat dropped with its load of cork-blackened flymen, Challoner went down the ladder and aboard. Oars dipped. The quarter boat shot forward.

The *Lerida's* rail was lined with a sunflower row of worried faces—among which, sandy-haired Captain Ortego-Patrick. Was he one of those sons of Irish *émigrés* to the South American possessions of Spain or Portugal? He bellowed in Irish-accented English, "What is the meaning of this outrage?"

Challoner did not answer until he'd set foot on the *Lerida's* deck.

"I am informed that you have gold aboard, sir. Hand it over and I'll allow you to proceed."

"Gold? I have no gold! I am carrying passengers to Lisbon."

"Sir, you lie," said Challoner. "Either you hand over the gold or we'll search and take it."

"I tell you, I have no gold!" spluttered Captain Ortego-Patrick.

At this, a beautiful woman in great hooped skirts and a black mantilla stepped from the companionway and swept down-deck.

"What do these ruffians want, Captain Ortego-Patrick?" she asked haughtily. "If it is ransom, pay them, so that we may continue our journey."

"This ship is carrying gold, Madam," said Challoner stepping up to the lady.

She spun around, her eyes fastened first upon the iron glove in the gilt bandolier. "Who are you?" she gasped, a ringed hand pressing her bosom.

"Captain Ironhand of the privateer the *Paramour*," said Challoner. "May I ask who *you* are?"

"You are addressing the Marquesa de Valalodad Hermoso, sister of the Viceroy of Bolivia!" answered the lady with icy dignity—at which Captain Ortego-Patrick struck his forehead with his palm in a truly Latin gesture of despair.

"Excellency! Why did you reveal your identity? These cutthroats will kill us all and take Your Excellency for ransom."

"Oh, no!" said Challoner. "All I want is the gold."

"And I declare, with our good captain, we have no gold!" said the Marquesa.

Challoner gave Flymaster Maunday the signal he was eagerly awaiting. Swift and silent, the flymen ducked into hatches and companionways, held the *Lerida's* crew at bay and established battle rule over the captured ship.

They began a search that ended in futility. There was no gold aboard the *Lerida*.

Challoner knew what he must do in order to make the threat of Ironhand good.

"Seize the women and transboard them to the *Paramour*," he said in low tones to the flymaster.

A pack of screaming, weeping, scratching, kicking women were placed in one of the *Lerida's* boats and lowered into the sea while her crew stood at bay under the menace of the flymen's cutlasses and pistols.

But Maunday's sharp eye did not find the beautiful Marquesa among the lot. "Lower away!" he ordered. "It seems we're short a passenger. I'll bring her aboard with my own hands."

Where had she disappeared? Maunday conducted the search singlehanded—going from deck to deck and from cabin to cabin, looking under bunks and tables, throwing open wardrobe doors. The perfume of the women lingered here. Silks, furbelows had been strewn about at the moment of panic. His zeal was rewarded at last. A gasp coming from a dim corner of one of the cabins betrayed the fugitive hiding in a garderobe.

"Come out, lady," said Maunday gently.

The Marquesa braced herself against the walls of the garderobe. "Kill me! I'd rather die than be captured by you savages."

What a beauty she was! "Lady," said Maunday, "you'll be safe aboard our ship, I swear it. Captain Ironhand is a fine gentleman. He'll defend you with his life!"

The Marquesa stepped out of her hiding place. "Will *you* defend me with *your* life?"

"Why . . . yes . . . for certain, I will!" stammered Maunday.

"Then I commend myself to your care, bold one." The Marquesa held out her little white hand.

Challoner blinked when he saw his doughty flymaster handing a lady on deck with all the gallantry a storybook prince would bestow upon a princess.

"So . . . our runaway has been found?"

"Aye, sir," said Maunday, turning lobster red. "She agreed to trust herself to me."

"I see!" Challoner concealed a smile. "Get her to our ship, lock the lot in my office and stand by to scuttle the *Lerida*."

He watched the *Lerida* sink with a sad heart. Some of the crew went overboard but redheaded Captain Ortego-Patrick went down with his ship in the best tradition of men of the sea. What must one do in the name of King and Country. What atrocities must one commit? Three ships and their crews sunk, and a dozen women of noble birth taken hostage? Where would it end? "I must get Kit off *this* pirate!" he thought. "Who knows when it may be my turn to go to Davy Jones' locker with all hands aboard."

The Turk hailed from the *Jewal*. "Have you found the gold?"

"No gold. Where away?"

"Make after me, Ironhand effendi."

6.

Reputation that Reeks to High Heaven

A BOATLOAD OF MALE SURVIVORS FROM THE "LERIDA" GOT to the coast by dint of oar and sweat. Their report of the sinking of the Bolivian and the abduction of women by a pirate wearing a hand of iron was transferred to Lisbon by semaphore. His Majesty's Envoy to King Joseph of Portugal dispatched the news to the Admiralty, in London; and that same day, Admiral Lord Wilmington brought the news to his friend, Admiral Lord Frawley.

"Seems to me our chap is going a bit too far, Greg."

"Not at all!" chuckled Lord Frawley. "He acts in our best interest. You'll notice . . . he hasn't sunk an English ship."

"Mark my word, he will!" retorted Lord Wilmington. "He'll do the very devil's work in order to win!"

The same day the two admirals were conversing in a quiet study in Chelsea, London, the subject of their conversation was sailing into the Bay of Tangier, in the wake of the *Jewal*.

The Moroccan city, bathed in royal purple of sunset, presented a grandiose vista from the sea, rising gradually in the form of an amphitheater, with the citadel on the left, and the ruins of York Castle and the English Mole on the right.

The waggoner said of the Bay of Tangier—"Extensive harbor and good in all weathers except during a strong east wind, but vessels of any size have to anchor a mile or so out, as the shore to the west is shallow and sandy, and to the east, rocky and shingly."

Suddenly, the *Jewal* was no longer in view. Where had she vanished?

The *Paramour's* sails hauled, and anchor down, Challoner trained his glass on the beach. Night was falling fast, the heat like a pall and the stars glittering in a sable sky, when a craft resembling the oared ships of ancient Egypt put away from the shore and headed out to the *Paramour.* She was long, at least sixty foot. Challoner counted twenty black-skinned men at the oars, and four helmsmen, bow and stern. She'd a roof like a canopy, midship. Her sides were painted yellow and blue and the canopy was yellow. She'd one sail, a lateen square. This sail reefed. At her masthead, the green flag of Islam, and a second ensign. A lion in red on a field of white.

Challoner was surprised to see Captain Hassan on her foredeck.

"Captain Ironhand, the *Paramour,* ahoy," called the Turk when the oared craft neared. "Captain Hassan and friends wish to come aboard."

"Captain Hassan and his friends are welcome," answered Challoner.

The ladder was lowered. Four white-robed, turbaned Moors followed on the Turk's heels. A silent quartette! Shown to chairs, they squatted, Arab style, on the bare deck and stared at the metal glove hanging from Challoner's epaulette.

"What can I do for these gentlemen?" Challoner asked the Turk.

"Answer a question or two, Ironhand effendi."

"Ask away!"

"First . . . the gold? Are you certain there was no gold aboard the *Lerida?*"

"My men went over her inch by inch."

"And . . . then you scuttled her. Why?" said the Turk sharply.

Challoner answered in the same manner. "Because I chose to scuttle her."

A murmur ran from Moor to Moor when this piece of bombast had been translated into Arabic.

Had he, Challoner wondered, created an illusion—loud-mouthed, simple-minded, thick-skinned fighter of the sea? Would they take him for what he purported to be, undisciplined hothead and renegade? He added a purple touch for good measure.

"Gentlemen! We of the Caribe Sea are brethren of the man-eater shark, who has teeth like saws and an appetite like the elephant. And as for women! Bah! They say Solomon's harem numbered six hundred. I have forgotten the number of my wives, only that I sold my harem for ten thousand sterling to a slave trader when I departed."

Another murmur.

"Ironhand, effendi," said the Turk, "tell my friends how you disposed of your plunder in the regions of the Caribe?"

"How I disposed of my plunder? In excellent fashion, I assure you. And it is the problem, now, how to dispose of plunder, that caused me to consider joining with you Moroccans. A stranger in foreign waters must proceed with caution. Take the treasure I already have aboard my ship, where can I market it?"

"You cannot, sir," said the Turk. "Not without our help. Such treasure must be coined or worked into jewelry before it can be forwarded to the proper agents."

Challoner assumed an air of surprise. "Coined . . . yes, if you have the moulds, but . . . geegaws? I sold my bar gold to go-betweens of the King's Governor in the Caribe."

"The North Atlantic is not the Caribe, Captain Iron-hand," said the Turk. "My friends also wish to know why you deem it necessary to sink your captures? Such is not our mode of operation. We seize cargo and crew and passengers. We leave the vessel afloat, able to sail another day."

"Gentlemen," said Challoner, lifting one eyebrow. "You do your way, I'll do mine. No hard feelings, eh? The women I have aboard . . . take 'em. I've no time for petticoat trade. I'll up anchor and sail my own course."

This proposal was the subject of another whispered conference between the Moors.

Then the Turk adopted a more conciliatory tone. "Ironhand effendi, my friends and I . . . the Lion himself . . . would regret losing an ally of your mettle, who sails a ship the likes of your *Paramour*."

"The Lion himself! Now there's an idea!" exclaimed Challoner. "Let me talk to the Lion himself. Perhaps *he* could win me over to his way of thinking . . . make me see the wisdom of your methods, in contrast to mine."

"You'd go to the Lion?" exclaimed the Turk.

"I was King's Governor's friend in the Caribe," Challoner answered boastfully. "I can be Lion's friend in Morocco."

After another whispered conference, the Turk again turned to Challoner.

"We shall have to dispatch a messenger to the Lion."

Challoner waved his hand. "Dispatch! Dispatch! Time is not the essence. I'll visit Tangier while awaiting the Lion's invitation."

"No!" said Captain Hassan quickly. "It would not be healthy for you or your crew to visit Tangier."

"Oh? Why?" asked Challoner.

"Because, sir, the Caliph welcomes only those to whom he gives freedom of the port."

"And why should the Caliph refuse *me* freedom?"

"For many reasons, Captain . . . one of which is that you have not yet been accepted by the Lion."

"I see," said Challoner, yielding the point with a shrug. "The Lion is my passport to Morocco. Very well, I'll wait aboard the *Paramour*."

"Excellent idea," said Captain Hassan, "and should anyone question your right to lie here, my ship will be within hailing distance. Now, effendi, since you have no use for the women, we'll take them off your hands."

A voice said at Challoner's shoulder, "Sir . . . will you not keep the women aboard?"

Challoner turned in surprise. "Maunday! You . . . asking to keep a covey of women aboard?"

"Sir, I feel for them."

"Your sentiments are noble," said Challoner concealing a smile. "I cannot refuse the Turk."

"Sir . . . do not hand over the Marquesa?" stammered Maunday.

"Sorry, Flymaster!" said Challoner crisply. "The Marquesa goes with the rest."

Maunday made a little gesture. "Aye, aye, sir." He turned and went below with a long face.

A sad lot of females filed out of the companionway. All
their starch and pride, gone. Challoner felt pity for them.
But this was one of the accidents of war. Some won. Some
lost! Some lived. Some died! He watched the jolly boat
pull away. The women were pictures of dejection.

He'd scarcely opened his office door when a lady appeared in silhouette. She was carrying her head high under
a mantilla of black lace. Her full skirts billowed around
her. (A little too long, those skirts!) She had red-gold hair
and sea-green eyes. Kit McKenna!

"How did you get out of the inside cabin?" he gasped.

"I picked the lock with a pin," she answered saucily.

"Those Spanish fripperies?"

"The Marquesa lent 'em to me."

"You spoke to the Marquesa?"

"I did. She offered to smuggle me off this ship. I refused, saying I was your wench. Her manner changed after
that. She regarded me with pious scorn. Oh! those grand
ladies! But my friend Lady Artis Grantley is different. She
is not proud."

"Different indeed!" mumbled Challoner. He'd caught
sight of his cabin lad's face down the companionway.
Cricky had seen the girl! Soon it would be all over the ship
that the Captain had a woman in his quarters!

And now the Turk appeared.

"Ah! I see one of the ladies has been left behind!" he
said with a smug smile.

Challoner took the only way out of his dilemma.

"You vixen!" Seizing Kit by the arm, he said sharply,
"Inside!"

"Effendi!" protested the Turk. "You gave *us* the women!"

"This one is *my* wench," said Challoner. "She must have
thought she could escape by mingling with the others. What
a wildcat!"

"A wildcat . . . but a pretty one," murmured the Turk.
"Well . . . if you say she is your woman . . ."

Calmly seated at his desk, the "wildcat," in mantilla and
a silk skirt, was nibbling the Captain's goose quill. So fair!
So impudent!

Challoner closed the door, locked it and slipped the key
in his pocket. "Now, young lady!"

"Wait!" murmured Kit, narrowing her green eyes as though to take a better focus of the scene. "I dreamed it would be like this. You'd lock the door, put the key in your pocket, then you'd come to me and sweep me into your arms and kiss me."

"I'll turn you over my knee!" said Challoner with shortened breath.

Her laughter tinkled like a music box. "Dear, dear, Mr. Challoner, I forgive you, because, you see, I knew what you would do. Precisely what you did! Claim me for what I wish to be . . . your wench."

Challoner kept a tight rein on his temper.

"See here, Kit, don't make things more difficult for me than they are now!"

Suddenly she was in his arms, planting tear-wet kisses on his cheeks. "Dearest! Dearest! I'll never leave you. Never! I love you! I love you!"

He felt the very marrow of his bones turning to liquid. Pulses pounding, he gathered her into his arms. One more kiss . . . he'd wipe Miss McKenna off the slate . . . and embrace a pirate's wench! Soft . . . soft! Lips like warm dew! Green eyes crackling with amber lights!

"My Ironhand," she whispered.

Knock-knock at the door!

Challoner put her away. "Sit down in that corner and behave," he said harshly. His hand shook as he fumbled in his pocket, found the key, opened the door. It was the first mate. Boggs' gaze turned to the lady, demurely seated in a corner. "Sir, the men have wind of it . . . that you've kept one of the ladies aboard."

"I know," said Challoner. "Cricky saw her before I could lock her inside."

"It'll mean trouble, sir."

"I fear it will. We'll face the issue when it comes to a head."

"Aye, sir," said Boggs. "I'll do my best to make light of the whole thing."

Challoner heard little fists softly pounding the cabin door as he locked Kit in her quarters.

"James! James! Shall I see you tonight?"

Her whispered query sent a tremor through his nerves.

Did Kit understand, fully, with what kind of fire she was juggling? How weak the male? How very weak?

Ill at ease in his improvised quarters, Challoner opened the tome by Yarborough and turned the pages, reading a little here, a little there. Wrote the author on page sixty-seven:

> We Europeans hold Moorish rovers in high contempt, deeming them bloodthirsty robbers. However, to the Moors [Yarborough used the term Moslims], they are religious warriors whose duty it is to punish the Nazarenes for having rejected Mahomet and adhered to Christ.

If this were true, the conspiracy of the Moorish sea rovers would take on a new color and dimension—not merely a handful of rogues—resolute fanatics—thirsting for Nazarene blood. The Lion? What kind of man was he? What race? A Moor made of the conquering stuff of the Abencerrages? A European cut to the jib of a Drake or a Hawkins?

Restless, perspiring from the heat, Challoner shut the book and went on deck. A spirit of power brooded o'er this African land. Out of the Continent, there outlined in dark masses against the starry sky, had come the harassers of Europe. Mahomet's disciples. Islam's cohorts. Pushed back after bloody centuries, were they biding their time? Would another Mahomet arise? Would Christendom again feel the sword of the Faithful?

Who was this African satrap who flew his own flag with King Lion in red on a white background? Could he claim descendance from the Prophet of Mecca? Call himself Defender of the Faith? Explainer of the Greater Law? Where did he lurk? Tangier? Rabat? Taraisk? Darel-Beida? Tetuan? Fedala? Agadir? Names as old as Shem. Or did he hide behind the rocky wastes of the desert? Meknes? Fez? Challoner spent the rest of the torrid night slumped in a chair, eyes turning from the dark sea to the galaxies of heaven. But he saw neither sea nor heaven—only a girl's face. Kit's green eyes, taunting him. Kit's dewy lips reaching to his.

Her image followed him into the land of sleep so that

when a hand shook him awake, he heard himself mutter "Kit!" under his breath.

The sun had come up with a fury unmatched by dawnings in northern climes. It was Will Boggs who had shaken him awake. The first mate seemed to have something on his mind.

"Well, Mister Boggs?"

"I shouldn't speak, sir."

"Well then, hold your tongue," grinned Challoner.

"I can't, sir. It's something you should know."

"In that case, limber your tongue."

Boggs lowered his voice to a froggy whisper. "Sir . . . I 'as it in strictest confidence from Cricky who was cabin boy aboard Lord Grantley's yacht, *Seabird*, three years this spring. The lady you've locked in your quarters is Lord Grantley's widow."

Challoner blinked, moistened his lips, said slowly, "Has the sun given you a brain stroke, Boggs?"

"No, sir," said Boggs soberly. "It's the ruddy truth. Cricky spent six months aboard the *Seabird*. He says he'd know her ladyship among a thousand . . . as 'oo wouldn't, if they'd ever set eyes on her?"

"Carry on, Boggs," said Challoner. At the moment, he was too dumfounded to say anything more.

7.

Fine Knacks for Ladies!

ARTIS OR KIT, LADY GRANTLEY OR MISS MCKENNA, you had her measure. Dimity and challis or silks and satins? Horse trainer's daughter or Diana huntress, you paid your penny and took your choice. Challoner laughed bitterly as he thought of little Kit's defense of her school friend and patroness, Lady Artis Grantley. Defendant and counsel for the defense at one and the same time!

Angry bewilderment pursued him as he walked the hot

deck, that he should have been so blind as not to have detected the aristocrat under the skin of Kit. Swallowed the lies she'd fed him, swallowed them whole!

What was this curse on James Challoner that decreed he should be made a fool by two—not one mind you—two women of high birth? Given wealth, power and their choice of men, why must they bend to an impecunious Navy captain? He'd gone, minding his own business, until they'd crossed his path.

Putting down his anger, Challoner tried to think what course to take with Lady Grantley. Should he let her know *he* knew she was Lady Grantley or go on addressing himself to Kit McKenna? "Lady Grantley or Kit McKenna, I'll keep out of her way," he muttered under his breath. For he knew in his bones that if she continued as she had been doing—teasing him with kisses, caresses, soft words— some day he'd throw reserve to the winds! "And what if I should?" he argued with himself. "Where's the harm? I'd not be ravishing a virgin! I'd only be taking what my predecessors have taken—and thank you kindly ma'am."

Memory dredged up anecdotes and remarks heard over after-dinner wine, and the images they presented to the listener.

"Lady Grantley . . . Courtesanerie lost when Lady Artis was born in a blazoned cradle!"

"They tell about Lady Grantley. . . . Once she'd put one lover in one closet and another in the other. Her soubrette set the paper basket afire with a singeing taper. Lady Grantley screamed 'Help'! Out jumped the two and at each other until both were felled . . . all bloody . . . on my lady's carpet. And that's how Number Three found 'em when he came in."

"These high-born Jezebels . . ."

Some of this might have been froth of slander. Some of it must be true. How much, good Lord?

As the long day wore on, Challoner was aware of a change in the attitude of the crew. They stood around in knots, talking among themselves. They cast underbrow looks at the bridge.

Boggs gave the explanation.

"They say, there were twelve women. Enough to go

around if they took turns. They say it's in their contract.
No women. That stands for captain as for crew."

"Who's the loudest talker?" broke in Challoner.

"A gunner, sir. Big Harry he calls himself. He wanted
to lay over in San Carlos . . . have a bit o' fun with the
girls. He was left with 'is powder dry."

"Speak to Gunner-Captain Jack Scotland, Mister Boggs.
If this Big Harry keeps wagging his tongue, he'll end up
in the brig on a mutiny charge."

"Sir . . ." said Boggs, pulling a long face. "Big Harry
is the best wrestler aboard. He's givin' the young-uns les-
sons. They swear by him. They'd turn restless if he goes
to the brig."

"Wrestler, eh?" Challoner grinned. "Mister Boggs, set
up a match to be held as soon as the sun has gone down.
Tell the men I'm offering a belt of ten guineas to anyone
who will take *me* on and drop me, two out of three."

Boggs scratched his bullethead, saying, "Sir . . . you're
quick. You're strong. But Big Harry is a half head taller
. . . and two stone over your weight."

"Carry on, Mister Boggs," said Challoner.

Captain's bridge is the watchtower of ships—a sound-
ing board for rumor. Not an hour passed before Challoner
knew that the spirit of his crew had altered. Promise of
sport, action, a change in the deadly tempo of waiting in
kettle-hot waters, with sails furled—above all, their Captain's challenge had charged them with fresh interest and
energy. Lines were being tested, decks whitestoned, guns
cleaned. Captain's lad, Cricky, was washing Captain's table
linens.

"They're fair pleased, sir," said Boggs when he returned
to the bridge.

Challoner nicked his head in the direction of a giant of
a man briskly wielding an oiled rag on the mechanism of
one of the truck guns. "Is that Big Harry?"

"Yes sir."

"Has he dropped the subject of our lady passenger?"

"Sir," grinned Boggs, "who'd think about a petticoat
when there's a match ahead?"

"About the lady, Boggs. Has she been served with
proper food?"

"Her meal was sent in at noon, sir. She took only a lemon and a cup of tea from the tray."

"She'll eat when she gets hungry," said Challoner with a shrug.

Boggs cracked the knuckles of one hand, then the other. "Sir . . . Cricky says 'e 'eard 'er cryin', sir. 'E's fair took with the lady's looks."

"She has plenty to cry about," muttered Challoner. With all his heart he wished he could put Lady Artis Grantley ashore and consign her to the British Crown Agent in Tangier. But the Turk had warned him against setting foot in the Moroccan city, and if this warning were not sufficient, author Yarborough also had *his* say.

"Crown agents have no standing in Morocco," he wrote on page 120 of his African tome.

> They are but shallow observers who do not understand and are not allowed to investigate; mere stampers of invoices for the merchandise that flows between Morocco and the Continent. When they appear before the Caliph at public functions, they must go bare-headed and on foot, while he sits on a white horse under the imperial umbrella. And do not think it does not delight him to keep them sweltering in the noonday sun!

Well, turn and turn about. Where was the poor Caliph when the English conquered Tangier? In flight—white horse, imperial umbrella and all!

Day had almost waned before an idea struck him. Have Lady Grantley on deck to witness the wrestling match, thereby killing three birds with one stone: relieve Helmsman Peters of the need to keep his big mouth shut, destroy the Kit McKenna legend, and set Lady Artis Grantley squarely on her own two little feet, vis-à-vis the men of the *Paramour*.

Proceeding to his quarters, Challoner ordered the door opened and sent the guard away.

Dressed only in a shift, the lady presented a charming and pathetic picture stretched upon the bunk in the torrid afternoon heat. Her petticoats and mantilla lay on the floor. Her amazing hair curled in damp coppery ringlets around her brow. Her cheeks and chin and bare shoulders were highlighted with mother-of-pearl tints. She stared at him without blinking an eyelash.

"Lady Grantley?"

She sprang to her feet, stammering. "Y . . . you called me . . . Lady Grantley. Why?"

"Because you *are* Lady Grantley."

Her green eyes seemed to film over as she received the full impact of his words.

"So . . . you know. How did you find out?"

"Intelligence from London," said Challoner acidly.

"How could anyone know where I am, Mr. Challoner?"

"Need I answer you, Madam?" said Challoner.

"No!" This, sharply. "But I am curious. My solicitor thinks I am visiting friends in Touraine. McKenna thinks I am in Scotland."

Challoner steeled himself against the appeal of her eyes and voice. "Will your ladyship please dress, and come with me?"

"Come where? What are you going to do with me?"

"If I did what I would like, I'd lash you to the mast and give you the cat-o'-nine-tails."

She drew herself up to the last quarter inch of her diminutive height. "You wouldn't!"

"No, ma'am," said Challoner. "Damaged goods fetch low prices. I intend to collect handsomely for your return to the arms of . . . whom shall we say? Who is your current heartbeat?"

She sidled up to him. "Captain Ironhand. I remember an old saw . . . 'Sticks and stones can break my bones but words' . . ."

Oh, lure of fair women! Challoner picked up the rag of green silk at her feet.

"Your ladyship's attire."

While she slipped into the gown, he retrieved the black lace mantilla. She stepped to the door and used its glossy panel for a looking glass.

"Have you a comb, Mr. Challoner, or Captain Ironhand, or whatever you like to call yourself?"

He handed her his pocket comb and she arranged her ringlets in more orderly fashion, then gave it back with a murmured "Thank you."

"I suppose I *have* been horrid," she said, "but I've been no more horrid than you. First you said you were James Challoner. Then you turned into Captain Ironhand . . .

as black a pirate as ever lived! I saw you sink three vessels with these eyes! *These!"* She poked two indexes at the plump of her cheeks. "You had the crew shot like sitting ducks. You handed twelve Christian ladies over to the Moors. *All this I saw with these eyes!* And now you affect tremendous indignation for *my* supposed sins? Were they sins, Captain Ironhand? What is a woman made for, if not for love? And who taught me differently, I pray? Not my stag-hunting father! Not my governesses who were busy with their own little fornications! Not my husband . . . himself a rip of the best! We matched loves . . . who'd collect the most! We'd tally 'em on the bed head. My lovers? They were out for what *they* could bag! Then *you* came along. Ex-Navy Captain, James Challoner! Oh, yes! I took the trouble to find out who you were. What I found pleased me. 'Here's one who hasn't a penny or a hope to his name,' I said to myself. 'All he has are handsome looks and a residue of human dignity that clings to him like ravelings of silk. He believes I am a horse trainer's daughter,' I said to myself. 'He loves me for . . . *me!* Not for my million pounds. Not for my castles and hunting boxes and wine cellars and all the rest that money can buy.' You kissed me as you'd have kissed a maiden, Mr. Challoner, and my heart nestled under you like a fledgling under its mother's wing."

The pearly luster of her face so near his, the rose of her lips!

"Madam," said Challoner hoarsely. "What you have just said will read well in your Memoirs. Write them! They'll sell better than Pepys' Diary!"

"Oh, how good we are at the retort *mordaunt*, Captain!" she cried, clapping her hands in mock applause.

He stopped the gesture with a cold, "Madam! Listen to me!" and, stepped back two paces—not to be within the aura of her person. "My crew resents your presence on our ship. I am seeking to pacify them, and in order to do this I shall have to make your identity known. They'll respect Lady Grantley while they would not respect a red-headed wench without handle of nobility. Please behave as the precariousness of your situation demands."

Saying neither aye nor nay, she adjusted her mantilla and followed him.

Another scarlet and purple sunset was blazing over the African sea when Challoner, stripped to the waist and in stocking feet, faced an ox of a man! Ox with a grudge. He'd wide, muscled shoulders with the forward droop that comes of lifting ball and hauling iron cannon. Bullethead! Fists like battering rams.

The crew of the *Paramour,* barring none, were mustered for the match. Even Cook had come out of his galley. Challoner could hear bets fly.

"Three bob on Big Harry, three to one."

Mister Boggs' worried face!

"Cumberland style?" said Challoner, flexing his arms.

"Aye!" Big Harry answered, forgetting the "sir." And why shouldn't he forget. Were there not limits to a pirate's royalty? That limit reached, the dividing line between captain and crew was so thin as to be invisible.

"Remember, Big Harry," said Challoner. *"Two* falls out of three . . . and as Lancashire Dan would say, 'no kneeing or kidney blows. Fight fair and may the best man win.' "

Striving for a first "trip," thick welts sprang up along the arms of the big gunner and Challoner's shoulders purpled under the iron pressure of his adversary's biceps. Nimble footwork was soundless on the smooth deck— only Challoner's ear heard the creak of a backbone, a sob crushed from collapsed lungs. Throwing off the Lancashireman, Challoner glanced at Lady Grantley, who was leaning on the rail of the quarter-deck. Her expression was intent, alert, the decorum of a sportswoman, almost the cool demeanor of a referee.

Big Harry was trying for a back-heel maneuver to get a leg behind his opponent's heel on the outside. Failing this, he tried the "hank," lifting the opponent off the deck after a sudden spin.

But Challoner met him with a countermove—deftly he kicked Big Harry from behind, where the knee bends, and threw him backward, falling him, shoulders down, and holding.

"One fall!" counted the Lancashireman from where he lay. "The fall's fair."

Released, he bounded to his feet and grappled for a second bout.

This time Challoner took the offensive with a cross-buttock throw. Big Harry landed on fingertips and knee-caps. Seeing his opponent so strong and sure, Challoner put the pressure on.

Down went Big Harry on a lucky "chip" but he rebounded . . . caught the downer unprepared . . . floored him! "One fall each!" he counted. "It's still two out of three."

Challoner's most successful trick was the swinging "hype" he'd learned from a Westmoreland man—lift the opponent, swing clear around, get the left knee under his right leg and carry it high for a throw. He made a try, and failed.

"Westmoreland?" grunted Big Harry. "I knows that 'un!"

The salt of the Lancashireman on his lips, Challoner tossed rules overboard and let fist and knee go to work for victory. For a moment, Big Harry's surprise gave him an advantage, then . . . ! He was thrown clear and out of reach of his opponent.

"Free-for-all, Cap'n?" said Big Harry, bullethead lowered and chin stuck out.

"No hits barred!" answered Challoner.

Two boxers put fists up.

A banging blow to midriff knocked the breath out of Challoner. He danced away, recovered, came back and let the Lancashireman have a bruiser under the heart.

The crew roared its delight!

In a clinch, Big Harry and Ironhand worked on kidneys and chinned clavicles.

"Ahah!" gasped Challoner, and disengaged himself. Big Harry's right fist ripped again and he reeled, but with footing regained, he raked the gunner's jaw in a catlike strike that snapped his head backward. Thinking to end the fight, he bore in with a bulldog charge, but Big Harry was ready.

Arms locked around heaving torsos, they punched and pummeled it from rail to rail, the watchers scattering before them like quail before bird dogs.

Challoner would have gone over the rail had the Lancashireman not seized him by one knee and hauled him back. The effort unbalanced him. Down went both men, head over heels!

"Five bob sez Cap'n'll never rise," roared a voice from the mob.

But Captain did rise! Challoner circled, sparred, feinted. If Big Harry couldn't be overcome by physical might, his chin button was certainly no harder than that of any other man! *Crrack!* snapped the paralyzing blow. Down went the big fellow like the ox he so strongly resembled.

Cheers broke the deathly silence that followed the Lancashireman's fall.

Challoner backed away from hands that would have lifted him on brawny shoulders. "Carry on, men, and let's hear no more about Lady Grantley! She'll remain our passenger until such time as I can collect ransom for her person."

"Aye aye, Sir. Ransom . . . and a fat one for Lady Grantley!"

8.

Into the Lion's Den

THE EVENING OF THE THIRD DAY OF ANCHORAGE OFF TANgier, the Watch sang, "Ship ahoy!"

It was the same oared craft that had rendezvoused with the *Paramour* before.

The Turk came aboard, salaaming low. "The Lion bids you welcome, Ironhand effendi."

"Oh?" said Challoner, affecting a calm he was far from possessing. "Has the Caliph arranged for my safe conduct into Tangier?"

"Not Tangier, effendi. Your ship will stay at anchor here. Fresh provisions and water will be brought aboard. You and the Englishwoman will come with me."

"The Englishwoman? No, Captain Hassan!" said Challoner firmly. "She stays aboard ship."

The Turk spoke softly but with persuasive tones. "Effendi. Where would your mistress be safer . . . here, or in *your* company?"

Challoner sensed a hidden meaning in the Turk's words. He was not asking, he was conveying the order of a higher-up.

"Why is the Lion so anxious that I bring the woman along, Captain Hassan?"

"The Lion is never 'anxious,' as you put it," the Turk answered with a bland smile. "Either you bring the woman with you or you make sail and . . . try to leave our waters."

"Meaning . . . that I would promptly have my head blown off by your shore batteries?" said Challoner with a grin.

"The words are yours, Ironhand effendi," murmured the Turk.

Challoner debated with himself. Leave the *Paramour* under first mate Boggs' command and comply with the mysterious Lion's request, or risk the ship's very life. He was still debating when Flymaster Maunday presented himself at the door left open because of the great heat.

"Sir, may I have a word with you?"

"Two, Maunday."

"Sir . . . word is going round that you're takin' a trip to where the Moors are hiding."

"Word travels fast aboard the *Paramour*, Flymaster."

"Aye, sir. Will you take me?"

"Is it the Marquesa, Maunday?" said Challoner with a smile.

"Sir . . . the poor woman! I can't bear to think of her in them heathens' clutches!"

"I think the Marquesa is well able to take care of herself," said Challoner. "You must remain aboard and give Boggs a hand, should trouble arise."

He did not then realize that Maunday had helped him to a decision. He'd go to the Lion.

With what glee Lady Grantley received the news that she was to embark upon a new adventure!

"Where are we going?"

"I cannot say."

She'd have made a captain of adventure in the grand manner, had she been a man instead of a woman. The robes of white wool that the Turk provided for the journey, even the camels, pleased her.

"My *camel* looks very much like my aunt, the Countess of Mitford," she giggled. "Auntie has the same lip!"

She found no fault with the wooden saddle, over which sheepskin was stretched, nor did she look askance at the camel driver who was to be their guide—a villain-faced fellow, with only one eye. When Challoner helped her onto her beast she clung to his wrists with a pretty, dependent gesture.

"Oh! You're so strong!"

"So says barmaid to sailor," laughed Challoner. How hard it was to withstand her ladyship's charm!

The tawny, humpbacked beasts following nose to tail, the camel caravan wound its way into the hills under cover of night. The only sound was the jangling of the bronze bells that hung from their long necks.

Her ladyship seemed to be enjoying herself. Never weary, she sat her mount with the ease of one who has always ridden a camel! Amazing little creature! For the life of him, Challoner could not see why the Lion had made it mandatory that she come along. The caravan moved on through the night, climbing slowly but surely into higher terrain.

At dawn, the eye beheld the sea, far, far, below. The scents were not only of dust and desert flora, there were trees on the hillsides, scrubby trees, to be sure, still—trees. The caravan then entered a valley where no green thing grew. Was this the region Yarborough described . . . "desertic like the valleys of the moon"?

Halting to take food, the Turk said, "I trust you do not find riding camels too fatiguing?"

"Not I," Lady Grantley declared in her spritely manner. "I find it exhilarating."

How like Kit McKenna she was! Kit would have put it thus.

The Turk frowned. He had addressed Challoner, not a mere female!

Challoner spoke in a quick aside. "If your ladyship would only hold her tongue! Mohammedans do not encourage garrulousness among their women."

"Ah, but *I* am not a Mohammedan!" retorted Lady Grantley. "By the way, who is that little man?"

"Captain Hassan is his name," said Challoner before he realized that he was again playing up to her curiosity.

She turned to the Turk. "Captain Hassan. How many wives have you in your harem?"

The Turk's brow beetled in a prodigious frown. He barked an order to the head camelman. Bells jangling, the caravan proceeded on its way.

The evening of the second day, the travelers came to a halt on a mountain pass.

"The Lion's castle," said the Turk pointing a finger.

Challoner aimed his glass upon a blocklike structure that seemed to make one with the cliffs. Was this "castle" one of those that the Knights Templar or those of Malta had built with the aid of captive Moors in times of the Crusades? He thought it wiser not to ask.

The way led on down into a narrow gorge. At the end of the gorge was the entrance to the sanctuary. A wooden gate with iron reinforcements opened and the caravan passed into a courtyard paved with stone, then on through a second ironbound door. There was yet another court to cross. The Turk escorted the Lion's guests to a large, airy room overlooking the gorge through which they had just ridden.

The furnishings were in Moorish style—the floors and walls of tile in beautiful color, divan bed, cushions for chairs, low tables with brass or ebony and mother-of-pearl surfaces.

Two veiled serving women took charge of Lady Grantley. A young lad with large, liquid eyes and slim bare legs attended Challoner. Other servants carried in the travelers' baggage.

"How cosy *we* are going to be!" said Lady Grantley with a smile that said volumes.

Challoner drew back the silk hangings that curtained off an adjoining room. "Your quarters, Madam. It is not the custom for male and female to co-habit, night *and* day, in these lands."

"Night *or* day. Which would please my lord the most?" she answered with a little smile that mocked him.

"My troubles with this one have only just begun," thought Challoner. Again, he caught himself wondering why he'd chosen to reject what Lady Grantley offered. Was it because he feared an involvement of the heart? Falling in love with Kit McKenna was one thing. Falling in love with Lady Artis Grantley was another. In the first instance, you'd occupy a new house. In the second, the room of a wayside inn!

She lingered with a hand on the door hangings.

"What? No bolts, no locks? Are you not afraid I will fall upon you in the dead of night, my lord?"

"That I am, ma'am," said Challoner. "That I am."

She switched the curtains shut with an angry gesture.

Keep her angry, maybe she'd sulk in her own Achilles tent! "You want her so, you know you'd be putty in her hands," thought Challoner. He could not afford to be putty, now, or ever! Yet the mere idea of her so near, only a silk curtain between them, made his mouth go dry. Danger shared was a bond as strong as iron! His safety was her safety. He'd have felt the same way about Kit McKenna. Then where did the difference between Kit and Artis lie? Why . . . in a long parade of lovers! In woman's fickleness! In a great lady's volatile spirits and unbridled passions! "Call yourself Parson Challoner and be done with it!" thought Challoner bitterly. So he was constituted, and by God, he could not come down out of Parson's Pulpit!

Challoner watched a lad filling a sunken tub of blue and gold tile with cool water. The water flowed out of a bronze lion's head. How did they bring water to these heights? By hand pumps? Or was there a natural spring that supplied the fortress from somewhere in its subterranean depths? The youth spoke only Arabic.

Challoner soaked off the dust of the long journey and, draped toga-wise in a woolen bath cloth, stepped out on the terrace. The view was of the narrow gorge through which the caravan had passed, and of fold upon fold of rugged hills beyond. The walls of the fortress were sheer with the cliff. He gained the impression that there was more, much more, to this place than met the eye from his present point of vantage. He also suspected that the fortress' north façade faced the Mediterranean, for, although there was no visible evidence of it, from here, his seaman's nose could detect that faint saline aroma in the air which always betrays the presence of a large body of salt water.

Turning to the task of dressing, Challoner shaved, brushed his dark hair to a fine luster and donned pirate garb. A highly polished brass disc serving as mirror, he scrutinized his reflection critically. How far had he come? Quite some distance in miles, but there were many more miles ahead. Standing *inside* the stronghold of the chief of the Moroccan pirates, he stood on a most precarious base. One slip of the foot and all his work would be undone. The thing was—how to learn what he must learn in order to fulfill his mission—and be permitted freely to depart. What was the key to the Lion's favor? Dash? Daring? Or was it subtlety? Sagacity? Damn Yarborough! Why had he not keyed the Moslem nature with more clarity? Architecture, landscape, anecdote and personal incident were favorite ingredients of writer-travelers, but how seldom they bothered to dig deeper into those mines from which the ore of character is extracted.

Challoner placed the gifts he'd brought for the Lion on a brass tray—a handsome gold timepiece with jeweled case and a pair of dueling pistols—part of the loot taken in San Carlos.

A Moor entered and, salaaming, beckoned "Come."

Challoner handed him the gifts and was guided through a dark, twisting passage, the walls of which were made of roughhewn stone. Here and there, an oil wick shed some faint light but there were no windows in the walls and the air was close and hot. So hot that Challoner was glad when his guide unlocked an iron door and ushered him into a spacious court.

Here, another Moor became his guide, leading him into a large chamber with a vaulted ceiling, upheld by numerous pillars and walls of fretted marble.

Sparsely furnished in Moorish style, this chamber had an opulence and beauty which was in great contrast to anything Challoner had seen so far. The floor was of marble inlay, covered with silken rugs. There were niches in the walls, these decorated with vases of different shapes, sizes, color and glaze, each one a masterpiece of the potter's art.

An archway at the far end of the room gave access to a terrace. It was there that the guide directed his charge.

At first Challoner saw only the glow of a scarlet sunset on the wide, blue Mediterranean and straightway congratulated himself on his topographical acumen. The fortress *was* situated above the seashore. Then he saw a man seated cross-legged on a pile of cushions. Majestic Moses!

His broad shoulders were erect and his white silk robe, open at the front, disclosed a bronzed chest of herculean width and depth. His massive head of iron-gray hair was crowned with the green turban which marks pilgrims to Mecca and confers upon them the title of Hadji, or Holy. His iron-gray beard was close-clipped at the chin. His nose was a great, willful beak. His eyes, under thick black brows, flashed with the brightness of supreme self-confidence. Here was a Lion indeed!

The Moorish guide salaamed deeply and placed the gift tray on a low table, then, turning to Challoner, "El Hadji," he murmured in reverent tones and withdrew.

"Welcome to Castle Akbar, Captain Ironhand," said the Mosaic personage in perfect English that rumbled out of his deep chest like thunder.

"I thank you, Hadji," said Challoner, bowing.

The Holy One smiled benignly and waved the visitor to a pile of cushions on his right.

Settling himself, cross-legged, Challoner handed his host the gold watch. "Accept this small token of my esteem, Hadji. Also these pistols."

The Hadji examined the objects with nods of satisfaction. "I am informed that you made the journey from the coast in splendid time, Captain Ironhand."

"Captain Hassan set the pace. I had only to follow."

"Did you find the heat oppressive?"

"No, Hadji. I am accustomed to heat."

"Heat of the Caribe?"

"Yes, Hadji."

"I'm told you transferred to our waters by reason of need rather than by choice?"

"The Hadji's informant is not quite accurate. It is true, the day of the freebooters is almost at an end in the Caribe Sea, but it is not true that I was *forced* to leave. I could have given up my calling and settled down as a planter and gentleman, had I wished."

"Gentleman, perhaps. Planter, never," said the Hadji with a courteous smile. "We of the sea are not at home on dry land."

"Is the Hadji also a lover of the sea?"

"Ten generations of my name have sailed the oceans, Captain."

The conversation remained general in tone while servants placed knee-high tables before the Hadji and his guest
and passed brass platters heaped with food. No lamb and
rice monotony here! Wild game and meats of several
varieties were served with delicious side dishes, succulent
melons and candied fruits. No wine or spirits were served,
only the sirupy coffee of Araby that Challoner had come
to enjoy.

The meal finished, the Hadji rose and Challoner followed
suit.

"I'm fond of walking in the garden after dinner, will you
join me?"

"With pleasure, Hadji."

The garden was beautifully green and planted with a
great variety of shrubs and a few dwarf palms.

"These palms were brought from a desert oasis some
two hundred leagues to the south," said the Hadji. "I had
hoped their dates would ripen, but they fall off beforetimes.
I think it is the salty air."

Strolling beside the majestic figure in trailing robes,
Challoner maintained a provocative silence. Let Moses
speak first. After some moments of silence, he did.

"Are there date palms in the Caribe, Captain?"

"No, Hadji. There are coco palms and breadfruit trees
and many other trees bearing edible fruits and nuts. No
date palms."

The Hadji leaned on the parapet and gazed at the moonlit sea.

"Tell me, Captain Ironhand, what do you hope for, joining with us?"

"I hope to carry on in the life I like best. Sailing my
ship for gain."

"Ah! I've another question, Captain. Sooner or later
you'll come to grips with an enemy belonging to your own
natural kingdom . . ."

"I beg the Hadji's pardon. I do not consider myself to
be an Englishman in the narrow sense of the word."

"Indeed? What kind of Englishman *are* you?"

"I've been called many names, Hadji," smiled Challoner.
"Rogue. Pirate. Thief. Gallows' bait. I like to call myself
. . . a free soul."

The Hadji's glittering eye fixed Challoner.

"As a free soul, would you go against the Cross of St. George?"

His use of the name "Cross of St. George," instead of the more familiar word "Jack," put Challoner on the alert. There was hatred in the Hadji's voice as well as in his eyes. His bronzed hands gripped the parapet so tightly that the knuckles whitened.

"I've sunk the Jack before, Hadji."

"Indeed? When? In the Caribe?"

"Yes."

"It serves, but only in principle, sir."

"Only in principle?"

"Yes, Captain Ironhand. Not in practice. We never sink our captives . . . whether English or of other flags. We free them, to sail for us again and again."

"So I've been told by Captain Hassan," said Challoner. "Let us suppose some Englishman refuses to be captured. What then? Must I withhold the fire of my guns? And if I fire, must I not aim to kill?"

The Hadji spoke slowly. "If you join us, Captain Ironhand, your first duty will be to obey the Lion's orders, *blindly.*"

Challoner challenged him. "*If* I join with you. Let me defer my answer until after we've taken more stock of each other."

The Hadji toyed with his beard and eyed him from under heavy brows.

"You're a brave soul, Captain."

"Why do you call me brave? Because I'm in your . . . shall we say . . . custody? Remember the *Paramour's* guns. Ask Captain Hassan how the *Coira* and the *Nina* and the *Lerida* were sunk."

The Hadji laughed heartily.

"By the Prophet! I like you, Captain Ironhand! Sleep on it. Let me know your decision tomorrow . . . whether you will sail under my supreme command or . . . alone."

"And if I decide to sail alone, Hadji?"

"You are free, Captain. You are free. I might add that freedom is a relative thing in *my* point of view."

"I see. You'd do your best to destroy me."

The Hadji's glittering eye fixed him.

"You'll have safe conduct back to your ship . . . then, beware!"

"A duel, eh? My guns against the Caliph's guns?"

"Who can tell how you will be destroyed, O Ironhand," said the Moor eying the spiked glove. "You might even scratch yourself to death!" He gave another hearty laugh that covered the threat his words implied and then he changed the subject abruptly, asking, "Do you play chess, sir?"

A first game—the Moor winning—was followed by a second, that Challoner won. The checkmate arrived at, the Hadji swept the pieces off the board.

"We'll break the tie another time, O Ironhand."

Escorted back to his quarters, Challoner dismissed the Arab lad who proposed to aid him in undressing, and prepared for bed.

What was the Moor's hurry? Were not the peoples of the East given to slow ponderings?

> Moors and Arabs in general indulge in interminable bouts
> of bargaining over the purchase even of a gourd!

wrote author Yarborough. And here the Holy One, the Lion of Morocco, was forcing his would-be ally's hand with a yes or no, as early as tomorrow!

Challoner consulted his timepiece. Midnight. The moon's rays fell in a bright, silver band across the tiled floor. Why the Hadji's great haste? Suddenly, Challoner was brought upright in his bed. A sprite in wide skirts and fluttering laces had come dancing in from the terrace. It pirouetted on dainty feet. It curtsied low.

"Captain Challoner, I bid you good evening."

Challoner leaned over and scratched tinder to his bedside taper.

"What in the world?"

The sprite's gown, made of pale green taffeta, was mounted over a petticoat of fine lace. The bodice was cut daringly low, the waistline laced to waspish proportions. She wore a trimming of flowers in her red-gold hair and pearls on her white bosom. Her little shoes were made of green satin and her stockings of pale green silk.

"Look!" she exclaimed, pivoting again. "Look what they gave me. And two closetsful more. I've gowns for morning, for evening and for afternoon. I have coats and bonnets and deshabilles. A whole wardrobe! Can you explain it, James dear?"

Her use of the term "dear" had the effect of breaking down barriers.

"No, I cannot," said Challoner, keeping his reserve with some effort.

"But . . . those with whom you dined . . . did they not speak of me?"

"No."

"Not a word?"

"No."

"It's very strange. What does it mean, James? Why are you keeping secrets from me? Surely you must know? Tell me the truth, are you a pirate as you pretend to be? Or are you something else?"

Astute lady!

"What do *you* think I am?"

"You might be a secret agent, sent to discover what these Moors are up to?"

"What makes you dream of such an odd idea?"

She eyed him obliquely. "Well, for one thing, my informer told me you visited Admiral Lord Frawley at his Chelsea home. And Admiral Wilmington and other Admiralty bigwigs were there."

Challoner twirled his index finger. "Turn about, ma'am, so that I can pull on my breeks."

Laughing, she did as he asked. "That's what McKenna calls 'em."

Clad in "breeks," Challoner felt abler to deal with his fair enemy. She followed him out to the terrace.

"You have such beautiful muscles, Challoner!" she said, staring boldly at his nude chest. "Tell me, handsome . . . why did you go to Chelsea?"

Challoner gazed at the moonlit wilderness. Good Lord! What to tell? What not to tell? He wasn't dealing with a featherbrain, but with a clever woman.

"I might answer you, saying it was my business, not your ladyship's, that took me to Chelsea."

She gave a twitch of her silk skirts. "This clothing? What

has *it* to do with your business, Challoner? I cannot agree
that it was given me, merely to oblige me and afford me
change of dress. In my room there's a lady's baggage . . .
trunks, boxes, wearing apparel. Everything is marked
H.O.H. There are jewels, as you see. They took *my* Spanish
rags away, leaving me no choice but to wear the finery . . .
or go naked. Why? If you know, tell me!"

"I cannot," he said lamely.

"Is it that you *will* not?"

"Use your own judgment," he retorted with some heat.

She drew back and eyed him. "Are you afraid of me,
James Challoner?"

"Yes."

"Why in heaven's name?"

"Call me eccentric, if you will."

"Eccentric?" she quizzed with a crooked smile. "In what
way, James darling?"

"In that I prefer to make *my* choice. Not be chosen."

"You were choosing when you pursued Kit McKenna."

"I was pursuing a dream that had no reality."

She touched his arm. "Look at me and say I am not
real!"

"Not to dream all my dream . . . let's act the rest,"
muttered Challoner.

She gave a little cry. "Ah! That's John Donne! *'Love is
weak where Fear's strong!'* he says. *'Tis not all spirit pure
and brave, if mixture it of Fear, Shame, Honour have.'*
I know the ending, too.

> *"Perchance as torches, which must ready be,*
> *Men light and put out, so thou dealst with me."*

"A pretty Jezebel, spouting John Donne!" said Challoner sarcastically.

Suddenly she gave a heart-rending sob.

"I'm no Jezebel! I'm a woman who never knew love
until she met you."

The inclination he'd felt for a girl named Kit McKenna
and the turbid sensation that a lady well versed in gallantry
had inspired seemed to merge into one overwhelming wave
that bid fair to roll him under . . . under. Said one part of
him, "She's not for you." Said the other part, "What man

would step away from a moment like this?" Fool! Prig! Why could he not put love to the touch . . . gain small advantage rather than lose all?

She seemed to sense the tug-of-war that was tearing him in two.

"James, can't you see? Would I have followed you? Would I have lived in that pigsty of a galley . . . done Hercules' labors . . . had I not loved you sincerely?"

He held her at eye's length.

"Dear lady . . . what stories you'll have to tell at your dinner parties! Adventures of a Noble Lady on a Pirate Ship!"

Tears coursed down her cheeks. "How cruel you are!"

"They roll poison into sugar pills," he said with a fixed smile. "Eat and you die!"

Her tears ceased and her eyes flashed with anger.

"You're Death's constant companion, now, Challoner! Right here in this Thousand and One Nights scene, you're corn for the Reaper! Oh, do not think me such a fool as to believe you are an accomplice of pirates. You are risking your neck . . . for a purpose. And I am with you in risk. With you all the way."

He clasped his hands behind his back so she would not see their trembling.

"Remember, I did not ask your ladyship to stow aboard my ship."

She made a little sound under her breath, half sob and half angry "oh," then she turned on her green heels and flitted away like a moth, taking wing.

Who said, "Let each man his hell explore"? Challoner wondered that night as he thrashed about in his lonely bed. His present hell was a varied abode. In it were rooms of all sizes and colors. A bedroom named Regret. A game room—You lose. A dining hall—I Starve.

Restlessness dragged him from bed to open air. He paced the terrace on bare feet, stopping now and then to lay his hands on the stone parapet, then clapping cooled palms to his burning forehead. To bed again, but not to sleep. Morning found him dry-tongued and with eyeballs bulging.

He'd scarcely had time to shave, bathe, dress, when a messenger came.

"The Hadji will receive you and the Englishwoman as soon as you are ready."

So . . . the Holy Man of Mecca had decided to uncover his hand in regard to the "Englishwoman." Challoner stepped to the portières.

"Madam?"

"Yes, Captain Ironhand?"

Had she been lurking behind the curtains? She looked like Kit McKenna as she stepped forth, gowned in white, with a blue sash and lace at the bosom.

"Our host wishes to see us . . . together."

"Yes, my lord."

She might as well have said, "Yes, Idiot!"

The Hadji was seated on the terrace, dictating to a scribe. He waved to cushions.

"Pray be seated, Captain." No mention of the lady. But Challoner saw that no detail of Lady Grantley's person was lost to those eagle eyes.

The Moor dismissed his scribe and turned graciously to his visitors.

"Captain Hassan informed me correctly when he said your female companion was a person of grace and distinction, Captain Ironhand. May I ask who she is?"

"You might ask," said Challoner with studied impertinence. "I cannot see why I should answer."

His words made the Moor's heavy eyebrows beetle, but he chose to use a conciliatory tone in reply.

"You may be right. The lady has all the requisites that I need. Manners, bearing, looks, even the proper stature."

"All the requisites you *need?*" echoed Challoner.

The Moor smiled broadly. What white teeth he had!

"Perhaps the moment has come to lay subterfuge aside and speak outright. Believe me, I had strong reasons for bringing you and this woman to Castle Akbar." The Moor rose. "Come with me."

He led the way through courts and passages and down tortuous staircases into the very foundations of the castle. Here, armed guards opened barred and locked gates. Challoner could feel Lady Artis' little hand reaching for his hand as they kept pace with the fast-striding Moor.

"What do you suppose . . ." she whispered at a turn of a corridor.

"Shhh!" he warned.

Two armed guards threw open a heavy ironbound door. One of them went ahead with a flaming torch. The way led down narrow stone steps that smelled of the sea.

"We've not far to go, Captain," said the Moor. His voice echoed hollowly against the vaulted ceiling.

Rounding a turn at the bottom of the steps, Challoner found himself in a vast, stone cavern that was also a harbor —for a yacht was anchored there! White of hull, rakish of lines, she was both a pleasure craft and ocean-going vessel, combined. He'd never seen a ship of her exact build and proportions, before. On her bow, the name *Atlanta*. Her prow carried a figurehead representing a savage redskin, wearing a war bonnet of feathers like those described in romantic tales of Captain Smith and Princess Pocahontas.

"Well, Captain Ironhand? What do you think of your new command?"

"My command?" exclaimed Challoner. "She's a pretty toy, but I'd not trade her for my *Paramour.*"

"No trade's involved," said the Moor. "Come aboard. Look her over." He led the way up the plank with a plunging stride that made his white robes flap like sails in a calm.

Lady Artis hung back when Challoner motioned her up the plank. "What does all this mean?"

"I don't know."

"I've a premonition of terrible things to come!"

"I hardly think we're picnic bound either," grinned Challoner.

The Moor having called from above, "Well, Captain Ironhand?" Challoner boosted Lady Artis up the plank with none too gentle a hand. What a strange sensation to stand on the deck of a seagoing vessel and look up at ceiling of stone instead of open sky!

"Where was she built, Hadji?"

"In Charleston, in the Colony of Carolina," answered the Moor. "Her master and owner was a wealthy planter from Georgia, named Henry Oliver Hunnicutt. He and his consort were on their way to present an extraordinary gift to the King of England."

"You say *were*. I take it they are dead?"

"Yes, Captain Ironhand, all except one man of the crew. Come. Let me show you about."

The vessel was a jewel of the seas. Every detail of her was studied for beauty as well as comfort. The woods used in her trimmings were rare hardwoods, such as teak and mahogany, and the inlay of her paneling was the work of skilled and patient craftsmen.

"How many were in her crew, Hadji?" asked Challoner.

"Fifteen, including a lady's maid and a valet. Would you like to see the *Atlanta's* cargo?"

"Let me stay here," whispered Lady Artis in a quick aside.

"No!" Challoner gripped her by the wrist. "We're in this together."

Preceded by a guard carrying a lantern, the Hadji led the way down into the ship's hold. Challoner's nose and ears told him this was no ordinary lading. The air reeked of the wild and the sounds that issued from the darkness were howls, whimpers, whines, barks, snarls, coughs, growls!

Stepping into the hold, he saw cage after cage around the sides, a narrow aisle between. Each cage contained one or a pair of beasts, most of which were species he had never seen. Here was a tawny-colored, lionlike creature, who stared at the light of the lantern with amber eyes. A mountain lion, the Hadji called it. Here, were a pair of silky black lynxes with tasseled ears and thrashing tails. Here, a great gray wolf with tremendous fangs. Here . . . a creature, half wolf, half dog.

"Its name is . . . coyote," said the Hadji. "It comes from the western plains of the North American continent." He directed Challoner to the last two cages. "Observe these animals, Captain. This one with the mane and short curved horns is a bison. And here is the largest mammal found in North America. Its name is grizzly bear."

Lady Artis uttered a little cry of fear at sight of the great furry monster that stood on its hind legs and gripped the bars of the cage with front paws over a foot long.

"Please!" she gasped, holding a handkerchief to her little nose. "Take me away or I'll swoon!"

She'd scarcely finished speaking when a creature—seeming more beast than human—stepped out of the shadows.

He was nude to the waist. His skin was copper-colored. His long, coarse hair was pulled into two braids that hung down over his ears. His expression, fierce, hard, animalistic, was that of the untamed savage. But his manner was gentle.

"This redskin is keeper of the menagerie," said the Moor. "He speaks not a word of any language except his own tongue. I let him live because he knows what the animals eat . . . and how to cope with them. For the rest, he takes orders from me as readily as he did from his erstwhile master."

The redskin's glittering black eye fixed upon Lady Artis. He put out his hand as though to point to her gown and then he smiled. The pantomime was fairly clear. He'd recognized the gown, and linked the wearer with his mistress.

Lady Artis had not flinched. She also seemed to understand that the redskin meant her no harm.

The Moor had made no comment. Leading the way "ashore," he guided his guests back to the terrace room.

"The woman may withdraw," he then said with a quiet firmness that brooked no argument. A servant showed Lady Artis to the door while another servant brought caffè.

"Now, Captain Ironhand," said the Moor when he had taken a few sips of his cup. "I presume you would like the answers to the questions that are nibbling at your mind?"

"I would indeed," said Challoner.

The Hadji's voice deepened as though a graver tone would better convey his meaning.

"When first the *Atlanta* was captured, I had no clear idea what her worth would be to me, but on examining the log and owner's papers it became clear that Allah himself had given her into my hands."

"Indeed?" said Challoner by way of comment. Let the Moor tell the whole of it!

"Yes," exclaimed the Hadji. "Allah never works halfway. Not only did he give me the ship, he also inspired me with an idea . . . what to do with her and with the strange cargo she carries."

"Really?" remarked Challoner, sipping coffee.

His murmured response seemed to stimulate the Moor to further revelations. His dark face began to glow.

"Yes, Captain Ironhand. And if I had doubted the

Divine Will, Hassan effendi's meeting with you would have given me positive proof. *Wa la glaliba . . . illa . . . Allah.*"

Echo of author-traveler Yarborough! The Moor had voiced the war cry of Islam. "There is no conqueror but God, and Allah is God."

Challoner launched a question. "Hadji . . . are you perhaps a descendant of Mahomet the Prophet?"

The Moor's reply fully revealed what his listener had desired to know.

"I am!" he said proudly. "Not the present usurper, Mahomet XVI . . . I, sir! I, Mohammed-ben-Dar, alone have the right to call myself Son of the Prophet and King of the World."

"Now I have it," thought Challoner. Here was the keynote Lord Frawley had sounded and Yarborough had put in the pages of his work on Morocco. Mahomet's followers of today had not relinquished their dream of world power! Their raiders were not mere pirate ships. The Islamic brotherhood—Turks, Moroccans, Arabs, and the peoples of Persia were all united under the Half-Moon banner of the Prophet of Mecca. Their purpose—to destroy the Christ idea and elevate their materialistic deity to the throne sublime. And what more fanatic leader of the new crusade of Islam than this fiery-eyed Moor who proclaimed himself Mohammed-ben-Dar and Son of the Prophet and King of the World? But . . . how would a Captain Ironhand and an English lady and a yacht—her hold packed with wild beasts—fit into his plan?

The Moor seemed inspired as he said, "What would you say, Captain Ironhand, if I told you I have a way of dealing a death blow at the very heart of the Christian world?"

"I'd say, let's hear more about it," retorted Challoner.

The Moor leaned forward and fixed him with glittering eyes. "I take it you're not a convinced follower of the Christian faith?"

"I?" Challoner's laughter sounded a note of contempt. "No, Hadji. I am not a convinced follower of the Christian or any other faith."

The Moor smiled. "Good! You, who call yourself a free soul, can well afford to join forces with Islam for the purpose I will explain."

"Hadji," said Challoner. "I'll join with anyone . . .

Christian, Mohammedan, Hindu or Jew . . . who will offer me a sound protective alliance and good hunting upon the seas."

The Moor rose from his cushions. "Then, sir, kindly return here at sunset. It is time you met my Council of Twelve."

9.

Plot Royal

THE STAGE WAS SET AS CHALLONER WALKED INTO THE Hadji's chamber. Eleven men in Moorish dress and Captain Hassan, wearing well-fitting Navy blues, were seated on cushions around a long table, sipping caffè and conversing with each other.

The Hadji entered by a door on the other side of the room and there followed a ceremonial introducing of the company.

"My Prime Minister, Abu-ben-Ali, my Minister of Justice, Achmed," and so forth and so forth. Finance and War, Interior and Foreign Affairs. They were all here, including Secretary of the Navy, Hassan. Mohammed-ben-Dar, the Ruler of the World, had more ministers than King George.

Shown to a cushion on the Hadji's right, Challoner submitted to the bombardment of twelve pair of eyes. He was uneasy. What were these dark-faced, long-nosed men up to? In vain he'd tried to tell himself that it was very likely some plan for a more daring and concentrated raid than in the past, but, the Hadji's remarks apropos of "striking at the heart of Christendom" seemed to imply *more* than a mere raid by land or by sea.

The Hadji addressed his Council in Arabic and a short exchange of remarks was made, then he turned to Challoner.

"No more delay!" he said abruptly. "I'll come to the

point. What would you say, Captain Ironhand, if I told you I have a plan whereby I shall assassinate the King and Queen of England and their children?"

Challoner was at first conscious only of the furious beating of his heart, then those sentiments of loyalty to the Crown he had served and longed again to serve welled up in him like an irresistible tide. He was tempted to spring at the throat of the Hadji! But discipline conquered the impulse.

"I'd say . . . you're mad!" he answered scoffingly.

Deep silence followed the remark.

"You'd be right, Captain Ironhand," the Moor agreed. "However, there's a 'but.' "

Affecting an air of insolence, Challoner said, "What is your 'but,' Hadji?"

The Moor rubbed his hands with a gesture—self-congratulation? Exultation? Anticipation?

"Listen well, Captain Ironhand! Listen well! On the morning of June twelfth, King George and his Queen and the royal children will visit the North American animal collection which Planter Hunnicutt of Carolina will bring as a gift to the English monarch and the people of England. Pleasure-loving mobs will line the streets along the way of the royal progress. Troops in gala uniform will keep mock guard. Can you not see the King and Queen and their children entering the exhibit pavilion to the plaudits of their loyal subjects? Can you not hear the roar of our captive wild beasts? Now . . . what would be the result, should our grizzly bear, our mountain lion, our wolf, our bison, escape from their cages? The result would be the most terrible confusion imaginable! The crowds would panic. Of what avail soldiers' discipline against wild beasts on the loose? Ironhand effendi, can you imagine a more propitious moment for the King and his family to die?"

Challoner had been shocked at the first hint of a plot against the Crown. Now he was struck with the simple perfection of the plot. Its elements were novelty, surprise and fear. Formidable combination. Panic in a holiday mob would abet the Moor's diabolical scheme. What guardsman or gentleman-in-waiting would brave a grizzly bear, a shaggy horned bison, a cougar, a giant fanged wolf, to save his sovereign? And even equipped with all the courage of a Christian martyr, how could his efforts prevail against so formidable an adversary as a pack of wild beasts? He drew a cautious breath and spoke quietly.

"I can imagine no more propitious moment, O Hadji."

His approval seemed to encourage the Moor to go on to further revelations. "Now do you see why it was imperative that I use you and your English wench for my plot? Planter Hunnicutt and his wife will be royally entertained in London. The newspapers will carry advance news of their arrival and the order of ceremonies attendant upon the presentation of the North American Zoo to the King. There has to be a Planter Hunnicutt and his spouse to make the illusion complete. I was fortunate in finding you and the woman . . . your mistress. You will act as decoy for our unsuspecting game. You will attract the eyes of the guards, whilst I and my assassins do our deadly work. Oh! I'm leaving nothing to chance. I shall be there in disguise, directing every move of my men."

"A question, Hadji!" said Challoner. "I understand your prime motive for regicide. But . . . exactly what do you hope to gain besides the working out of an age-old grudge against the Crown of England?"

"Ah!" exclaimed the Moor. "Vengeance is sweet, as your poet says, but vengeance would not be a sufficient prize! No! This majestic act of assassination of seven royal persons will work confusion among the nations of Christianity. It will loosen the faith of the peoples in the invulnerability and Destiny-bestowed life of the King. It will set the chancelleries a-buzzing. It may even start wars. We of Islam can draw vast profit from all this. Our agents, working in all corners of Europe and in the Far East, will foment trouble between the Western Colonial powers. The ground spaded for Moorish dominion over the Mediterranean, I shall strike and strike again against the ships of the Christian world! Allah is great and Mahomet is his prophet! Islam will triumph!"

Challoner made a show of rising and pacing the floor as if in conjecture, then turning to the Moor he put a blunt question. "What will be *my* reward for going along with your scheme?"

"Twenty-five thousand pounds," answered the Moor, "and remember, Captain, those who serve the Lion gain not only gold but also power and glory."

Challoner had always been able to assess his adversary's strength in the moment of crisis. The Moor's position was that of a man needing help.

"Add ten thousand to the twenty-five and I'm your man," he said as if on the spur of a decision.

Murmurs of satisfaction went around the table. The twelve nodded and smiled their approval.

"So be it," conceded the Hadji. "Thirty-five thousand pounds it is."

Seeing how readily the Moor had granted his demand, Challoner pressed him still further.

"The money *now*, O Hadji."

"Now? Why?" protested the Moor. "I'll pay when the raid is successfully concluded."

"Then so far as I'm concerned, there'll be no raid," said Challoner flatly. "I want no part in the rulership of the world. I only want to sail the seas, fight, enjoy life. Pay me now, or we'll part in good friendship."

Again the Moors consulted with each other and it was Captain Hassan who broke the Gordian knot.

"I think we may safely grant half of Captain Ironhand's demand, O Hadji," he said in conciliatory tones. And turning to Challoner, "You, on your part, will see fit to accept half, will you not, Captain?"

Challoner thought a moment, then, with an air of a man granting a favor, "Very well," he said. "Half now and the other half when our mission is completed."

The Hadji clapped his hands. A steward appeared from behind a curtain. After some whispered words, he disappeared and soon returned with a neat packet of English hundred-pound notes, which he placed on the table in front of Challoner.

Challoner counted the banknotes one by one, slipped half into one pocket of his tunic, the other half in the other, then he rose.

"With your permission, O Hadji, I'll repair to my ship and bring her down to Castle Akbar."

The Moor smiled.

"Look out the window, Captain."

Challoner looked. There was the *Paramour,* sails furled, lying at anchor under the castle walls! Flushing angrily, he turned with a terse question.

"How dared you order my ship to your waters without consulting me?"

The Moor spread his heavily ringed hands in a gesture truly oriental.

"I only wanted to save you time and trouble, O Ironhand."

"You took too much upon yourself. What if I had refused to enter into an agreement with you?"

"But you did *not* refuse, O Ironhand," said the Moor softly. He rose from his cushions. "Come morning, you shall go aboard your ship and assure yourself that she is in good order."

"I prefer to board her now," said Challoner.

"Tomorrow, effendi!" murmured the Moor. "Be not so hasty to desert the delights of your bed and waste hours of the night that are meant for love."

Angered to the very depths, yet impotent to resist the Moor's will, not to speak of his army of guards, Challoner withdrew without further argument, or even a goodnight, but a hundred questions seethed in his mind as he walked the long corridors back to his rooms. How had the Moor decoyed Boggs here? What false orders had he presented? A forged letter? No! Boggs would not be deceived by a forgery. Then how?

Reviewing also the preposterous yet simple plot of the Moor, he understood at last why an intruder from the Caribe Sea and his "wench" had been suffered to come to the stronghold of Mohammed-ben-Dar! Lady Artis would play the role of Mistress Hunnicutt as well as she had worn her gowns. He, himself, would fill Planter Hunnicutt's boots to perfection!

Lady Artis Grantley had marked a path for her pacing of the terrace. Cross the center pattern of blue and rose, then turn, walk along the border made of tile flowerlets, click heels, turn and walk the same route back.

"I'm not the least bit frightened," she'd told herself again and again. "Challoner will get us out of this fix." But she knew in her heart of hearts that it was fear she felt—a creeping, horrid thing! How difficult now to cling to childish hope that "all wad turn out right," as Nurse McKenna used to say in olden days. She'd even come to doubt the one whose predicament she shared. What was Challoner . . . man of honor or thief? There was need of a stouter heart than the one which beat so unevenly in her breast.

Cross the center pattern, walk along the flower border, click heels . . . she was making the turn around when Challoner stepped out on the terrace.

"You, here? Why are you not in bed?"

"I could not sleep."

"Well, go to bed and try again."

She ran to him, seeking to read his expression by the light of the stars.

"James, something's gone wrong. I can tell from the way you speak. It makes me afraid."

"Fear's no good," he said, chopping out the words from between clenched teeth.

"I can't help it," she cried, and suddenly he was holding her as he would have held a frightened child.

How much of the truth dare he tell? The plot to assassinate the King? No!

Cheek nestled against his shoulder, "James," she said, "what do these Moors want of you and me?"

"Mohammedans respect the right of the male to have his woman," he said parrying the question.

"Ah, but I am not your woman!" she retorted. "Even the servants who wait upon me must know that we spend the nights apart."

"According to the habits and customs of Mohammedans, that would not surprise them," said Challoner in the same light tone of voice. "We could be making love by day . . . sleeping the nights through."

Lady Artis' doubts spoke louder and louder until they shouted.

"You haven't answered my question. What do they want of you? Of me?"

"I'm beginning to believe that they may want me to act as go-between for a peace between themselves and England," he said, lying outright.

She stepped back. *"I'm* beginning to think you have gone over to the Moor's side, James Challoner!"

He shook his head, left to right, as though in amazement at a child's bad temper.

"Think what you will, your opinion of me will not change things."

How lovely she was in her disarray as she pleaded, "James! I want the truth!"

He laughed. "You, the lighthearted, the daring, the careless of danger, should trust your fellow adventurer!"

"I trust you one moment, I mistrust you the next."

"Do you love me one moment . . . unlove me the next?"

"Perhaps I never love you . . . really," she cried defiantly, and turning she ran into her room.

Seeking to formulate some plan by which to wreck the Moor's plot, Challoner paced the terrace and gazed at the wan hills under the moon-pale sky. It was not long before he had the solution to the dilemma. The plan was simple in concept. The mystery yacht *Atlanta* must be destroyed. A self-styled ruler of the world and his fanatic followers must go down to a watery death—this, even if it entailed the deaths of one James Challoner and a lovely woman named Artis. Yes, the North American animal collection, the Moors and the pseudo Mr. and Mrs. Hunnicutt must disappear in a strange and outlandish sacrifice.

The thing now—prepare Boggs to do his part. Instruct him to fire at and sink a pretty, white-hulled yacht the moment it set sail, then turn and blast Castle Akbar to rubble. And, having wrought her ruin, the *Paramour* must return to England and report to Lord Frawley—"Mission accomplished."

Challoner had gone to bed and fallen into fretful slumber. A light touch roused him. A voice murmured, "Dearest." A hand caressed his cheek. He kept his eyes closed, not to banish the dream. Soft lips brushed his bare shoulder. "Dearest James!"

This was no dream. Artis was kneeling at his side. Her delicate flesh showed through the gauze of her night robe. Her hair seemed to flame in the morning light. Her expression, her whole being reflected the gentle, unmistakable presence of love as she whispered, "Dearest one. I'm sorry I spoke as I did."

Adam must have fallen to sweet music like this—to the soft touch of hands, the caress of a swelling bosom. Poor Adam! But who would not have relinquished Paradise for Artis' kiss!

A thoughtful Challoner edged, inch by inch, away from his lovely mistress. So, Captain Morality had added his distinguished head to Lady Grant-em-All's trophy collection!

She was sleeping, bare limbs in a charming pose, right arm thrown up and tucked under her head, the breasts surging into snowy sunrise-tinted peaks. One tiny foot hung over the edge of the bed. Bright Venus so soon to perish 'neath the waves.

He rose and dressed. Would the Moors allow him to board the *Paramour* without further delay?

"James?" yawned Artis. Seeing him fully clothed, she sat upright in the bed. "What time is it?"

"Late," he answered.

"Late for what?" she laughed. "Now that you are mine and I am yours, I'd as soon stay here forever. Yes! What lovelier life than to be the favorite of a pirate captain here in this Aladdin's castle by the sea? You, dear James, will sail for booty. I'll wait for you. And when you return, think what kisses we'll share!" She leaned back against the cushions and, her mood changing, "James," she said thoughtfully, "perhaps it would be better after all if we returned to England where we could be married and live merrily, spending my fortune in a thousand delights!"

Oh inconsistency of woman!

"Yes!" she cried, as if, having made up her own mind, all others should bow to her decision. "We'll return to England, James."

He went to her and planted a light kiss on her lips.

"Dream on it, my dear. Dream."

He'd scarcely set foot in the corridor when two robed figures sprang at him. A cloak was tossed over his head and shoulders, his arms pinioned to his sides. He kicked, fought, struggled with a savage will to resist—all in vain. Some sick-sweet scent emanated from the cloak, a narcotic scent. He felt the dulling impact it made upon his musculatory system and powers of reason. He was becoming lethargic, will-less. Suddenly he went limp in the grasp of his assailants who lifted him by the ankles and shoulders and bore him away.

10.

Boggs' Choice

ACTING CAPTAIN BOGGS OF THE "PARAMOUR" WAS HONING his rugged cheeks smooth in anticipation of his Captain's coming aboard ship. From time to time his eye traveled to an iron glove that lay on top of his locker, then it shifted to the letter of orders that had been presented with the glove.

> Bring the *Paramour* down in this pilot's wake and stand by Castle Akbar.
>
> > Ironhand

Having completed the job of shaving, Boggs doused his face with water, dried it, examined it in the mirror atop the toilet stand. He was glad that the waiting was over—glad to relinquish command of the *Paramour* to her real captain. The crew had been restive in the heat and idleness of forced anchorage off Tangier. Given a few days more, some might have gone overside in defiance of orders to stay aboard.

Boggs went on deck where he found Flymaster Maunday leaning on the rail, staring at Castle Akbar.

"It's a mighty mass, all right," said Maunday.

"Aye," said Boggs. "But a few shot of our big guns could make mincemeat of it."

"Will Captain let us go ashore?"

"I'd say, yes."

"Good. Just to touch foot on land will do the men good."

Boggs accepted a mug of lukewarm tea from the cabin

boy and drank it without pleasure. Then, each thinking his own thoughts, he and Maunday resumed their survey of Castle Akbar.

"I could enter from a dozen places," said Maunday, thinking out loud.

"Where's the Captain?" thought the worried Boggs. There was a quietness, a mystery about the place that bothered him. No sign of life anywhere. Not a face, not an eye!

"Sir," said Maunday, "look sharp! Do you see what I see? Since when do ships sail out of the rock?"

Boggs' gaze followed the direction of the flymaster's pointing finger. "There must be a harbor inside that rock!" he exclaimed. "That, or the ship we see is a toy."

"She's one hundred foot if she's an inch," said Maunday. "Look at her sails as they break out! Her decks are manned with blackamoors."

They watched the yacht's sails take the wind and veer seaward in dumfounded silence. When she was no more than a speck on the wide blue waters, Boggs pushed back his cap and scratched his head.

"I don't like it, Maunday! I don't like it at all!"

"Nor I," Maunday agreed, with a frown. "What'll we do about it?"

"I'll give the Captain another hour," said Boggs.

"You mean . . . we'll go in after him?"

"Yes."

"I'd like that, and so would my flymen," chuckled Maunday.

The hour ran out and there was still no sign of the *Paramour's* captain. Boggs gave Maunday a whispered order.

"Slip overside with ten of your best men and filter into the hills behind that perishin' castle. See what you can see from the other side."

"Aye, sir!" said the smiling Maunday. He would have swum around the globe in hopes of finding a lady whom he named "Sweet Pilar" in his dreams. And shortly after, ten flymen and their leader dropped soundlessly into the sea and swam underwater for a rocky promontory some five hundred yards to the north of the stronghold.

The little band lay dozing or resting in the shade of a stubby cliff, while their chief Flymaster Maunday and his first lieutenant, a rugged youth named McNamara, surveyed the scene.

There below were the walls and battlements of a medieval castle—toylike in size at this distance. In front, the blazing sea. In back, shark-tooth ridges extended into the distance. A winding mountain trail led from some wild backland to the coast.

"What are our chances, Chief?" said McNamara.

"Poor," said Maunday. "We're too few to assault the place by day. Try it by night? See those sheer walls? See the drop into that gorge?"

"There's the portcullis," said McNamara. "Couldn't we go in by the front door?"

"It's a chance we *could* take," Maunday agreed, "but not without orders."

The morning wore on and the heat increased until the men were panting with thirst. Even McNamara had succumbed. He lay dozing, openmouthed, in the scant shade of a rock while Maunday kept vigil on the castle and the sea, and a lookout posted on the ridge watched the approach from the hills behind. He was mopping his perspiring brow with the butt of his hand when suddenly, his keen ear caught a faraway cry, "Caravan to the south!" Instantly he was up and racing to the lookout post.

The Watch had been right. A caravan of ten camels and their cameleers was winding its way over the mountain trail. It wasn't long before the jangling tones of the bells could be heard. Ten camels! Waterskins! Food!

Maunday went leaping down the mountainside where the flymen were waiting. They'd roused out of their doze. What was it that made their chief bound along like a goat?

"Boys? How would you like to ride a camel?"

They crowded around him. "We would! We would!"

When the caravan wended its way around a bend in the mountain path, the Moor cameleers did not expect an assault at this, the final half-mile of their long journey from the oasis town of Wadi-Zouf. Castle Akbar was just out of sight, but rest, fresh water and food were within minutes. Women, too. The Hadji always had a surplus of captive women. The ten camel drivers dreamed of pleasures to come, also of profit, for the Hadji sold guns, ball, shot, slaves male and female, and Turkish tobacco to desert traders at reasonable prices. The trail-weary Moors dozed in the saddle, swaying to the shiplike roll of their humped beasts.

Maunday, balancing on an overhanging rock at the turn of the trail, made a flying leap. The tail-end man in the caravan train never knew what hit him! Dragged from his sheepskin-covered saddle, a hand clamped over his mouth, an elbow crooked around his gullet, he died of strangulation before he could say Allah!

Up ahead, another flyman was dealing with the next to the tail-end driver, and so on until all ten had been accounted for.

"Lucky fellows," grinned Maunday. "They've gone to their kind of Paradise where beautiful houris abound."

"What's a houri?" asked McNamara.

"A black-face Polly!" laughed Maunday. "Come, men! Break out those saddlebags and sample the water. We'll rest here until dusk and practice playing Moor." He wiped the sweat from his brow and regarded the ten camels with a doubtful eye. They hadn't attempted to run away when separated from their drivers—were standing bunched together like statues made of sand. "I've seen how they make those smelly devils kneel . . . they tap 'em on the snout with their whips, or whatever they call 'em." He retrieved one of the drivers' sticks that had fallen among the rocks. "Now watch out! I'm going to have a try."

He was right. The camel obeyed the light touch of the stick and lowered itself to its knobby knees.

There were a few dates and some coarse cheese and a small sack of raw millet in each of the cameleers' saddlebags. The water was brackish but drinkable.

"We'll stay here until dusk," said Maunday. "Gather up all the robes and turbans and fit yourselves out to play the Moor."

Maunday, a stickler for detail, was not satisfied that his men should *dress* the part. They had to assume the attitudes of those whom they were impersonating. He saw to each detail, even to the darkening of faces with a mixture of earth and water. When dusk began to fall, it was a very authentic band of cameleers who stood by their kneeling beasts, sticks in hand.

"Now . . . about getting aboard these ships of the desert,"

said Maunday. "Watch me. You sling a leg over and you hold on . . . so." He gripped the wooden bow at the front of the saddle, the camel rocked, rolled, got to its feet and gave a snort. Even Maunday seemed surprised that he had brought off what he intended to do. "We'll advance easy-like. Keep the edge of your head-cloth well over your faces. Make no hostile move until I give the signal."

Bells jangling, the caravan wore its way down the trail with the sinking sun at its back.

Those inside the castle were evidently awaiting its coming. No sooner had it hove into sight than the drawbridge came down and the gates were opened.

Each flyman listened to his own heartbeat as he rode into the inner court. Each pair of eyes was riveted on the flymaster.

The three guards who advanced to meet the travelers noticed nothing amiss, uttered guttural greetings. A fourth guard ambled to the inner gate on the opposite side of the courtyard and lazily drew the bolt, and the caravan went through.

Maunday gave the signal—a leap from the saddle onto the back of the nearest guard. Quick as lightning, three flymen took on their men. The dusk was deepening. Had anyone seen what had happened in the courtyard? Maunday scanned the windows and the walls above. He saw no one. "Drag 'em under that arch and follow me," he whispered.

The sudden desert night had fallen like a bolt from the sky as the little band crept up a flight of stairs that led into the fortress. Not a challenge! No one interfered. But suddenly Maunday understood why when he heard the chant of the Muezzin.

"Wa la glaliba . . . illa . . . Allah."

The guardians of the castle had been at sundown prayer. "Take cover!" he whispered.

The flymen had had barely time enough to flatten themselves against the wall when a face showed at an upper window and someone shouted in Arabic and pointed to the camels. Instantly, with a scuffling of soft-soled shoes, a dozen Moors came running down the stairs.

Maunday and his men were ready for them. It was wonderful to see the somersaults the Moors performed as they hurtled onto the stones of the courtyard. But the silence was now broken by their hideous screams.

"We're in for it!" said Maunday. "We'll have to fight for keeps!"

It was like trying to stem an avalanche! Moors and more Moors poured down the staircase.

Maunday was quick to see the advantage the gloom of night might provide for the invaders. He sent an order down the line of flymen. "Mix with 'em!"

So dark it was now, the Moors could not tell their own kind, one from another, much less the Infidel in their midst!

In the confusion that ensued, Maunday was able to elbow, wriggle, crawl, up the staircase. Several of his men followed—just how many he could not tell until he found himself on the threshold of what appeared to be a guard room. It *was* a guard room! Spears, scimitars and muskets hung on the walls. The room was dimly lighted by torches set in torchères. Where were the rest of the castle guards? He was soon to find out. A mob of unarmed men surged through a side door and went running for their weapons. Maunday saw at a glance that his meager force would never suffice to beat their ever-increasing number. "Rat tactics! Lock 'em in!" he shouted in a voice of thunder.

Was it the voice speaking a strange tongue that caused the soldiers to halt in their tracks? One moment of hesitation was enough. Maunday and his men raced to the doors in the zigzag "rat tactic" way he had taught them and before the Moors knew what had happened, they found themselves behind bolted doors! But the strategy had also separated the flymen—some were inside of the castle, some were on the staircase.

There wasn't time to deplore their loss. Maunday led the way down a corridor. He must, he knew, find a window or a terrace on the sea side of the castle, and there, send light signals to the *Paramour*.

This door? He tried the latch but it was locked from inside. Then suddenly the door opened and a veiled woman put her head out. Maunday acted on instinct when he grabbed her to prevent her from screaming. His heart leaped into his throat when he heard a staccato rattle of Portuguese from the woman's lips. That voice! "Pilar, is it you?"

"Maunday!" gasped the Marquesa. She drew him over the threshold and closed the door. *"Querido!* The Saints answered my prayers! You've come to save me!" Maunday found himself wrapped in soft arms. Warm lips pressed his. "My love! My darling! They were going to sell us to a slave trader arriving by caravan this very day!" And again the lady fell on his neck with endearing words and kisses so that it was some time before the bemused flymaster could ask the question that he wanted most to have answered.

"Where is the captain of the *Paramour?*"

"Gone," cried Doña Pilar. "They took him aboard a pretty, white sloop that sailed away at dawn. The lady went also, but she *walked* to the ship."

"The captain did not walk?"

"No. He seemed to be unconscious. They carried him."

"They?"

"The Moors. Their head man is named Hadji. His council of twelve rule this castle and sail for plunder."

"And how does it happen that you know so much about these heathen?"

"I got in the good graces of the head eunuch who guarded us. He would sell his soul for a bauble in gold."

"Did he tell you where they were taking Captain Ironhand?"

"No, *querido.* I'm sure the eunuch did not know or he would have told me."

Maunday, a worried man, asked another question. "Which is the quickest way out of this fort . . . to our ship?"

"This way." Doña Pilar led Maunday to a window opening on the sea. The drop to the rocks was a good thirty feet.

"We'll need a line," said Maunday, and suddenly he thought of the yards-long turbans he and his men were wearing.

The five surviving flymen and the twelve ladies of Lisbon made knots as fast as their fingers could tie.

Maunday lowered the improvised line out of the window. "You, Mack. Try it out."

"Aye, aye, sir!" His eager lieutenant leapt the sill and climbed down the rope hand over hand. The rope's tug went slack. McNamara was well away! Maunday couldn't see him but he could visualize his progress—first touching foot to the rock, then slithering into the water and making for the goal as silent as a fish.

"I pray he will succeed," murmured the Marquesa. Her shoulder brushed Maunday's arm, sending a thrill through him.

"I too," he muttered. It was sheer delight to have such a beauty near.

For a time that seemed an eternity, they waited. What would Boggs decide? Order a landing in force? Suddenly a cannon roared!

Maunday leaned out of the window. No, not Boggs firing on the castle, the castle was firing on Boggs! A cannon on a tower was belching flame and smoke. He could follow the trajectory of the balls. Some fell short of the *Paramour*, others landed on her decks. "By God! They'll sink her!" he shouted. "Why doesn't she answer?" Then, realizing that if the *Paramour* fired on the castle they would all be in jeopardy, he could place himself in Boggs' shoes!

Quickly he hauled up the turban rope and pressed the arm of Doña Pilar. "We must vacate. Keep a good hold on my neck. I'll take you down. You men . . . bring down the other ladies as quickly as you can."

He'd undertaken no more pleasant feat than this one! The lady's soft body pressed to him, tightly. Her arms encircled his shoulders. Her breath warmed his neck.

"Don't be afraid!" he whispered.

"I'm not afraid with you, *querido.*"

That light touch of a woman's lips on the nape of his neck! Maunday set toe on the rock with regret and gave a tug on the line.

"Pilar, you'll have to swim for it!"

"I am a good swimmer."

"Those clothes . . . take some of them off."

"Very well, *mi amor.*"

Never, no never, had Maunday enjoyed a swim as he did this one, even though cannon balls *were* whizzing over his head! He prolonged the delight by swimming to the port side of the *Paramour* where he was sure he and his lovely, white-armed partner would not be detected by those manning the castle walls.

"Hold onto this line, Pilar. I'll go aboard and drop a breeches buoy."

She floated closer, murmuring, "I love you."

Her kiss gave him wings. He hauled himself up the line, leaped the rail and ran to the bridge.

"You! Thank God!" exclaimed Boggs. "What's happened?"

Maunday gave him a quick report, then said, "In just a few moments you can open fire on those demons!"

"But . . . our Captain?" demurred Boggs.

"Our Captain is sailing the seas in a white sloop, destination unknown," answered Maunday grimly. "You need only wait to fire until my men and a parcel of women are aboard."

It was not long before Boggs could send an order thundering down to the gun captain.

"Fire on the castle!"

Soon the truck guns were blazing, while inside the stronghold, a determined band of Moor soldiers were doing their best to carry out orders received from the Hadji before he'd sailed.

"Sink the infidel's frigate!"

But they hadn't counted on the power of the *Paramour's* great guns. Nor had they foreseen that intruders would have assaulted them from *inside* the castle walls, even locked some twoscore of their number inside the guard room.

Salvo after salvo hit the castle broadside. Chunks of the façade split off and fell into the sea. Stone blocks and masonry flew like pebbles. Boom! Boom! The very hills shook!

A lucky cannon ball hit the ordnance room. Powder kegs went off like bombs. The structure of centuries-old walls was being reduced to the same dust from which it had been created by the Crusaders.

"Prepare to land and destroy all survivors!" bawled Boggs through the mouth horn.

Armed to the teeth, the men of the *Paramour* swarmed ashore, and soon the bloody battle was over. The cannonade had ended. Calm settled over the Mediterranean night, made furiously bright by the fires that were consuming Castle Akbar.

But Boggs was in no mood for rejoicing. Where next? What was the destination of the sloop that had sneaked

away at dawn, bearing Ironhand as passenger? In what
direction should one search? Spain? Portugal?

It was a heavyhearted Boggs who went below, locked
himself in quarters and opened a packet wrapped in oilskin that hung around his neck by a greasy thong. Inside
the wrapping was a letter and a code book.

Boggs placed letter and book under the light of two
candles, found pencil and paper and sat down to the hardest task given a slow-writing, slow-reading man.

Admiral Lord Frawley's message when decoded, read:

> In case of extremity and seeing no profit in holding your
> position, repair to nearest friendly port and contact our
> Crown Agent with the password *Buttons.*

Sadly, Boggs burned the original and the decoded mes-
sage and dropped the code book into the fur of his chest.
Then he turned to his sea charts. The nearest friendly port?
A small one, some ten miles south of Lisbon, named Viga.

11.

Ladies' Choice

DOÑA PILAR DE VALALODAD HAD BEEN EXPEDITED TO FAR-
away Bolivia to marry the Governor of that land when she
was a slip of a girl of fifteen. Traveling under the protection of a stern-faced *dueña*, seeing something of the world
outside the convent where she had been raised, young Pilar
was all agog to discover what fate had in store for her in
shape of a bridegroom.

Imagine her disappointment when, decked in her finest,
and awaiting the Governor's call, she saw a man who
looked like a basset hound enter the drawing room.

The Marques Gubernator was Autumn to her Spring.
Fifty, pitted against fifteen. Bald, gaunt-faced, sad-eyed,
with huge ears, he nevertheless possessed some qualities
that compensated for his lack of physique. He was a kindly,

even-tempered man. He liked to play the flute while she played the harp.

The Marques had set ideas about marriage and the duties of a wife toward her husband. First of all, she must give him children. Of romantic love he knew nothing, though he maintained an official mistress in an elegant *apartamiento* near the gubernatorial palace. This able lady set a rich table and provided him with all the pleasures of the flesh, so that his relationship with his immature wife remained of a purely biological nature—so many tries a year, at getting her with child.

His efforts had failed. Pilar had remained sterile. Also, her capacity for love dried up as time went on. She'd become accustomed to the frivolous life of the society in which she reigned as vice-queen. Had she been more alert to the delights of romance, she might have decorated her uninteresting husband with many a fine set of horns—that she did not was not for virtue's sake. The lady simply could not understand or enjoy *"le sport amoureux"* as His Excellency the Ambassador from France called love. Her nature remained cold even after the death of the Marques.

The great change had come when Doña Pilar had found herself confronting a young Apollo with red hair, named Maunday. Pilar fell in love.

Parted from the object of her affection during her short term of captivity in Castle Akbar, she would willingly have cast herself into the sea and swam to where he was. His reappearance in the role of rescuer had sent her to high heavens of joy.

All during the cruise of the *Paramour* from Africa to Portugal, she seized every moment to be alone with him. What man could have resisted her blandishments? Surely not Maunday who, himself, was head over heels! Aware of the distance between himself and the grand lady that was the Marquesa, he did not press his luck. It was she who did all the pressing. She wanted to involve him and she did.

"Mi querido, you will see what plans I have in store for you and for me when I reach my native Lisbon!"

What these plans were, Maunday, a simple man, could not have guessed even in his wildest dreams.

The *Paramour* had sighted the coast of Portugal. Captain Boggs was on the bridge. Much to his surprise, a lady joined him without by-your-leave. The Marquesa.

"Señor Capitan! I wish to speak with you, alone."

Boggs sent his first mate below. "Ma'am? What have you to say?"

"This, Señor Capitan, I wish to marry the Señor Maunday. I desire that you dismiss him from your ship. Give him his . . . how do you say it . . .?"

"Discharge, ma'am?"

"Si! Si! Discharge!"

"Impossible, ma'am. Maunday is a member of this ship's crew. An important member. We have not finished our cruise, ma'am."

"Dear Señor Capitan," said the lady sweetly, "your cruise might finish sooner than you think unless you do what I say."

"Might finish?" said Boggs in amazement.

"Yes."

"But why?"

"Because I, myself, will swear out a warrant for your arrest as a pirate and a murderer and an abductor of women. You'll never leave Portugal, alive."

It took Boggs some time to digest the meaning of the Marquesa's astonishing speech. But he finally understood.

"You win, Marquesa. I'll give Maunday his discharge."

"And also his share of the gold and jewels?" said Doña Pilar with a lively smile. "I am a rich woman but I do not think it is good for rich women to marry poor men."

"So . . . Maunday blabbed to you about his wealth!" Boggs scratched his head, but he finally said "yes," because, as he later put it, "the lady had the big end of the stick."

The morning the *Paramour* dropped anchor in Viga harbor, His Majesty's Consul Douglas Selkirk was breakfasting on his vine-hung terrace. Two soft-boiled eggs, a pot of hot milk, laced with brandy, and a basket of crusty peasant bread were being served by a buxom middle-aged woman name Tia. He'd devoured one egg and was starting on the other when his man-of-all-work came out on the terrace.

"Excellency! A man wishes to speak with you."

"Let him speak to Señor Peewick," said Selkirk, knife poised over the crown of the egg.

"Señor Peewick is painting boats," said the servant.

"Señor Peewick can cease painting boats until I have finished my breakfast," said Consul Selkirk.

The servant leaned over the terrace rail and called, "Señor Peewick! Señor Peewick!" in a shrill voice.

A man clad in white linens was seated on the sands in front of an easel. A wide-brimmed straw hat shaded his eyes. His hand paused in the act of conveying a brushful of cobalt blue to the canvas on the easel.

"What is it?" he answered.

"The Señor Peewick will be pleased to come," shrilled the servant.

"I don't want any breakfast."

"Not for breakfast. It is official, Señor Peewick!"

Kevin Peewick glanced at the quickly shifting color of the waves. Oh, well! Tomorrow at the same hour the effect could probably be recaptured. Leaving his painter's materials on the strand, he trudged up the beach and climbed the wooden stairs on bare feet. Once in a while one must humor Consul Selkirk and do a little "official business" or one might lose one's sinecure . . . bed and board in beautiful Viga in exchange for a few secretarial duties.

It was a strange trio that waited in the anteroom. A stockily built man in the dress of a sea captain, an Englishman by the cut of him. A tall, handsome redhead, dressed in plain seaman's clothing and carrying a heavy sea chest—also an Englishman. The third member of the trio was a beautiful woman with dark eyes and raven hair—certainly not English! And if Kevin Peewick had doubted his judgment, the lady's Portuguese-accented English confirmed its worth.

"Are you the British Consular Agent?" she said, throwing back her veil.

"No ma'am," said Peewick. "He is Mr. Selkirk."

"Then take us to Mr. Selkirk," said the lady in tones that brooked no argument.

"One moment, Madam, Sirs," said Peewick, I'll announce you. What names shall I give?"

"Never mind our names," said Boggs, intervening. "The matter is urgent. Please hurry." Boggs turned to the Marquesa as soon as the door closed on Peewick. "Ma'am, let me finish my business first. Then you may attend to yours."

"Very well, Señor Capitan, since you have been so kind to Maunday and me, I consent," said Doña Pilar graciously.

Wiping a spot of egg from his lower lip with the tip of his pinky, Consul Selkirk came through the door.

"Your servant, ma'am," he said bowing to the beauty of a lady. He eyed Boggs. "Mr. Peewick says you wish to speak with me on a matter of urgency. Please come this way, sir."

Boggs waited until the door of the inner office closed then he saluted, Navy style. "Captain Boggs on special duty. The password is Buttons, sir."

"Buttons?" Selkirk consulted a memo book that he carried in his inside waistcoat pocket. "Ah yes, Buttons. At your service, Captain Boggs."

"I wish to send a code message to His Majesty's Envoy in Lisbon. Can you provide a fast, reliable carrier?"

"I can do better. I can send a carrier pigeon. Use my desk, Captain. While you are composing your message to His Excellency, I'll speak to the lady."

Doña Pilar wasted no time in small talk. "Señor Consul, I am the Marquesa Valalodad. This gentleman is Lieutenant Maunday."

Selkirk's excellent memory began to stir. The Marquesa Valalodad? "Were you not the victim of a pirate kidnapping, Madam?"

"Yes," said Doña Pilar. "And this brave cavalier, Lieutenant Maunday, rescued me from a pirate castle where I and my eleven companions were imprisoned."

"Were you not captured by the notorious Ironhand, Madam?" exclaimed Selkirk.

"I was," the lady answered. "And now I must call on you for help. We need conveyances to take us to Lisbon. Four coaches will suffice."

"Four coaches, Madam? Where would I procure four coaches in Viga? You are welcome to use my carriole. It will hold two . . . three people in a squeeze. Then there is the public stage. It comes through Viga in about a half hour."

Doña Pilar spoke to Maunday. "The ladies can take the

stage. You and I will accept the gentleman's loan of his carriole." She turned back to Selkirk. "Señor Consul, I thank you in the name of my uncle, the Minister of Foreign Affairs. He will report your courtesy to your superiors, and who knows, you might someday find yourself wearing an ambassador's falucca!"

"I . . . an ambassador? Oh, no, Madam!" protested Selkirk. "Take my vehicle but do not recommend me for promotion. I love the quiet life in Viga."

Doña Pilar laughed. "Very well. I shan't recommend you . . . merely give you my thanks. Now, sir, hurry that carriole. Lieutenant Maunday and I are in haste to repair to Lisbon."

His Majesty's Envoy to King Joseph of Portugal, Sir Mathew Houghton, received a message by carrier pigeon, that when decoded caused his pale-gray eyes to sharpen. Within less than an hour, the same message was speeding to London by pigeon and semaphore and light signal.

The Lord High Admiral, Lord Wilmington, received the message from the hand of his code officer and straightway entered his carriage and drove to Cheyne Walk, Chelsea, where he routed his old friend Lord Frawley out of his afternoon nap.

"Greg! Your chap's either played us false or fallen into a trap."

"What chap?" Lord Frawley sat bolt upright in his wing chair. "Trap? What trap?" He donned his spectacles and read the message Wilmington handed him, half to himself and half out loud.

Challoner and Lady Artis Grantley abducted by Moor pirates, sailed aboard sloop, name unknown . . . destination unknown. Boggs aboard *Paramour* in Viga, Portugal.

"Lady Artis Grantley? I don't understand."

"I do, Greg," sputtered Wilmington. "It is my belief that your chap threw in with the pirates and that he's abducted Lady Artis Grantley aboard her own sloop."

"Preposterous!" exclaimed Lord Frawley. "Challoner would die before he'd turn traitor."

"You forget whom he's turned traitor with," said Wilmington.

"But . . . but what would Lady Grantley be doing in African waters?" protested Frawley.

"Searching for adventure if I know the lady," grinned Wilmington. "She owns a seagoing sloop, the *Thetis*. I saw her at Cowes last year."

"All this sounds like a seaman's yarn to me," said Lord Frawley. "We'll soon find out the truth regarding Lady Grantley. I know a man who is well informed as to her comings and goings . . . "

"Quite a number of men are well informed about Lady Grantley," said Wilmington with a cool smile. "By all means, find your man, let's hear what he has to say."

Sir Henry Fox was taking a stroll in the afternoon sunshine after having spent several exhausting hours in Court. Still dressed in his robe and periwig, he was congratulating himself on having won a particularly difficult case involving rights of succession. The fee would be handsome, his prestige enhanced. He was crossing the Inner Court of the Temple when a man, decently attired in black, came hurrying toward him.

"Sir Henry, your clerk pointed you out to me through the windowpane. I am Admiral Lord Frawley's secretary, sir. Lord Frawley requests that you call on him immediately. His carriage is waiting. He said to tell you it's a matter of great urgency."

Sir Henry had only a nodding acquaintance with the retired admiral, but deeming it expedient to obey the summons, he followed the secretary to the carriage that was stationed at his door. A matter of great urgency? Was the Old Man in need of legal advice?

He'd no sooner stepped into Frawley's library and sighted the Lord High Admiral, Wilmington, than he was aware that serious business was on the docket. Frawley was retired, but Wilmington was not only master of England's sea power, but a good hand at statecraft and politics as well.

"Fox . . ." mumbled Lord Wilmington in his chins. He'd no love to waste upon "ravens" as he called members of the legal profession.

"I'm in your debt for coming here," said Lord Frawley rising to exchange a handshake with his caller.

"My pleasure, your lordship," said Sir Henry. He took

the chair his host indicated. "What can I do for you, gentlemen?"

"Answer a question," said the Lord High Admiral bluntly. "Where is your client, Lady Artis Grantley?"

Fox's tufted, white eyebrows rode upon his forehead. "May *I* ask a question, your lordship? What business is it of yours where my client is?"

"Don't take the pepper to your nose, Sir Henry!" said Lord Frawley in conciliatory tones. "The whereabouts of Lady Grantley may be a matter of state."

"State!" exclaimed the nettled barrister. "Lady Grantley has never dabbled in politics."

"Never is a big word when you allude to a woman, Fox," snapped Wilmington. "Especially when you allude to Lady Artis. We do not wish to pry, but we *must* know the approximate whereabouts of your client. Is she in London or at one of her country places? Is she in England?"

"It so happens, she is not in England," answered Sir Henry, taking on a somewhat pompous air.

"Ah? Ah? Where is she?" asked Lord Frawley sharply.

"She is visiting the Duchess d'Ivencourt in Touraine," said Fox. "I can't see why this should be a matter of state. We're not at war with France."

"You're *certain* she is in Touraine?" insisted Wilmington.

"Certain . . ." Sir Henry shifted uncomfortably in his chair. "She *said* she was off to Touraine."

"She said . . . but could she have gone elsewhere?" objected Lord Frawley. "Perhaps for a cruise?"

Lord Wilmington took snuff, sneezed, snapped the lid of the box shut with a loud click. "Have you any way of finding out precisely where Lady Grantley might be?"

The barrister looked first at the Lord High Admiral and then at Lord Frawley. "My lords, may I ask why Lady Grantley's whereabouts should concern you?"

"You may," said Wilmington. "We've intelligence that the lady may have been kidnapped by the terrible Captain Ironhand, the pirate of whom you have doubtless read in the press, and that she finds herself at sea . . . and at his mercy."

Sir Henry laughed a dry little laugh. Artis kidnapped? It would serve her right! His mirthful expression changed suddenly. "Come, come, my lords, you must be mistaken."

"We hope we are, Fox," said Lord Frawley curtly. "Will you do what you can to discover the lady's whereabouts? We, on our side, will leave no stone unturned."

Sir Henry Fox was a troubled man as he rode back to Town. A hundred times over, Artis had played the same trick on him—saying she was going south when she was going north! Causing him endless bother to trace her from castle to country house, from country house to castle. Would her household staff have heard from her? He directed the coachman to take him to Park Lane, but at the corner of Great Stanhope Mews, he called out of the window, "Stop here." The best man to talk to would be Artis' trainer.

McKenna was working on a filly that he had brought home from Tat's auction rooms earlier in the morning. She needed a liniment compress for a left front fetlock that she had barked on a stall post. So intent was he that he hardly heard Sir Henry Fox's voice hailing him from the stable door, "Pat McKenna! Oh, McKenna!"

When a stableboy called his master's attention to the visitor, the trainer threw over his shoulder, "I'll be with you in a moment, Sir Henry." The compress bound on the barked fetlock, McKenna came to greet the barrister who was pacing nervously up and down in front of the stable door.

"Good day to you, sir."

Sir Henry cut amenities short. "McKenna, where is Lady Grantley?"

"Visitin' my sister in Ben Lachda," said McKenna shifting his unlighted clay pipe from one corner of his mouth to the other. He never smoked in the stables but he liked the taste of tobacco on his tongue.

"Are you sure she's in Ben Lachda?" insisted Sir Henry.

McKenna scratched his red head. "Well now, I'm as sure as mon can be . . . but where Kit . . . I mean Lady Artis is concerned . . ."

"Well?"

"Well now . . . I saw her off for the Highlands, sir."

"Have you heard from her since?"

"No, Sir Henry. She said she'd send letters to you in case of need."

"I've not heard from her, but rumor has," exclaimed Sir Henry.

"Rumor?" McKenna cocked a rusty eyebrow. "We'd best go up to my rooms, Sir Henry."

The big North Irelandman climbed the stairs with considerably more haste than usual. Sensing trouble, he was anxious.

"A drop o' Glenavon, sir?"

Sir Henry tossed down the whiskey at one gulp.

"McKenna, I'll be frank with you, but you must keep your mouth shut. Rumor has it, Lady Artis has been kidnapped by a notorious pirate named Ironhand and that she is presently cruising the Mediterranean in his company."

"A pirate?" The big Irishman knocked the ash out of his pipe, packed it with fresh tobacco, ignited a spill from a coal on the hearth and lighted the tobacco. "D'ye believe the rumor, Sir Henry?"

"The rumor came from a high-ranking naval officer," snapped Sir Henry.

McKenna affected a calm he was far from possessing. "Well now, I think ye'll find Kit's takin' her ease at Ben Lachda with my sister."

"I'll find . . . I'll find! I've got to *know!*" snapped Sir Henry.

McKenna's quick mind was busy piecing bits of evidence together to produce a pattern—one he would rather not have seen! Kit, up to her tricks again. Gone to sea, was she? Gone . . . not with a pirate named Ironhand . . . but with a man named Challoner? Oh, the naughty!

Astute Sir Henry Fox saw the trainer's expression change—the alert tobacco-brown eyes cloud with speculation.

"Come, McKenna! You know something! Tell me what it is?"

"Well now," said McKenna, "ye ken how Kit is . . . full o' fancies. I thought when she invited the man here, it was just another of her whims."

"Man? What man?"

"His name was James Challoner, sir."

"Challoner, who went before Courts Martial on a charge of criminal conduct and lese majesty?"

"Aye, Sir Henry."

"Good Lord! How . . . where did she meet *him?*"

McKenna shifted his pipe from one corner of his mouth to the other. "She rode 'im down, in a manner of speakin', sir. It was in the Park. She was out exercisin' Daemon. Rode 'im down, then invited 'im to call. A fine gentleman, in spite of it all. No harm was done, either way. He went on a trading voyage . . . or so he said."

The barrister had heard enough. The picture was clear as crystal. Artis with her usual flouting of the laws that rule the weaker sex, had taken her newest male fancy to sea! But how had she gotten from Challoner to a pirate named Ironhand?

"You should have warned me, McKenna!" he said angrily.

"Warned ye, Sir Henry? How could I have guessed? Challoner refused to have anything to do with her."

"He refused?"

"Aye . . . backed out of the stall when Kit tried to put the halter on."

Sir Henry clapped his palm to his forehead in a gesture of despair. For a man to say "No" was all Artis needed! She thrived on negatives! Nothing pleased her better than a reluctant lover!

"Will she never learn?" he groaned half to himself.

"Give her time, Sir Henry," said McKenna indulgently.

"Give her time? She's a woman grown," exclaimed Sir Henry. "The scandals, her excesses of conduct, cannot be explained away as youthful pranks! Now she's run off with a man broken from rank! It's too much!"

"Well now," said McKenna placatingly, "some women are like some thoroughbreds in the spring of their days . . . high-strung, skittish, unruly . . . good for nought except to be flattered, caressed, fed, pampered, groomed. But I've seen many such as have turned into prime racing queens, and when their wild-oat days are done, into gentle brood mares of fine offspring. The knack is to find the right stud, if I may make the comparison. Would you believe it if I told you, Kit fell in love, heart and soul, with this Challoner? Never saw her so hard hit."

"Love!" snorted Sir Henry. "What does Artis know

about love? She collects men as entomologists collect butterflies! Oh, this time she's gone too far!"

Driving back to Chelsea, Sir Henry Fox tried to frame some plausible defense of his client . . . without success. Artis was indefensible. Her caprices were inexcusable. Her morals? Who would attempt to uphold them in a court of law?

His feet dragged as he climbed the steps of Number 16 Cheyne Walk. His face sagged in heavy lines as he again faced Lord Frawley.

"Your lordship's supposition was correct. Lady Artis is . . . presumably . . . not in Touraine . . . nor is she in Scotland."

"And where is she . . . presumably?" asked Lord Frawley coldly.

"There seems to be a person named James Challoner involved, your lordship," said the barrister lamely.

"Challoner?" Lord Frawley jumped from his chair. "Did you say Challoner?"

"I did."

"How came you to link the two . . . Challoner and the pirate Ironhand?"

"You spoke the name Ironhand," said Sir Henry, irritated by his lordship's pre-emptory tone of voice. "I heard about this Challoner from Lady Grantley's trainer, Pat McKenna. It seems she was on the . . . well . . . she knew the man quite well."

Frawley seized the barrister's coat by the lapels. "See here, Sir Henry! Not a word of this must go any further."

Fox glanced down his long nose at the speaker's clutching hands. "It is part of my profession to hold my tongue, your lordship. And I think I can vouch for McKenna's discretion. He serves Lady Grantley with more than a trainer's faithfulness."

Lord Frawley released him. "Forgive me, Sir Henry. I'm upset. You can deduce what you please, but I can tell you only one thing! Lady Artis is in over her depth, this time. Will you give me the *Thetis's* specifications? We'll do our best to find her."

"I'll have to get them from her ladyship's papers on file in my office," said Sir Henry. "I'm not a sailing man, myself. Don't know a sloop from a frigate."

"Find them as quickly as possible," urged Lord Frawley. "I'll have a man standing by to pick them up. And . . . thank you, Sir Henry. Good day."

The door had scarcely closed upon the bewildered barrister when Lord Frawley called for his coat, hat and carriage. An hour later he was seated opposite the Lord High Admiral in Seething Lane.

"It's as reported! Lady Grant-em-All and Challoner, alias Ironhand, have hoisted the Jolly Roger in a love cruise!"

"You don't say, Greg!"

The two Sea Lords regarded each other in a slow savoring of the idea just communicated. Then they broke into gusts of laughter.

"By Jove! That Challoner!"

"I say, old chap, what a pity we can't share this morsel with the Club!"

"Pity, indeed. Have you any idea how to lay hands on Challoner and his aristocratic paramour?"

"Paramour!" chuckled Lord Frawley. "Challoner rechristened the *Royal Acre* the *Paramour!"*

The two gentlemen exploded in fresh gusts of merriment. But their mirth did not last.

"As soon as you have the description of the sloop, order every ship to seek her out. I have my own theory. Challoner hasn't turned traitor. He himself is prisoner of the Moors . . . forced to do their bidding whether he likes it or not."

"Time will tell," said Wilmington. "Guilty or innocent, I rather envy him his cruise with a woman like Artis Grantley."

Frawley said with pinched lips, "Hasn't it occurred to you, Fred, that Lady Grantley may be the plaything of the Moors, rather than the lovelight of Challoner's eye?"

"I never thought of that horrendous possibility!" grinned Wilmington. "The poor, poor lady! Moors? I say, Greg, we'd better get on with the search."

Lord Frawley turned at the door. His face was stern. "If Challoner *has* gone over to the Moors, I'll spring the trap that'll hang him, with my own hand."

12.

Knight of Ghosts
and Shadows

With a heart of furious fancies,
Whereof I am commander;
With a burning spear,
And a horse of air,
To the wilderness I wander . . .

ROBERT HERRICK'S POEM, "TOM O' BEDLAM," HAD
haunted Challoner as the yacht *Atlanta* had borne up
from the African coast in perfect June weather. Phantom
ship! Her captain impersonating a dead man. Spying Moors
watching his every move by day or night. Let him but raise
his glass to scan the horizon, the Hadji was at his elbow.

"You betrayed my trust in you!" Challoner had flung at
the Moor when wakening from drugged sleep he had seen
the giant Moor standing at the side of the bunk.

"I made certain nothing would alter my plans or deter
them," Mohammed-ben-Dar had retorted.

"I would have come with you of my own free will."

"Would you? You had a powerful weapon of argument
at your disposal. Your frigate and her guns."

"We made a pact, Hadji!"

"So we did. But would you have ordered your ship to
stay behind, had I not taken strong measures to prevent you
from giving her her sailing orders?"

"I most certainly would not!" Challoner had answered
hotly. "The *Paramour* would have insured my safety."

"Just as I surmised," smiled the Hadji. "You would not
have stopped to consider that Planter Hunnicutt would not
have had a frigate as escort and that the *Paramour's* pres-

133

ence would have surely been suspicioned and challenged by some member of the English fleet."

"The *Paramour* could have sailed under false colors," Challoner had answered, knowing all the while that the Moor had bested him from every side of the argument. He hadn't dared let his captor know how worried he was for the *Paramour's* safety.

The chief masquerader was Artis! He was watching her at dinner, on the fourth night at sea. Gowned in Mistress Hunnicutt's best furbelows, she was "dear husbanding" it, right and left. How the evidence of the eye could fool the casual onlooker. Here in these luxurious dining quarters, amidst glistening white paint, gilt trim, shining mahogany and silver plate, a gentleman from South Carolina and his lady dined leisurely. A stately butler and his two black-face aides attended to the service. One could almost deceive one's self into thinking it was all true, legitimate, authentic!

"I am eager to hear the news of Mayfair," says Mistress Hunnicutt. "Are skirts full, this season? What color is à la mode? Dear husband, I fear I'll seem provincial, dressed as I am."

That was Artis' method for maintaining calm, poise and good humor in face of what she must guess was a "situation" to say the least.

"I know what happened there at the castle," she'd said the day they had sailed. "Some member of your crew must have told these pirates who I really am. Not the Captain's wench at all! A woman of means."

"And?" he'd prompted.

"Well, can't you see?" she'd retorted. "They're taking me back to England where they will claim some preposterous sum for my ransom." Then she had giggled like a schoolgirl. "Oh, James, I'd like to see Foxy's face when he hears he will have to 'dislocate' some holding of mine in order to meet the pirates' demands."

Did she *believe* the myth she'd cut out of the cloth of imagination? How easy to be deceived by a soft voice murmuring from across a dining table.

"Dear husband, will you pick me a good steeplechaser at Tat's next auction?"

Challoner spooned his trifle in silence. The meal having

ended, the Moor entered the dining saloon and seated himself at table. A servant brought a water pipe.

"I trust you enjoyed your meal, O Ironhand?"

"I did indeed, Hadji," answered Challoner. He lighted a cheroot and puffed in silence while considering a means of divorcing Lady Artis from the pseudo marriage in which they had been entangled by the Moor's efforts.

"Is there something on your mind?" asked Mohammed-ben-Dar.

"Yes," said Challoner bluntly. "I am concerned whether my woman will perform her role in London with faithfulness or whether at the crucial moment she may not fail us both. I am reminded that she twice sought to run away. Once, in Porto San Carlos and a second time when the women of the *Lerida* were taken off the *Paramour*."

The Moor's face darkened. "Will she not do what you require of her?" he asked tersely.

"The Hadji judges all women by those of his nation," said Challoner. "This wench is English born."

"She is a woman in love," said the Moor. "Command her, and she'll obey."

"Perhaps. But I'd rather avoid the risk . . . leave her out of the serious business before us."

"No!" said the Moor sharply. "A Carolinian planter and his wife are to have audience with the King. They will keep that audience, or . . ."

"Or what?" said Challoner with equal sharpness of tone. "Suppose at the critical moment our fake Mistress Hunnicutt should betray us? I've as much staked on this venture as yourself!"

The Moor thought a moment before he answered, his face taking on a look of sternness.

"My plan is complete, Captain Ironhand, it cannot be changed. Say to your woman, 'Do what I command.' She'll obey."

Challoner emptied his glass. "Very well! But should something go wrong, I'll take no blame, for I have warned you."

"Nothing will go wrong, O Ironhand," the Moor retorted. "I have weighed every possibility, even that you, yourself, should be of a mind to betray me!" His flashing eyes said the rest.

"Dagger in the ribs?" smiled Challoner. "In England, murder is a hanging matter!"

"Come, come, Captain," laughed the Moor. "I'd be a poor general indeed, were I not able to arrange for my own safety. I promise you, no English hemp will ever be about *my* neck!"

It was not a vain boast, of that Challoner was certain. If this fanatical Moor had a chain of receivers of stolen goods in England, he must also have trustworthy accomplices upon whom he could count in an emergency.

Baffled, still uncertain how to deal with "his woman," Challoner joined Artis in the drawing room. She'd gotten out Mistress Hunnicutt's playing cards.

"A game of bezique, dear husband?"

"Need you pound at the name *husband?*"

She waved him to the chair on the opposite side of the card table. "Yes, I do need. Merely to say 'dear husband' gives me courage."

"*You* lack courage?" exclaimed the astonished Challoner.

"Of course," she answered in her spirited way. "Do you think I do not question? 'Is the man I adore a scoundrel? Has he come to the conclusion it were better to join with the pirates than to play a lone hand against them?' Certainly I'm afraid, for I have much to lose!" She dealt the cards. "You see, James, pirate or no pirate, I hope to make you my husband for keeps, when we get to London."

"Indeed?" he said, affecting a calm that was not real. "How do you plan to hold onto a pirate long enough to make him your 'for keeps' husband?"

"Never mind," she said coolly. "I have a plan."

Challoner's heartbeat quickened. "Really? May I inquire what it is?"

"You may not," she answered with a laugh. "I am different from most women. I do not say all that is on my mind."

"Surely you wouldn't keep secrets from your 'dear husband'?" said Challoner coaxingly.

She threw down her cards, rose, came around to him and tipped across the arm of his chair onto his knees.

"James! When *you* say 'dear husband,' the goose flesh rises. I feel a faintness inside. Joy! Terror that it might not be true. Oh, darling! Tell me my hope isn't vain? Say you'll

desert this perilous career at sea and be all mine? I've
money you know. A great deal of money. I can buy you a
peerage. There! Wouldn't you love it to sit in Lords, take
snuff and mumble 'Hear, hear,' into your neckcloth?"

Bare white arms about his neck! Seeking lips!

"James! I love you so very much."

How she could make shambles of his resolve to be stern!

"Come, dearest."

Bezique forgotten, she led him to the master cabin, like
a lamb to the slaughter . . . but what a delicious way to die!

Challoner wakened in the dead of night. Near him, so
very near, Artis' small body was curled up like a child's—
knees and fists to chin. How beautiful she was! How readily
she could change caprice into near-acceptable coin. "I'll
buy you a peerage," she'd said. He could almost see himself, dozing, taking snuff, "hear hearing" it in his carved
pew in Lords. Ridiculous picture!

The deep stillness of the night let every shipboard sound
be heard with startling clarity. Sway of spanker in the shift
of the wind. A sighing of timbers. And there . . . the low
growl . . . the bark . . . the cough . . . the whine of wild
beasts in the hold. Merely to know that the *Atlanta* was a
carrier of death in animal form was to be deeply concerned!

A light sweat broke out on Challoner's body, so that he
found it impossible to remain abed.

Rising, he pulled on breeches and a linen shirt with lace
cuffs and the initials HOH embroidered in blue on the
front. The shirt of Mr. Hunnicutt.

Going topside, he began pacing the afterdeck in an effort
to calm his nerves and cool his overheated blood. Where
lay the path of wisdom? What loophole was there in this
web in which he was caught? How much dare he tell Artis?
The truth? No! No! He must bear that burden alone. But
some device was needed, some charming, implausible lie!

A steady wind from the south filled the *Atlanta's* sails.
She moved like a swan through waters that were just beginning to change from night-black to pre-dawn gray. On
her bridge, the Turk.

"Ho there, Mr. Hunnicutt!" hailed Captain Hassan.

"Ho, Captain!" answered Challoner.

"Will you take a cup of caffè with me, Mr. Hunnicutt?"

"With pleasure, sir."

The Turk was in a talkative mood. "This has been one of the most delightful cruises I have ever undertaken."

"Yes," Challoner agreed, and he added, "I only hope it is not the calm before the storm."

"Storm? The sky is without a cloud and the barometer stands firm," said Hassan.

"You never know, in the Bay of Biscay," said Challoner.

"We're not bound for the Bay of Biscay, my friend," answered the Turk.

"Ah? Where *are* we bound?"

"For Viga, Portugal."

"I see. Are we going to be in Viga long?" asked Challoner with pounding heart. There was a British Consul in Viga! Would there be a chance to get word to him?

"I doubt if you will see much of Viga *or* Portugal," smiled the Turk.

"I've no interest in Viga or Portgual," said Challoner with a shrug. "I'm in haste to get to our destination on time."

"Have no fear," said the Turk. "The Hadji has calculated his timetable to the hour . . . to the very minute. All will go as smooth as oil. You'll see."

Challoner emptied his cup of delicious caffè. "I have complete confidence in our leader," he said matter-of-factly. "There's only one weak link in his plan that I can see."

"What is that?"

"My woman. She has a hankering to see London. She even threatened to desert me for a lover who would stay put . . . keep her like a queen in a Soho flat. If *I* were the Hadji, I'd lock her up, never let her set foot ashore."

"There is some wisdom in what you say," conceded Captain Hassan.

Challoner did not press his advantage and bidding the Turk a casual goodnight, he went below. Again he was sorely tempted to explain their whole predicament to Artis and ask her help in getting a warning to Lord Frawley. The urge was so strong that when he found her sitting up in her bunk, reading by the light of a lamp, he sat down at her side.

"I thought you'd never come," she said, patting back a yawn. "What in the world were you doing, on deck?"

"Thinking," he answered.

"What were you thinking, Mr. Hunnicutt?"

"Oh! Damn Hunnicutt!" he said impatiently. "You don't seem to realize that we are in an extremely delicate situation, aboard this sloop."

"Do you mean those dreadful wild animals in the hold, or do you mean the Moors and what they intend to do about my ransom?" she said, closing the book and tossing it onto a table near the bed.

"The wild animals are caged," said Challoner. "It's the Moors I fear."

"What? You, their partner, fear them?"

"You don't understand!" exclaimed Challoner.

"Very well, make me understand."

He was on the brink of confession when suddenly—

"No," she cried. "I'd rather you did *not* tell me. I like surprises. I like the thrill of the unexpected. Life would be so tame if one were always prepared, briefed, warned, in advance. You needn't fear, dear heart, Foxy will pay the Moors what they demand. Of course I hope you'll get your share of the ransom money as one of their band. But should they decide to cut you out . . . never mind . . . my fortune can stand some nibbling at the edges. Come to bed, my sweet. We've wasted the night in conversation."

Her incredible frivolity amazed and disheartened Challoner to such a degree that he vowed to himself never to breathe word of the plot against the King, but one thing he must do—find a way to win the Turkish pirate captain Hassan over to his way of thinking—get him for an ally in convincing the Hadji that "Mistress Hunnicutt" would be a liability, not an aid on their arrival in London.

"Ironhand, why are you so quiet?" whispered Artis against his cheek. Her little hand caressed him. "Have you no kisses for me, *chéri?*"

How could a man draw away? He gathered her into his arms.

But, tonight, Artis was not persuaded by her lover's caresses, nor was she so blind that she did not sense a tenseness aboard the *Atlanta*—a state of suspense, a menace that went far beyond a mere pirate's bid for gain. Challoner's reticence and nervousness? What could it all mean?

Artis Grantley had always known that someday Fate

would bring her face to face with a man whom she would
be unable to regard with her customary outlook of . . .
woman in search of thrills. That man was James Challoner.
The look of love he'd seen in her face was real. She *was*
in love. No retreat. No begging the gift of herself.

Eyes wide open, she listened to her lover's even breathing. How could his man's nerves let him sleep while she
kept anxious vigil? No, this voyage was not an ordinary
pirate raid. What was behind it all? Was Challoner being
coerced by the pirates? Was he forced to do their bidding,
lest she, herself, should be the sacrifice? The theory was
interesting—still, not altogether convincing. For what
would prevent Challoner from taking her with him in a
daring "abandon ship" as soon as land was within sight?
No . . . Challoner was being *made* to stick with the pirates. But why? What hold had they over him to persuade
him to masquerade as Planter Hunnicutt? She was still
wide awake when sounds on deck betrayed the unmistakable maneuvers of a ship coming to anchorage.

Artis slipped out of the bunk and ran to the porthole.
There were a few lights ahead, lights that suddenly went
out. Why? Then she realized that a brushful of black paint
had been smeared across the porthole on the outside. The
same with the other portholes. She ran to the door, drew
the bolt and tried to open it. Locked! Sudden terror struck
her. She ran to Challoner.

"James! Wake up!"

"Eh? What?" He sat up, rubbing his eyes. "What's the
trouble?"

"We're anchored somewhere," cried Artis. "They've
painted the portholes so we cannot see out and our door
is locked. We're prisoners."

Challoner rose and threw on his breeches, stepped into
his shoes, knocked furiously on the panel, shouting, "Hadji!
Open up! Open I say!"

In a few moments a guttural voice answered, "It's no
use pounding and shouting. You will stay where you are
until the Captain gives the order to let you out."

All the next day, Challoner's trained ear could detect the
sound of brushstrokes on the hull of the *Atlanta*. It did not
take a genius to understand that her color was being
changed for the purpose of concealing her identity. Scream

of pulleys, banging of hammer, *zzzz* of saw. Were they altering her masts? A pair of armed Moors brought food to the prisoners at noon and again at night.

It was a grueling test of patience during which Challoner's determination to get Artis off the ship crystallized. He hadn't fully realized how much he cared for her safety, how much he treasured her life until now. Every barrier of censorship and jealousy seemed to fall. "I love her, wholly and sincerely," he said to himself. "Who am I to judge her past? The present suffices to show how dear she is to me."

Never, though, did he allow himself to be lured by Artis' blithe promise, "I'll marry you." There was too much distance between them. There was a mountain of differences.

To add to the prisoners' discomfort, the weather had turned torrid. The cabin was like an oven.

"How long will they keep us locked up?" sighed Artis, fanning herself with one of Mrs. Hunnicutt's fans. She presented a charming picture in a thin, white *négligé* that did not quite conceal her lovely self. Her red-gold curls clung damply to cheek and brow. There were tiny beads of perspiration on her upper lip.

Challoner kissed them, tasting of their salt. "They'll keep us here until they've changed the *Atlanta* so even her builders won't recognize her."

"Why are they doing that?"

"Because it's part of their game."

"And why must they keep *you*, their partner, in the dark as to what they are up to?"

"I wish I knew," said Challoner evasively.

"But you *are* one of them!" insisted Artis. "I can't see why there should be secrets among allies."

Again, Challoner was sorely tempted to take her into his confidence, but just as he was about to speak, the door opened and the Hadji appeared on the threshold.

Artis bounded out of her chair. "You . . . you wretched African! How dare you keep us locked in this cabin all this time." She gave the Moor a push, brushed past him and ran down the companionway.

"By the beard of the Prophet!" exclaimed the Hadji in an angry voice. "You were right, O Ironhand, your woman *is* a vixen."

Challoner was quick to take advantage of the Moor's irritation. "I'm glad you saw with your own eyes. I tell you, she'll hinder, rather than help us. Why not put her ashore, here . . . anywhere. For all her imitation fine manners, she's only a peasant girl. Let her go back to where I found her . . . in a Portuguese waterfront tavern. I would a thousand times rather put her ashore before we reach English waters than risk some new outburst that could compromise the success of our endeavor."

"And where do you think we are now, Ironhand effendi?" said the Moor with a sharp, underbrow look.

"I take it we're off the coast of Portugal."

"And what makes you think we're off Portugal?"

"Because I have good ears," grinned Challoner. "You brought a man aboard for carpentry. I heard him talking Portuguese as he hammered."

The Hadji smiled broadly. "By the Prophet, Ironhand, you're a man who would be hard to beat, if I had the ill luck to meet you in the enemy camp."

"You treat me as if I *were* in the enemy camp," said Challoner sharply. "What need was there to lock me up with that vixen of a woman? I'm sick of her, do you hear? Sick! Put her ashore. I'll make excuses to the King and Queen, say, Mistress Hunnicutt is suffering from fatigue of the voyage. Believe me, Planter Hunnicutt's royal hosts are not interested in his wife, but in the wild animals from America that he brings, as gifts."

The Moor seemed to hesitate. Would he consent? Challoner's hopes had begun to rise, when they were again dashed.

"Come," said the Hadji, "they're hauling anchor. Soon we'll be at sea again."

Following him on deck, Challoner watched the distance widen between the sloop and land. That village with its distinctive church and extensive shipyards was indeed Viga. He knew it from having put in for repairs to his ship some years ago.

He went to the rail. Yes, they'd done some altering! The white-hulled sloop was now a black-hulled sloop. And they'd changed *Atlanta* to *Hesperides*. They'd even removed the Indian warrior head from the prow.

That night, the cabin door bolted, Artis held close in his

arms, he said in whispers, "You asked me many questions. Now I am prepared to answer you. Listen!"

He told of the Moor's plot to assassinate the English royal family, and the role the wild animals were to play.

When he had finished she lay back in the hollow of his arm and gave him a strange look. "What are you afraid of, Ironhand? That the Moors will turn against you when their plot has succeeded?"

"Artis! Do you really believe that I am working *with* these devils?"

"You yourself convinced me," she retorted.

"I was keeping you in the dark to protect you."

"Really? If you had wanted only to protect me, there were other ways."

"How?"

"You could have escaped, taking me with you."

"How could I have escaped? They had me under twenty-four-hour guard."

"Methinks thou dost protest too much, Ironhand," she laughed. "I see another picture. James Challoner, a disgruntled man, without fortune or position, sees his chance to win a fortune in loot. He joins the African pirates. Then by a stroke of fortune, I fall in love with him. Here, he says, is the richest booty yet. How much is Lady Artis Grantley worth, in ransom money? Tell me, Ironhand . . . where do you and your accomplices plan to make rendezvous with Sir Henry Fox?"

"You've mentioned this Fox . . . Foxy . . . several times. Who is he?" said Challoner who had managed to conceal the upheaval her words had caused in his mind.

"Come now!" smiled Artis. "Don't tell me that you are not aware of Foxy's role in my life. Sir Henry Fox KC . . . my administrator and legal counsel?"

"I am aware of it now," said Challoner, softly. "I am also keenly aware that I should not have taken you into my confidence . . . let you continue in your role . . . to the bitter end." He put her away, rose and pulled on his coat. On the way out of the cabin he paused. "You said once that there was nothing you wouldn't do for me. There is your chance. Jump ship the next time we make land. Send word to Lord Frawley. I'll give you a token which you will present to him. Describe the *Atlanta* as she looks now. Black hull, no Indian head on the prow. The name . . . *Hesperides*. Give the word danger, danger, danger . . . repeated thrice."

Artis regarded him with doubt. "Do you really believe I would jump ship and leave you in jeopardy, James?"

He was tempted to pick her up bodily, carry her on deck, cast her into the briny deep.

"Wait!" she cried, rising and coming to him. "What if I *did* believe the incredible fairytale you just told me? Why should I desert you . . . whom I love?"

He caught her to him. "Listen to me, Artis! With you aboard this ship, my hands are tied. With you gone, I'll set her afire . . . sink her!"

She wrapped her arms around his neck and lifted herself bodily so that her lips crushed his. "Let you go down for the sake of George III and Charlotte and their plainfaced children? What do you think I'm made of . . . patriotic pudding?"

Later, pacing the deck, he ground his teeth in rage and despair. How could you deal fairly with a woman? Headstrong as bulls for all their frailty.

He would have been surprised to see what the headstrong Lady Artis was doing at this very moment. Collapsed on the bed, she was weeping to break her heart.

13.

When White Is Black

A COUNTRY CARRIOLE WITH ONE HORSE BETWEEN THE traces was rolling sedately along the coast highway to Lisbon. A lady veiled in black lace and a young stalwart with red, red hair were its passengers. The man held the reins. The lady held his arm.

"Are you happy, *mi querido?*" said Doña Pilar.

"I'm happy, yes, but I think . . . isn't it all a dream?" said Maunday.

"It's no dream," sighed Doña Pilar. "We're safe on Portuguese soil, and we're together."

Maunday smiled fatuously. "True! True indeed."

"You saved me, my handsome one," murmured the Marquesa pressing her cheek to the broad shoulder that served her for a pillow.

Maunday, a modest man by nature, flushed. "It wasn't me alone, Pilar. There were my flymen, too."

"Ah, but you were the leader!" cried Pilar.

"Giddap!" Maunday slapped the horse's back with the reins.

"Don't hurry him," smiled Pilar. "I'm in no hurry at all."

She raised her head and opened lips that Maunday kissed without urging. The shock he received was so thrilling that his attention, which had turned a moment ago to a sloop lying offshore, now focused completely upon the business at hand. The horse's pace slowed to a walk, then to a crawl. Then he stopped.

"Well now, hadn't we better get on?" said Maunday after a long, long kiss. He again noticed the sloop with the black hull, heading out to sea, but Pilar turned his attention back to herself.

"You'll see what surprises I have for you when we get to Lisbon," she murmured softly. "There's nothing I would not do to honor my hero."

Her praises embarrassed and pleased Maunday at one and the same time. To be with her was like living a dream! The scenes of his former life seemed to fade like the passing landscape, he could scarcely remember Maunday the foundling and Maunday the chimney sweep's apprentice and Maunday the lad grown too tall and broad for sweeping, who had gone to sea, and Maunday the fighting man. Today's Maunday was the lover of a grand lady. Beloved of her! Incredible? Yes. But it was truth. She planned to make him her husband! He . . . Maunday . . . husband of a noblewoman? How long would the dream last?

"You told me you had no first name, my love?" said Doña Pilar in the little silence that had fallen.

"It is true."

"Then you shall acquire one."

"How can I?"

"The King will give you a name when he gives you a title."

"I . . . a title? I wouldn't know how to deal with a title."

"Ah! I'll teach you, *querido*."

"I'd feel like a fool."

"No! It is easy to learn to like wealth and position. You'll see."

"Even when you've been poor as long as I have?" asked Maunday looking at her with doubt in his eyes.

"You have the bearing and looks of a prince, my love," murmured Doña Pilar. "I'll be the most envied woman in all Portugal when I take you for my husband."

"She's joking," thought Maunday. For a man the likes of himself, to make love to a grand lady was one thing but to be turned into a nobleman overnight was another.

The carriole entered into beautiful Lisbon and clattered over cobblestone-paved streets and drew up at the iron gates of a handsome *palacio*. Liveried servants ran out.

The inside of the palace was finer than the outside. A hall as big as a church. Coats of mail at every column. Pictures! Statues, like the kind you saw in parks. Servants at every step!

They escorted him to a bedroom with a bed as big as a jolly boat. They undressed him. They put him into a silver bathtub. A barber shaved him and clipped his hair and cut and filed his fingernails. A tailor brought a coat of scarlet and breeches of blue. A bootmaker fitted him with knee-high black boots. A hatter brought a grand tricornered hat with a gold cockade. But it was the sword that Maunday liked best. It had a gold tassel and chain and the scabbard was chased with battle scenes.

With a low bow the valet handed him a pair of white gloves. "Your Excellency."

Maunday liked the sound of "Your Excellency." Could Pilar be right? Could you become accustomed to wealth and power?

"Her Excellency, the Marquesa, awaits your Excellency in the Blue Room," said the valet.

Maunday threw out his chest, clapped his grand hat on tight and started for the door. He hadn't quite reached the threshold when he stopped in his tracks, exclaiming, "The black sloop!"

Instantly his mind's eye conjured up the vision of a white-hulled sloop that he'd watched sail out of the rock of Castle Akbar and head seaward. He remembered the lines, the slant of her masts and the way they were set. He remembered the color of her canvas—new white! And now his memory compared the lines, masts and canvas of the black-hulled sloop that he had seen out of the corner of his eye, whilst his lady was kissing him in the carriole. The abduction ship—painted black—that had carried , away Captain Ironhand and his lady, prisoners!

Maunday's muscles tautened for action. He ran down the grand staircase of Palacio Valalodad at top speed. "Where's the Marquesa?" he bellowed to a gaping footman.

Doña Pilar was not prepared for the catapult in scarlet and gold that erupted into the Blue Room, shouting, "Give me a horse! A horse!"

King Richard himself could not have made his meaning more clear, but Pilar stammered, "A horse? Why?"

"Because I must go back to Viga at once!"

"But . . . love!"

"Love will come later. Give me a horse!"

Vendors and carters' mouths fell open as they saw a rider in a scarlet coat, sword banging, gallop through the streets of Lisbon and out the South Gate.

But Maunday had made his bolt without taking his lady's passionate regard for his person into account. He was out the gate and racing down the highway to Viga when the crrrack of a pistol shot made him glance over his shoulder. He saw what appeared to be—and was—a troop of Lisbon's mounted guard in hot pursuit. The distance was narrowing between them, fast. A bullet would catch him soon! When he said, "Whoa!" and hauled on the reins, bringing his mount to a stop, the captain in command of the troop was polite but firm.

"I arrest you in the name of His Serene Majesty King Joseph. Follow me, Excellency!"

Guarded fore and aft, larboard and starboard, His Excellency rode back to Lisbon and was locked up in a grand, brocade-hung chamber on the third floor of the Palace of

Justice. The same apartment that served to "detain" Portuguese citizens of high degree.

The long day of waiting was nearly done—Boggs nervously pacing the floor of Consul Selkirk's anteroom—when the door of the inner officer opened.

"Please come in, Captain," said Selkirk.

"News, sir?" said the anxious Boggs.

"Yes," said Selkirk. "Please be seated, Captain." He handed a paper across his desk. "This came by carrier pigeon from Lisbon just now. Have you the code?"

Boggs fumbled for his code book. This was the hardest part of all! Better to fight three battles than decode one message from his chief. But after a time of sweating, it was done.

Buttons will proceed Shadwell and report.

Buttonhole

Boggs heaved a sigh. "It's done, sir. These are my sailing orders. I'm greatly obliged for your help."

"My duty, sir."

The two men shook hands.

"I trust all is satisfactory?" said Selkirk.

"Very satisfactory," Boggs lied with a brave face. What more would Old Buttonhole have to say when a certain undercover agent came to report?

If he is strong, the man who knows he is surely going to die can regard himself and his actions much as a spectator views the proceedings upon a stage. Challoner was at this point. His worried state of mind was giving way to a philosophical calm as he watched familiar landmarks come into view and disappear. Cabo Villano and Torre de Hercules were left behind. The newly christened *Hesperides* rounded Cabo Ortegal on winds that freshened as she entered the Bay of Biscay. Ortegal was her last Continental landfall. Then, Land's End, and the adventure would begin racing to its inevitable conclusion—destruction of the ship whose deck he was pacing as a prisoner of formidable conspirators and enemies of England.

Challoner had not reached his decision easily. He'd twisted and turned, seeking other ways. But because Artis had refused her help, there *was* no other way. The plan he had concocted was ready.

He'd wait until the sloop was in Thames waters, then touch off four fires in her vitals. She'd be a torch in minutes. He'd hidden combustible material in a leather portmanteau in the closet. A tinderbox was ready. He'd a life ring for Artis. But what chance would there be of escape for himself? The fanatic Hadji would kill him if it took his last, dying effort!

Challoner leaned on the rail and stared into the blackness of the night, wondering what had become of Boggs and the *Paramour?* Had they fallen victim to a combination of pirate ships—perhaps the *Jewal* and two or three lesser craft? It would take a numerous enemy to best the *Paramour,* but strong as her fire might be, she wouldn't stand a chance in a concerted attack by night.

Challoner sharpened his eyes to try and see a light that had appeared on the horizon. It blinked with the rise and fall of the ship . . . disappeared.

The bosun was sending the men aloft to trim sail. The wind had increased in velocity and the sloop was pitching and bucking as she drove head on into the storm. What if the elements were to be the decider? What if the *Atlanta* were to go to Davy Jones' locker without the assist of one James Challoner? His grin widened as he pictured a new kind of Ark—wild animals spewing out of her hold. Had Noah a bison? A lynx? A grizzly bear? He must have had them or they wouldn't be in the hold of the *Atlanta,* now.

There! That light, again! It was traveling in the same direction as the *Atlanta.*

Little did Challoner know that the pinpoint of brightness upon the black, wind-riven sea was made by the *Paramour's* running light. He was startled to hear Artis' voice at his elbow. She looked pale and shaken.

"Are we in danger?"

"The Bay of Biscay is a touchy passage in weather like this," he said, throwing a protective arm around her.

She laid her cheek against his shoulder. "James. Are you sorry I did not go ashore when you asked me to?"

"Very sorry."

"I'm glad I refused. What would my life be worth without you?"

"It's blowing up quite a gale," he said lightly. "Go below, my dear. Go to bed."

"And you?"

"I'll be down presently."

He watched her sway and stagger along the corridor, hands pressed to the walls to steady herself. Were ever two lovers in a worse predicament than they?

Acting Captain Boggs, having received his orders from London, had taken the *Paramour* up from Viga under full sail. The weather had been fair the first two days but a sultriness in the air at nightfall of the second day warned of a change and the barometer was falling. The morning of the third day, the sky was foul with rain clouds and gusts plucked at the canvas like nervous fingers. It began to blow hard at dusk. Boggs sent his men aloft to take in canvas, and set a course well away from the Spanish coast.

Pacing the bridge and keeping an eye on the cox'n, he reflected sadly that the *Paramour's* homeward voyage was not to be compared to her voyage outward bound. True, she had bested every enemy ship that had dared give her a fight. True, she had blasted a Moorish stronghold off the face of Africa. True, she'd netted rich booty, and rescued a dozen of females, but she'd lost her Captain—not to mention her most beautiful passenger, a lady named Artis. Could not the Portuguese Marquesa have been mistaken? Could Challoner and Lady Grantley have perished in the bombardment of Castle Akbar? Boggs flinched at the thought! Challoner alive might have a chance to escape from his captors, but a dead Challoner? What a waste!

The *Paramour's* watch sang, "Ship's light on the port bow."

Boggs squinted through the rain—a small craft, from the way her light jigged. She was soon left behind by the faster-sailing frigate.

The sloop's timbers creaked and groaned. The wind howled in the shrouds. Challoner clung to a handrail, feeling the lace of his stock beating against his cheek. Lucky to have a Captain Hassan on the bridge, he thought. And again he thought, I'd rather be in real command of this sloop than be a mere supercargo.

Hit by a giant wave, the *Atlanta* shipped water over her prow and went down into the trough where she lay shuddering. It seemed to Challoner that minutes passed before she nosed up out of the spume and began to ride the crest of a second giant roller.

He was handing himself down the stair when he heard the first raucous shout, followed by a chorus of yells in Arabic. They came from below—bedlam seemed to have broken loose in the hold.

He was about to turn and seek an explanation when suddenly the Hadji loomed in the door of the saloon. With him, the *Atlanta's* swarthy Moorish first mate. They exchanged words in their native tongue and the first mate hurried below.

"What's wrong down there?" asked Challoner.

For once the Moor's calm seemed to have deserted him. "The grizzly bear cage has broken loose from its moorings and the beast is fighting to get free."

"A grizzly bear . . . free on this ship?" Challoner seized the Moor's sleeve. "Arm yourself! Arm several of your crew. I'll go warn my woman to stay behind her locked door."

The Moor shook his arm free and drew a pistol from his sash. "The devil take your woman! I'm thinking of my enterprise. I'll let no mere animal foil a plan that has taken months . . . nay years to lay. You'll come with me, effendi!"

Faced with a pistol, Challoner could do no more than precede the Moor down the stair but he tore an axe from its rack.

Nearing the bottom of the stair he caught the strong scent of wild animals. The din—shouts, bumpings, jarrings—was terrible! The hold of the *Atlanta* presented the strangest sight he had ever laid eyes on. A half dozen of the crew were skipping, dodging the great iron-barred bear cage that had turned upside down with the roll and pitch of the ship. Inside, the grizzly clawed, roared, fought to escape from his tumbling prison. So far the bars were holding, but Challoner could see that at any moment, the weight of the cage might crush one or several of the other cages, thus freeing some other wild beast. The crew seemed too frozen with fright to do anything except get out of the way of the cage as it started on its cross-hold run.

"Where's the Indian?" shouted Challoner in the Moor's ear.

"Injured, trying to secure the cage," the Moor answered.

Challoner saw a possibility—thread lines through the bars of the bear cage and tie them fore and aft. But where was the man of the crew bold enough to execute such a maneuver? It flashed through his mind, "This may be the natural and logical way to destroy the *Atlanta* and all aboard! Let Nature take her course! She'll perish twixt a zoo and the storm!"

It was then that the ship took another tremendous downward plunge. The bear cage bumped, rolled, lurched to port and then teetered on its side before beginning the starboard run. Deafening screams of men! Animal roars! Crash! Bang! Splintering of wood! Challoner saw by the light of a swinging lantern, a sleek black shape slip out of one of the cages, saw amber eyes staring into his—then a lithe beast leaped past him and up the stairs.

He was aware of the Hadji's expression—stark fear written on his rugged features as he wrenched the pistol from his grasp.

"Try and get that bear cage battened down! I'll go after the panther." The Moor made no move to stop him. Axe in his left hand, pistol in his right, Challoner paused at the top of the stairs. Which way had the panther gone? Fore? Aft? He proceeded cautiously, praying as he went that Artis would stay safe in her cabin.

Suddenly he knew he had prayed in vain. The cabin door was swinging on its hinges. "Artis!" he shouted. "Artis, where are you?"

A piercing scream from the direction of the dining saloon answering, he made an about-face and fighting the buck and roll of the ship, managed to reach the saloon doorway.

The black panther was perched atop the dining table, big claws dug deep into the wood. Backed into a corner of the wine cellaret, Artis in her dressing gown. Mouth open wide, she screamed again and again.

The shrillness of her voice, the pitch, made the hair stir on the nape of Challoner's neck. "Stop screaming!" he shouted. But the screamer did not seem to hear, or if she heard, could not obey. Steadying himself against the door lintel, Challoner laid the pistol muzzle across his arm, took aim at the panther and fired! The ship rolled. The ball spent itself in the woodwork. The panther turned amber eyes and glared. What must it be thinking . . . Shall I first silence that shrill female din or shall I deal with the man?

Challoner dropped the pistol and shifted the axe to his right hand. "Come on, cat! Come on!"

Did the gleam of the axe provoke the feline? He made a leap into the air, turning as he leapt—then using the table for a springboard he launched straight at his taunter.

Challoner saw the muscular black shape streaking through the air—saw enormous claws spreading, white fangs gleaming. Using the axe with a swinging under blow, he embedded it deep in the panther's belly. Hot blood sprayed him like a fountain. The impetus of the beast's attack was not stopped. He landed on his intended victim —but on landing he was dead! Thrown to the floor with two hundred or more pounds of black panther across him, Challoner gasped . . . groaned.

Suddenly the screams ceased. He heard Artis crying, "James! James, are you hurt?" Her little white hands tugged at the great black carcass. She dragged it clear of him, knelt beside him. "James! Speak to me! Are you all right?"

"I'm all right," he said, getting to his feet. He grinned. "I'd like a bedside rug made of that black pelt!"

"How like a man!" cried Artis in relief which bordered on hysteria. "I'm shaking with fear and you dream of a fur rug."

This time, Challoner locked the door of Artis' cabin. "You stay there. I'll give a hand, below."

"Be careful!" cried Artis through the panel.

The frightened Moors were still trying to cope with the bear cage. All they'd done was to get a line around it. Seven men were bracing their strength against the pull and roll. The bear was beginning to weaken from the jolting he'd received.

Challoner strung lines through the bars and directed the battening of the cage. It had to be secured upside down. Would the bear know the difference?

"See to it that the other cages are tight," he said to the

Atlanta's first mate. He turned to Mohammed-ben-Dar. "I think we may safely leave this pesthole."

"You are a brave man," murmured the Moor. "If you were really with me, O Ironhand, not for money but for belief . . ."

"That is not my game," laughed Challoner, and added to himself, "Not my game at all."

14.

A Ball for
Captain Ironhand

NO COMBINATION OF COURIERS, SEMAPHORE, SIGNAL LIGHT or carrier pigeon could have forwarded the news of pirates, of captive females, of gun battles and a dashing buccaneer named Ironhand as fast and in such wonderful detail as did the clapping tongues of twelve Lisbon ladies. Their news traveled by word of mouth via Lisbon, Madrid, Paris, London! Baroness This gave it to Countess That. Countess That gave it to Lady So-and-so. Milady's maid gave it to his lordship's valet. The valet gave it to the groom of milord's stable. The groom had a cousin who worked in Fleet Street as a printer's devil. Printer's devil gave the news to Mr. Henry Pultock as he was returning to his desk at the *Morning Post* after a long and filling meal at the Side of Beef tavern.

"I 'eard 'as 'ow Lady Grantley, she as they call 'Lady Grant-em-All,' was captured by the notorious pirate, Captain Ironhand. Spirited awye she was . . . gone to parts unknown!"

Mr. Henry Pultock, a newsman of the best, hied himself to Seething Lane and there confronted a young Navy lieutenant with a series of questions.

"Is it true that the pirate Ironhand has captured Lady

Artis Grantley? Is it true that a dozen noblewomen of Lisbon were rescued by his efforts and brought to Lisbon in his pirate ship, named *Paramour?* Is it true that the Admiralty has not acted to seize this criminal? And if so, why not? Is the Lord High Admiral disposed to let a renegade Englishman run the high seas, taking prisoners and booty, and make no move to stop him?"

The lieutenant replied, "Sir, kindly wait," and went to next-in-rank, and next-in-rank went higher, until the question was posed to the Lord High Admiral himself.

· Lord Wilmington (already a worried man) banged his desk with his clenched fist. "Ironhand again! Blast him! Give me my hat!"

"But, your lordship?" stammered the lieutenant. "What shall I give out to the Press?"

"Blast the Press!" roared his lordship. And moments later he was on his way to Chelsea with a red leather dispatch case under his arm.

Now it was the turn of *two* worried men to ask questions of each other.

"Are you hiding something from me, Greg?"

"Fred! How could you think me guilty of subterfuge, with you?"

"Think . . . think! I'm casting about for the truth." Wilmington opened his dispatch case and took out a sheaf of papers. "Let's sift through these again. Your man Boggs says here . . . '*Paramour* at Viga Portugal. Greatcoat (code name for Challoner) and Lady Grantley forced aboard white-painted sloop . . . name unknown.' Here's my answer. You helped me write it. 'Return home.' Now comes a raft of rumors. Challoner, alias Ironhand, is still aboard the *Paramour* taking prisoners right and left. He seems to favor the ladies."

"Fred!" exclaimed Lord Frawley. "Are you out of your senses?"

"I'm as sane as you are!" retorted the Lord High Admiral.

"Where did you hear that Challoner was aboard the *Paramour?*"

"A gazetteer came to the Admiralty, giving me hints that he knew things I did not. I avoided him, but you know the Press. If you refuse to answer, they take it for granted

the rumors are true. Tomorrow, every rag in London will
be full of Captain Ironhand's newest exploits! They'll make
a hero of him! First thing you know he'll sail up the Thames
with Lady Grantley on his arm and ask to be knighted!"

"Poppycock!" growled Frawley.

"Greg!" pleaded Wilmington. "Are you aware that times
have changed? We of the Navy are none too sweet in the
public's nostrils as it is, and Parliament begrudges every
shilling they give us. I cannot jeopardize my high post for
the sake of your harebrained schemes!"

Lord Frawley threw up his hands. "What are you trying
to tell me, Fred . . . that we shouldn't have sent an undercover man to spy out the Moors? I wanted not victories, but
information. Who is the Moors' liaison in England? Names
of receivers? Ports of call? Channels by which the loot
reaches English markets . . ."

"And what have we?" broke in Wilmington with a grimace. "A hodgepodge about rescued Marquesas, a love
affair between a pirate and a peeress that will set London
on its ear."

"The *Royal Acre* is safe, though," muttered Frawley.
"She'll be here, soon. We'll hear the truth from Boggs."

"It will be too late to make the truth believable," retorted
Wilmington. "I need your help in framing a rebuttal for
the Press. Come, Greg! Put on your thinking cap!"

"Let the Press print the story as it sees it," said Lord
Frawley with a sour smile. "Let the subscribers read and
shake with vicarious thrills. I'll never give up hope that
Challoner will come through with the information we
need."

"Optimist!" said Lord Wilmington. "I'll wager a shilling
to a china horse you'll never see hide or hair of Challoner,
again."

"The wager is on!" said Lord Frawley grimly. "And I
shall ask you for your apology, to boot, when I win."

In days following, a series of spine-tingling accounts of
pirate ventures nudged all other topics off the front page
of London's gazettes. Even the forthcoming arrival of a
wealthy Colonial subject, bearing a zoo of wild American
animals in gift to His Majesty the King was relegated to
the back pages. What counted a new species of wild animal
compared to the appeal of a scandalous love affair between

a great lady and a pirate named Ironhand? Mayfair whispered over its teacups, Whitechapel argued over its alepots.

So much did Captain Ironhand intrigue the people—a duchess planned a pirate ball and a famed puppeteer composed a new puppet play entitled *Captain Ironhand* or *The Loves of a Pirate and a Lady*.

Among those invited to Her Grace's ball—Admiral Lord Frawley.

The Admiral dispatched a note to the First Sea Lord.

Dear Freddy,
    I think it wise that you accompany me to the Duchess of Somerset's ball. Wear navy dress of a hundred years ago, and a mask.

The two gentlemen, sporting much lace, gilt and embroidery, met for a quiet club dinner before the ball.

"Why did you deem it wise for us to attend this ball together, Greg?" asked Lord Wilmington.

"A faint hope, Freddie," answered Frawley. "The gazettes have been trumpeting this ball for days. Furthermore, rumor has it, Captain Ironhand himself will attend."

"Challoner, in London?" exclaimed Lord Wilmington.

"I did not say Challoner is in London," said Lord Frawley. "It was I who spread the rumor he'd be at the ball. I hope, perhaps without logic, that some of those who serve the Moors in England may come to see if Captain Ironhand is there. Imagine the stir the announcement must have caused among those pirate devils? If Challoner is *with* them, they'll ask themselves who is impersonating him. If he is *not* with them, they'll attempt to discover which side he is serving."

"My dear Greg," said Lord Wilmington in amazement, "you impute greater powers to these Moors than I would give them were I to see them remove the bells from Westminster and carry them away before my very eyes."

"You live in your ivory tower in Seething Lane, my dear Freddie," said Lord Frawley with irony. "You forget that I, poor old, decrepit Greg, am Chief of Secret Operations with express mission to run down these Moorish bandits who have been tweaking our noses, these several past years."

"I do not forget, Greg," said Lord Wilmington in haste,

to make amends for his seeming lack of interest . . . respect.
"I value your efforts highly. Why only yesterday I was
talking to Lord North. 'Wilmington,' he said to me, 'I congratulate you on the success of your war against the Moors.
They haven't raided our coasts or sunk a ship of our Navy
in three months.' "

"Hmmm." Frawley took a swallow of wine. "That is just
what worries me. Those fellows are too quiet. They're letting us alone too much. The Prime Minister may take this
lack of hostility as discouragement on their part, I take it
as a lull before the storm. Where . . . how will they strike
next? Gad! If only Boggs would bring the *Paramour* home!"

Lord Wilmington consulted his timepiece. "It's half past
ten, Greg. If we're to attend Her Grace's ball . . . let us
repair to Somerset House."

While the two Sea Lords were driving from St. James'
Street to Park Row, the *Paramour,* flying the Jack, came
to rest in Shadwell Basin as quietly as a gull.

Will Boggs set a guard of flymen at the rail with orders
to detain any man of the crew seeking to leave ship. Clad
in his well-brushed blues, he went ashore and threaded his
way through the dark maze of streets and alleys that was
Sailor's Town. At the Waterman's Arms he halted only
long enough to toss down a glass of ale and bitters and send
a boy for a hackney coach. A little over an hour later the
driver halted at the door of No. 16 Cheyne Walk.

"His lordship has gone to the Duchess of Somerset's
masked ball," said the Admiral's servant in answer to
Boggs' request to see Lord Frawley. "You'll have to come
back tomorrow morning."

"I could wait here," said Boggs. "Surely 'is lordship
won't stay out too late?"

The servant yawned. "Wait if you like, but his lordship
slept most of the afternoon so as to be fresh for tonight."

"Masked ball, eh?" Boggs eyed himself in the hall mirror. "I'll come back tomorrow morning, mate."

The hour was nearing midnight. Lords Wilmington and
Frawley were sore disappointed. There were pirates and
buccaneers and pirates' wenches of a hundred styles at the
ball. Blackbeard and Peg-Leg Harry, Black Bart and Long
John Silver were present. One ingenious young buck had

made his entrance hanging from a gibbet that he held over his own head! Ghastly pale face, lolling tongue. The effect was immense. But Lord Frawley, whose agents, garbed as lackeys, were generously sprinkled among the fashionable mob, hadn't turned up a single suspect, and he was beginning to long for his bed.

"Well, Freddie?" he said, approaching Lord Wilmington who was threading his way among the dancers with two beakers of champagne. "I think I'll retire."

"Dashed bad luck, Greg," said Wilmington. "Can't say as I regret having come though. The wife of the Spanish Ambassador is a charmer!"

Lord Frawley smiled bleakly as he reminded himself of the two decades' difference between his age and that of the First Sea Lord.

On his way down the grand staircase, his drooping eyelids suddenly opened wide, for coming up the stairs he saw a familiar, stocky figure in plain navy blue. "Boggs!"

"Your lordship!"

"Man . . . when did you drop anchor?"

"A little over two hours ago. I went to Cheyne Walk and your lordship's servant told me you were here. They gave me a bit of an argument because I had no card of invitation, but I got in."

Lord Frawley led the way to the Duke's library which opened out into handsome gardens. "We shan't be disturbed here and I happen to know where His Grace keeps his liquor."

A glass of Scottish comfort in hand, Boggs waited for his superior to fire his first question.

"Well, Boggs?" said Lord Frawley. "Suppose you begin at the beginning."

A half hour later, Lord Frawley leaned back in his chair. "You've told me . . . precisely nothing."

Boggs turned and turned his glass in his hands. "I know, your lordship. I've told you everything that happened in *my* ken. Where Captain Challoner is, I cannot say."

Lord Frawley leaned forward in his chair. "Could he have deserted with Lady Grantley?"

"In my opinion, no, sir," said Boggs firmly. "I never knew a man whose devotion to duty was stronger than Captain Challoner's."

"Then you, yourself, are persuaded that he was abducted by force, and the lady with him?"

"Yes, sir," said Boggs.

"But why? It's senseless! Could the Portuguese lady's eyes have deceived her? You know the unreliability of eyewitnesses."

"She has sharp eyes, sir," said Boggs quickly. "Beautiful, if I may say so."

"Never mind the Marquesa's beautiful eyes!" said Frawley. "Did *you* see them force a man and a woman aboard the Moorish sloop when it sailed out of the harbor?"

"No, sir," said Boggs. "The Marquesa saw it."

"And *you* did not?" pressed Frawley.

"No, sir. Neither did Maunday, and his eyesight is sharper than mine."

"Maunday?"

"Sir . . . Captain Challoner named him Flymaster. He was the leader of a special attack corps of daredevils named Flymen."

"And where is this Maunday?"

"Sir . . ." Boggs' leather cheeks flushed. "I gave Maunday his discharge in Viga."

"You gave?"

"Sir!" said Boggs who saw the tempest brewing. "The Marquesa forced my hand . . . said she'd denounce the *Paramour* as a pirate ship . . . have her seized by the Portuguese authorities. She was that gone in love for Maunday. Bound to marry the lad!"

Frawley's lean jaws sawed up and down. "Gone in love? Marry? What *was* the *Paramour*? A bride ship?"

"No sir," said Boggs, choking back a cough.

Long after he had sent Boggs back to his ship, Frawley sat shaking his head and muttering under his breath. "Women! Women!" He rose with an old man's heaviness of limb. Gad! What would Wilmington say to all this? He must be told without delay. Lord Frawley began slowly to climb the grand staircase, up and down which a merry throng of young people were racing.

15.

Bridegroom's Escape

MAUNDAY IN HIS SCARLET COAT AND COCKED HAT WAS THE same man who had led his flymen to the assault of Castle Akbar. The hours he had spent in detention had not changed his nature in any perceptible way. He paced his prison chamber in his shirtsleeves, sweated, eyed the turnkey who brought him food and water and removed his pail twice a day.

Sometimes he talked to himself. "Maunday, which is better . . . let your Captain go to blazes and marry Pilar, or escape from this prison?"

Maunday also answered himself. "Escape? How can you escape?"

A steadfast loyalty to his Captain kept him on the alert for his chance. At the same time he looked forward to the daily visit of Doña Pilar, who came bringing wine and delicacies as well as the nectar of her kisses.

That day, Doña Pilar put the usual question. "Say you'll marry me and I'll have you set free."

Maunday wrapped his big arms about her and looked squarely into her eyes. "No woman has ever cracked the whip on Maunday as you are trying to do."

"No woman has ever loved Maunday as I love him."

"Free me, Pilar."

"And wave goodbye as you sail away?"

"I'll come back to you," said Maunday.

"I'll take no risks, *mi amor*."

"I might never marry you if you persist in keeping me locked up like a jailbird."

"Not marry me . . . and stay here until you are an old man with a long white beard?" Pilar caressed her darling's strong neck. *"Querido.* Let the padre come. He's been waiting so long."

Suddenly the light broke over Maunday. Of course! Pilar

161

had the key to his prison! He did not show his feelings of elation. "Marry you . . . well, perhaps, some day."

"Now, *querido!* Now!"

"Well . . ."

"I'll fetch the padre." Pilar ran to the door and rapped sharply for the turnkey to let her out.

Maunday shrugged on his scarlet coat, donned his cocked hat and belted on his sword. He was ready when the bride returned, bringing her maid, a monk and the turnkey with her.

"Here is Padre Assuncion. My maid and the turnkey will act as our witnesses." Doña Pilar also supplied the ring.

No sooner had Maunday kissed the bride than he drew his sword and pressed its point to the jailer's Adam's apple. "Stand against the wall. Girl! You, Padre! You too, Mrs. Maunday. Now, turnkey, your keys if you please. And you, Padre, I want the loan of your habit."

Not an eye turned when a hooded friar walked through the prison corridor and down the stairs and out into the crowded streets of Lisbon. Maunday the Monk stepped into a small church in a quiet street, stripped off the friar's robe behind a pillar, tweaked his hat into shape and walked out again with the air of a man who has paid his respects to his Maker. He was not without funds, having taken care to fill a silken purse, gift from Pilar, with some of his share of the collected pirates' loot.

The owner of a livery stable in a *calle* behind Playa Real was not at all surprised when a fine English gentleman walked into his establishment and asked to rent a coach and four fast horses. The stable owner was used to Englishmen!

Consul Selkirk was about to sit down to a leisurely supper on his flowered terrace when he heard a carriage brake to a stop at his door. He strode to the window and peeped at the vehicle through the shutters but he did not recognize the man who got out. The bell pealed. He heard his servant greet the stranger. Soon after, the servant entered.

"Excellency, there's a gentleman to see you. He says his business is urgent."

"Tell Señor Peewick to see him," said Selkirk.

"Señor Peewick is on the beach, painting a boat, Excellency."

"Oh, very well! I'll see him! Bring him in."

The visitor's face and general appearance seemed vaguely familiar but Selkirk did not realize who he was until he spoke.

"Sir, do you remember me? Maunday, who came here with Captain Boggs and the Marquesa Valalodad?"

Selkirk's eyes nearly popped out of their sockets. "I do, sir. I do indeed. It's just that you . . . you are changed."

"My clothes?" Maunday grinned. "It must be true, what they say, clothes make the man. Sir, my business is urgent and private."

Selkirk had recovered from his surprise. "Step into my office, sir."

Maunday came to the point, immediately. "Sir, when did my ship sail?"

"Why, she hauled anchor, let me see . . . it must have been Tuesday morning. Yes, it was Tuesday. I recall that your Captain Boggs received an answer to his dispatch Tuesday, and left immediately."

"Then you'll have to advise London," said Maunday.

"Advise London?"

"Yes, sir. The message goes to Captain Boggs, sir. I'll tell you what to say if you'll write."

Mindful that Captain Boggs of the frigate *Paramour* had given the all-important code word *Buttons,* Selkirk wasted no more time. "Sir, dictate your message. I'll forward it at once."

Maunday moistened his lips, thought a moment, and began. "Say . . . the sloop out of the rock was painted white and they changed her color to black, in Viga Portugal. Say . . . a certain man and a certain woman are aboard."

"And how shall I sign your communication?" asked the astonished Selkirk.

"Sign it . . . Flymaster," said Maunday. He put out his hand. "Thank you, sir."

"One moment!" said Selkirk. "Would you mind if I reworded your message?"

"I would, sir!" said Maunday firmly. "It must go just as I spoke it."

"Very well. But you realize, do you not, that I'll have to expedite this message to Lisbon by carrier pigeon?"

"And what happens when it reaches Lisbon?" asked Maunday, frowning.

"It goes to the hands of His Majesty's Ambassador, Lord Houghton."

"Can you add a word, sir?" said Maunday. "Just one word . . . *Rush!*"

Selkirk showed his visitor to the door and watched him drive away. Rush! Of course! Any communication from Buttons to Buttonhole must be rushed. Now . . . to the pigeon coop!

The runaway bridegroom was halfway to Lisbon when his coach was halted by a guard of Military. Maunday grinned out of the coach window at the young lieutenant in command. "At your service, Lieutenant! Take me back to Mrs. Maunday."

"Mrs. Maunday?" echoed the young officer in his Latin-tinged accent.

"She was the Marquesa, Doña Pilar Valalodad," smiled Maunday. "She's Mistress Maunday now."

Maunday's part in the cruise of the *Paramour* had read itself to a happy ending. Not so, the part of the *Paramour's* captain and her first mate.

Boggs received the flymaster's communication (not at all cryptic to his understanding) from the hand of Admiral Lord Frawley.

"Sir! Your lordship!" he said with a look of chagrin. "I saw that black sloop put out to sea while we were at Viga."

"You saw her, yet you did not recognize her as the same craft you had seen in Africa?" pressed Frawley.

"No sir. She was white-painted in Africa. Black, in Viga."

"Well, where, in your opinion, does she find herself now?"

Boggs looked blank.

"Where would *you* steer if you were a Moorish pirate who had captured a wealthy English lady and were intending to ask ransom for her delivery?"

Boggs thought a moment. "I'd head for the English coast."

"Precisely what *I* would do," said Frawley, banging the arm of his chair. "I'll alert the ports from the Channel to London Bridge and put a twenty-four-hour watch on Sir Henry Fox . . . his town house . . . his chambers in the Temple."

"And what would you do next?"

"I'd send a go-between to those responsible for the lady's welfare."

16.

Ship of Death

CHALLONER, HIMSELF, MUCH LESS LORD FRAWLEY OR Boggs, could not have divined the workings of Hadji Mohammed-ben-Dar's subtle mind. As the *Atlanta-Hesperides* bore up out of Biscayan weather and sailed into calmer waters off the Channel Isles, several of her piratical crew, armed with brush and paint bucket, let themselves down her sides in monkey seats and began to stripe her black hull with scarlet. Others of the crew decorated her superstructure with white paint. A handsome flesh-colored goddess was affixed to her prow. The named *Hesperides* was painted out and the name *Atlanta* painted in.

Watching the transformation with "Mistress Hunnicutt" at his side, Challoner was perplexed.

"What does it mean, Artis?"

"I should think it means that they are afraid of being identified as a black sloop," said Artis.

"You are right," exclaimed Challoner. "I see a ray of hope!"

"Kindly share your ray with me, dear heart?"

"Can't you see? It means our side is on the alert. I shouldn't be surprised if we were stopped . . . searched. If so, I'd know what to do."

"Wouldn't the Moors lock you and me in our cabin if a vessel were to challenge the *Atlanta?*"

"Likely they would," said Challoner, thinking of the materials he had readied for burning. "But even locked in our cabin, I have a method for drawing the attention of any vessel within radius of three miles of the *Atlanta*."

"Do tell me?" said Artis in her wheedling way.

"Why should I?" said Challoner. "You refused me when I asked you to go ashore."

"I refused you because I thought you were imagining this Moorish plot against the King!"

Challoner smiled to conceal the anxiety he felt. "I wish I could make you see that if you would only obey me, jump ship, make haste to London, you might be instrumental in saving *my* neck as well as the necks of the royal family."

"*Your* neck?" murmured Artis.

Challoner detected a weakening in her resolve to resist his will at any cost. "Yes, dear. For what it is worth . . . my neck."

"But . . . abandon you? I couldn't!" Artis declared emphatically.

"Yes you could! I've prepared the Hadji's mind, told him that you were becoming restless . . . advised him to leave you out of our plot . . . confine you to quarters whilst we are docked in London. I even said you might attempt to jump ship . . . that you were hell bent on finding a stay-at-home lover."

Artis' beautiful face was averted. Was she beginning to waver?

"Artis! I beg of you! Do as I ask!"

She turned to face him. "Where would you put me ashore?"

His heart bounded. "Let me decide. It will be as close to London as I dare so that you can warn Lord Frawley."

Her eyes searched his. "Dearest, should the Moors discover that I have gone, would they not do something dreadful to you?"

"No! Never!" lied Challoner. "They need me to carry out their plot." His *real* plan was set. Artis had no part in it. Destroy the *Atlanta* by burning! But Artis must not know!

"Let me think, James!" she murmured, her hand creeping into his palm.

"You've thought enough!" he said tersely. "The time has come for obedience."

She raised herself on tiptoe and offered her lips. "I'll give you my answer in time. I promise."

Challoner knew every reach of this, the Queen of Rivers. His practiced eye, piercing the June haze, found here a bell and there a buoy that he had marked on his study charts. Yonder squat light was Tripcock Ness. Woolwich lay on the north bank and then came the grand sweep of Bugsby Reach, you rounded the bend to Blackwall Reach and so, into Greenwich and Limehouse Reaches. To larboard, a point called Cuckold's Point, name to delight all Second Form boys, and then Shadwell, where this adventure had begun—old Shadwell wreathed in the smoke of a thousand poor men's chimneys. You left Wapping to starboard and there loomed the Tower in all its dour beauty, and beyond the Tower, like a horned yoke over the river, London Bridge.

The *Atlanta* in her brave red-black-and-white dress would reach her destination all too soon. No one had challenged her. She'd proceeded like the royal guest she was. What a handsome sight she must be to those inhabitants of shore towns and villages who saw her sail by.

Again, Challoner was struck with the Hadji's ability to plan in advance. Under his watchful eye, the *Atlanta's* crew had been busy since dawn, brushing and de-spotting liveries, combing wigs, blacking boots, polishing swords and buckles, cleaning firearms.

Only Artis was inactive ... inert ... unable to say yes or no. He watched her with mounting anxiety. Caresses, kisses, passionate love-making had not swayed her. She seemed to have withdrawn into a shell—hard, impenetrable and without rift.

He'd decided upon the exact place and time when she must jump ship—a sandbar off Deptford Inlet. The sandbar would give her a foothold and let her rest, should the tide be strong. She could make land in two efforts instead of one. In Deptford hamlet she would find transportation to London. He'd prepared a packet wrapped in oilskin that would go around her slim waist. Money therein. She'd need money, coming dripping ashore!

He waited as long as his patience would allow, then,

the cabin door locked, he faced her with the question that burned his lips.

"Have you made up your mind? Any further delay will bring my plan to nought."

"James . . . swear to me that you deem it wise . . . expedient . . . your only hope . . . that I do what you ask?"

"I swear!" he said, lying with imperturbable calm.

She came to him. "Then I'll do it."

"Thank God!" He kissed her. "Now listen carefully and remember everything I say. Tonight, at midnight, you'll skin through this porthole. You're petite enough. I'll let you down on a line. You'll swim without splashing . . . let the current take you downstream. There's a sandbar. Rest there if you are tired. Then make for the shore. The hamlet in Deptford. Go to the inn, hire a coach, you'll have plenty of money. Make for London as fast as you can travel . . . and go straight to Number 16 Cheyne Walk, Chelsea. There, tell Lord Frawley everything that has transpired and warn him against this sloop . . . the *Atlanta,* now painted red and white. A flesh-colored goddess at her prow. He'll know what to do."

Artis clasped him to her bosom. "When shall I see you again, my love?"

"Likely, as soon as the *Atlanta* ties up at her mooring, near the Tower."

"Are you sure that is where she'll moor?"

"The Hadji said so, himself."

"Then I'll be waiting on the dock in my carriage."

"Yes, love!"

"You're certain all will go as you say it will?"

"It depends upon you, Artis," said Challoner with a sincerity that seemed to win his point. "The quicker you make contact with Lord Frawley, the better my chances!"

"I dislike the word chance!" she cried.

"I only used the word for lack of a better one," retorted Challoner. Would she change her quicksilver mind at the last moment? How could one know with a woman like Artis?

He cautioned her to show no change of behavior during these, the final hours of the *Atlanta's* cruise. "Carry on your play-acting as Mistress Hunnicutt. Dine merrily. Make much of me as usual. Retire at the same hour you always do."

No sooner had Mistress Hunnicutt retired for the night, leaving her "dear husband" to his wine and pipe, than the Moor entered the dining saloon and seated himself.

"You and I must rehearse last-minute arrangements, effendi." He brushed the glasses and decanter aside and taking a crayon began to draw a plan on the napery. "Here's where we dock . . . on the right bank, just off Tower Bridge. We unload the animals at dawn. From then on everything is prearranged. You have but to follow my orders."

"The Hadji must know London well!" said Challoner.

"I've never set foot in London," said the Moor, "but there are those awaiting us who know every street and mews, every alley and court."

"Your contact in London?"

"Yes."

"Are you certain this man . . . or these men will not fail you?"

"Certain," said the Moor with a cryptic smile.

Affecting naïvete, Challoner said, "Then I take it you've heard from them recently, either by signal or courier?"

The Moor's smile faded. His lips tightened. "I've heard from them. How, is no regard of yours, Ironhand effendi. Your role is to play Mr. Hunnicutt exactly as you're told."

"I don't mean to pry," said Challoner quickly, "but what if this person *should* fail us at the last moment?"

"He will not fail," said the Moor in tones that warned Challoner his patience was at an end.

The questions he had asked were purely academic. The *Atlanta* would never reach her mooring under the Tower!

"I think I shall retire," he said, suppressing a yawn.

"Do so, effendi," said the Moor. "Tomorrow will be a day you and I will long remember."

Challoner found Artis seated at her mirror with a comb in one hand and a brush in the other. Her locks were loosed in a cascade of gold over her shoulders. She was dressed only in a thin shift. When he entered she swung around to face him.

"James! I'm afraid!"

"Nonsense! You said you're a strong swimmer," he retorted.

"It's not the swim . . . I'm afraid of what will happen aboard this ship."

"What *can* happen?" said Challoner lightly. "I had a talk with the Hadji. Everything will go according to plan . . . or so he thinks. He even drew a diagram to make his idea clear in my mind."

Artis rose. "James, what do you intend to do to stop this plot?"

The beam in her eye confounded him. He stammered, lost countenance. "I . . . I? Why, I'll think of something."

She rubbed a waistcoat button between her fingers. "I know you too well! You'll sink this ship and go down with her . . . *because, James Challoner,* that *is the only way you can save the King!"*

Suddenly Challoner's will stiffened. To have come thus far and now be thwarted by a woman's will? No! He seized her, stopped her lips with his handkerchief, pinched her between his knees, fastened the money belt around her waist. She beat him about the legs with her clenched fists, fought him with every fiber and muscle in her body, but to no avail.

"Listen, Artis . . . the time is about come. Shall I force you through that porthole or will you go by your own will?" Her wild eyes seemed to shout what her gagged lips could not say, "I will not go!"

Watching his timepiece, Challoner took last-minute precautions. A pillowcase provided the means for controlling Artis' lively, fighting legs. He pulled the pillowcase up to her thighs. No need to fasten it. She'd have to kick it off after the plunge. Her hands? They must be free!

"Now, Artis . . . remember all I said. Get to Deptford hamlet. Hire a coach. Drive like hell for London!"

She shook her head, "No, No, No!"

"Artis . . . I love you," he said brokenly, and bending down he kissed her eyelids, her cheeks, her throat. How lovely she was, the thin shift stretched taut over her straining bosom. For one mad moment he asked himself, "Is there no other way?" Then reason prevailed. He picked her up bodily, thrust her feet and legs in the pillowcase through the porthole, pushed her relentlessly outward until

her head was on a level with the rim. Then with a flick of
the wrist he pulled the gag from her mouth . . . pushed her
out . . . out . . . holding her wrists until the very last
moment. That she might scream had occurred to him.
Would she scream, knowing that the Moors could hear?
At last, only their hands were joined. He let go with a
suddenness that broke the link.

Ear set to the porthole, he listened. Knowing that a body
had gone overboard, he could imagine he heard the faint
splash as it entered the water. But it was only the push of
the tide against the *Atlanta's* hull. The sandbar was soon
far abeam.

He turned from the porthole, face dripping with sweat.
His knees buckled. He sat down heavily in the seat where
Artis had sat combing her hair. Numb with a despair he
could not combat, he bowed his head. "God preserve her!"
It had been the only way!

The sense of shock abated. He began his own prepara-
tions that would end the life of the sloop *Atlanta* and all
aboard. First, remove Planter Hunnicutt's evening finery
and dress in black. Black face, torso, arms, legs and feet.
There was no moon. He'd melt into the shadows. A square
of black, torn from a lady's silk petticoat, provided covering for his head. Tinderbox, fuse and two pistols in belt,
and the oily rags wrapped in a ball and tucked under his
arm, he stole to the door and pulled the bolt gently. His
hand almost cramped over the metal. Easy now! This was
no time for nerves!

He crept along the companionway and made his way aft
to the hatch that opened into the *Atlanta's* hold. There, a
quantity of animal forage was stored. He broke the tie that
held a bale of hay, scattered the hay, then knelt and
scratched flint to tinder. The spark caught the mesh and
the flame flared.

In the act of dropping the lighted mesh in the hay, he
saw, in a brief instant, a dark shape silhouetted against
the wall. Then his skull seemed to explode in a fireworks
display. He dropped to the floor like a stone.

Artis, Lady Grantley, had known apprehension, fear
. . . never the stark terror she felt now as the cold waters
of the Thames closed over her. Quick! Kick free of the

pillowcase that trammeled her limbs. She came to the surface striking out blindly until, sensing herself safe and afloat, her movements became less wild, more coordinated. She turned to look at the lights of the *Atlanta*. How swift the current! It bore her as in powerful arms. "Oh James!" she murmured, realizing that her terror was not for herself but for the man she loved. Even now, the hulk of the *Atlanta* was fading from view. She was alone . . . alone.

For a time, her will to survive lessened. She let her arms go limp, but instinct set them in motion again. She swam slowly, seeking to find the shore. Land and water blended into one. The pressing of the current beat about her face and shoulders. How long could she hold up? Her heart began to labor and she turned on her back and floated. But floating, the current would carry her too far downstream. She turned over again and as she did so, her foot struck a solid. The sandbar James said would be there. She waded, floundered, finally found herself on semidry land. Could those lights be Deptford hamlet? Hurry!

Hope gave her fresh strength and hardened her will to reach the shore. She made the last fifty yards to the shore and pulled herself onto a sandy ledge and lay there panting. It was some time before she could summon strength enough to pursue her journey. Finally she staggered to her feet and stepping gingerly on bare soles, began to pick her way towards the lights of Deptford.

The buxom cook of the River Inn was taking the air at her kitchen door. A fine June night it was! The herb garden she cultivated with such care was fragrant with the scent of flowering thyme and marjoram and mace. Somewhere a dog barked. The trees rustled in the night breeze. Cook heard a rustle of the privet that divided the inn yard from the house next door. Then a woman's voice cried, "Damn!"

" 'Oo goes there?" gasped the cook.

"Come help me get free of this damned hedge, woman," said the voice.

Cook ventured slowly—discovered what she afterwards called "a bare lady" caught in the hedge. Poor thing! Arms and legs all scratched. Hair in a tangle. "Eeee!" she squealed. "You're wetter'n a fish!"

"I know it. I fell off a ship and swam ashore. Can you help me? I'll pay you well."

The inn cook's ears sharpened. "You'll pay?"

"Yes. Five pounds if you'll find me some dry clothing, a pair of shoes and take me to a magistrate."

"Magistrate?" echoed the cook. "Wot kind of magistrate?"

"A judge. A constable."

"Come into my kitchen. Show me the money," said the doubting cook. She did not doubt long. A five-pound note tucked into her bosom, she guided the "bare lady" to a room. "Cuddle under the blankets, ma'am, while I look for some clothing."

Nude as the day she was born, Artis paced the floor and rubbed her wet hair dry for what seemed like an eternity of time.

At last the cook returned with a pair of small boots and a woolsey dress that would have draped an amazon, with room to spare. "There's this dress and me brother's cap and britches and boots and jerkin. Take your pick, ma'am."

Wrinkling her nose, Artis donned the boy's clothing, pulled on the boots and tucked her bright hair under the cap. "Now take me to the magistrate."

"Ma'am," said the cook rolling her eyes, "if I was you, I'd stay away from them gentry! 'Twas only last week they were beatin' the countryside for a female prisoner who'd jumped a ship bound for the Colonies. They might think you was her!"

"A coach?" said Artis. "Where can I hire a coach?"

"Don't know as there's a coach to be hired, hereabouts, but there's a horse in the stable if you can ride."

Artis did not take long to make up her mind. "I'll ride."

In minutes she was astride a big brute of a nag and going full tilt. Crouched jockey style over the horse's neck, she heeled him along quiet country roads. Once, at the rise of a hill, she pulled rein and scanned the horizon. There below, the Thames. Dark as the River Styx. On again! How many miles to Cheyne Walk, Chelsea?

Cut through Old Kent Road to Lambeth, then on to Vauxhall. Cross the river by Vauxhall Bridge and ride like fury along Grosvenor Road and Chelsea Road to Cheyne

Walk. What other woman in England would have haz-
arded that night ride through London's sleeping slums?
Night wagoners saw a big horse gallop by with a small
creature on his back—boy or elf? He was gone before they
could close their gaping mouths.

It was still dark when Artis drew rein at Number 16
Cheyne Walk, but dawn was not long away.

The peal of the bell wakened Lord Frawley's man out
of a leaden slumber. He got up slowly, taking care for his
rheumatic limbs, went to the dormer window, opened the
casement and leaned out. "Who goes there?"

"Open the door!" shouted Artis.

A light sleeper, Lord Frawley heard, stirred, sat up in
bed, tugged at the bell rope.

Hearing the summons, his servant pulled on his master's
offcast house robe and padded downstairs in scuffed slippers.

"Yes, milord?"

"What in thunderation?"

"Milord has a caller."

"At this hour?" Lord Frawley glanced at his timepiece.
"It's half past four."

The bell pealed and pealed again.

"It looks like a boy on horseback, but it's a woman's
voice that called," said the servant.

Frawley got out of bed as fast as his old bones would
permit. "A woman? Well, let her in! Hurry!"

A thought had presented itself—so outlandish that it
couldn't be true. The lady . . . Artis Grantley! For who
in the world would turn up on horseback at four-thirty
in the morning except Artis herself? Lord Frawley's guess
was correct. He met Lady Artis on the stairs. "Good Lord!"
was all he could say when he saw her wild locks and her
mannish apparel.

"Never mind the Good Lords, Frawley," said Artis
crisply. "There's work to be done and done fast if you
wish to save the life of James Challoner."

Only a few minutes were lost. Lord Frawley's carriage
came around to the door with a sleepy coachman on the
box.

"To Payton House, Portland Square!" ordered the old
Sea Lord. He handed his fair passenger in and drew the

folds of his cloak over his thin knees, for the dawn was cold.

Lady Artis had accepted the loan of a cape and a neck scarf that she'd tied over her disheveled locks. A beautiful woman, in any disguise!

"Now, Lady Artis, kindly tell me your story?"

Scenes of the past amazing weeks came sharply to Artis' mind as she talked. The day she deliberately ran a handsome vagrant down in the Park. The day she stowed away aboard the *Paramour*. The first night of love in Akbar Castle. Her voice broke in the middle of a sentence.

"Frawley, I love James Challoner!"

"Hmmmm."

"You doubt me?"

"Your ladyship has loved before."

"You're a horrid old man!" cried Artis. "But I'll forgive you if you save James. Now I'll tell you the part that matters to you."

Lord Frawley was stupefied at what his old ears took in—at moments he was at a loss for words. The King and the Queen and their children menaced by Moorish pirates?

"M'dear . . . are you sure you haven't dreamed all this?"

"Oh!" cried Artis tearfully. "Would I bother to tell you a tale of Thousand and One Nights at five in the morning?"

Lord Frawley leaned out of the window and called to his coachman, "Give those nags the whip! Make on at full speed!"

17.

Fate Is a Joker

THE PROUD SLOOP "ATLANTA" DOCKED AT A WHARF TO LEE of London Bridge on the morning of June 22nd, and a Customs officer in a blue coat and a three-buttoned hat came aboard. "Where's your Captain?" he asked of a giant black-faced sailor. His astonishment grew at sight of the *Atlanta's* commanding officer.

White broadcloth and gold buttons, gold lace and gold epaulettes, white plumes in his hat, white gloves. "Captain Ezra of the sloop *Atlanta,* out of Charleston. Owner, Mr. Joshua Hunnicutt," said the Turk, Captain Hassan.

"Yes . . . yes," stammered the Customs man who had never before faced an English-speaking person in so fanciful a captain's uniform. "We was expectin' you, sir. The morning papers spoke of you, yesterday, and about certain wild animals you have aboard for His Majesty, the King."

"The animals are in the hold and will be brought up immediately," said the Turk. "We have no dutiable cargo except the owner's personal liquor, and tobacco."

The Customs official put his cipher on the *Atlanta's* papers. "All's well, sir. I shan't trouble. Truth is, I care little for even dogs and cats, much less for wild animals. Your servant, sir." The Customs man skipped down the *Atlanta's* gangplank as though a lion pack were at his heels.

Challoner had regained his senses some hours after being hit on the head. Wakening out of the stupor, he found himself lying in his bunk in the master cabin—head bound with a cold compress. The servant who was tending him ran to speak to another servant at the door. Soon the Hadji entered. His tone was bitterly sarcastic.

"How fortunate that we found you, effendi. You must have fallen down the hatch . . . rendered yourself unconscious. We presumed you were searching for your mistress."

Fallen? He'd been hit on the head! "Yes," Challoner had muttered. "I told you she'd play me false."

"You were correct, effendi. She was nowhere aboard, but no matter." The Moor locked the door on leaving.

Challoner was in full possession of his strength but desperate, when the *Atlanta* tied up at London Bridge. Watching through the porthole, he saw five drays harnessed with powerful draft horses roll down to the wharf.

The transboarding of the animals from the *Atlanta's* hold to drays took place with a minimum of effort. Each cage was hoisted overside by pulley. He saw the five draymen pocket some money, handed them by the Moor's right-hand man, Aben-ben-Ali, who was garbed as a plantation slave. They vacated their drivers' seats. Their places were taken by men of the Lion's band of conspirators.

One individual seemed to be in all places at once. A portly fellow dressed in Grey's Inn blacks. Was he the Moor's contact man in London? Challoner took good note of every detail of his bustling person, thinking as he did so that all had happened exactly as the Moor had planned.

The *Atlanta* had tied up at her destination on the exact day set far in advance. The wild animals had been unloaded and dispatched to their destination.

Would he be left to cool his heels aboard ship whilst the plot rolled to its foreordained conclusion?

A knock at the door. It was the Hadji, garbed in his most resplendent major-domo's livery. "It is time the Master made ready," he said and he stood by to supervise the valet who helped Challoner dress.

Wrapped in rice paper, against the damp, and carefully stretched on wooden hangers, Planter Hunnicutt's finest apparel came out of the wardrobe uncreased and glorious. The coat was robin's-egg blue with wide white revers, stitched in silver. The breeches were white leather, tanned to the suppleness of a kid glove. The boots, slightly too wide for Challoner's foot, were in *cuir de Russie*. He belted on a sword, adjusted his tricorn hat at the proper angle and pulled on white gauntlets with silver stitchings.

"Mr. Hunnicutt will dazzle the eyes of London's fops," said the Hadji. Strange words—"fops"—for a Moor to use. And what hatred in his tone of voice. "Beware!" he said, "one false move and you will die. Of what avail, your death? My plan must go through to the very last detail . . . the final triumph of Islam!"

Challoner felt like a sleepwalker as he went ashore, his brain seemed to be in a state of suspension. He hadn't the vaguest idea how or when to take counteraction—nor could he think what action to take. Every step carried him closer to the dreadful denouement of the adventure. There was no sense in hanging back. Of what avail his own, immediate death?

"Well, Master, shall we keep our rendezvous with the royal family?" smiled the Moor. He led the way to a handsome open carriage harnessed with two bays, seated himself, opposite.

The driver and footman on the box and the two lackeys up behind were all Moors wearing the liveries of Planter Hunnicutt's slaves.

The crowds, alerted earlier by the sight of animal cages lumbering through the streets, were out in force. The Strand was lined to the very curb. Windows and balconies were full of smiling, waving onlookers. But the mob was thickest along the Mall where vendors of pinwheels and sweets and children's toys mingled with the crowds, hawking their wares. While the mob came to marvel and stare, there were not a few informed spectators who admired the rich trappings and entourage of Planter Hunnicutt and spoke enviously of the good fortune of Colonials as compared to stay-at-homes like themselves.

Challoner saw only a blur of faces that could be compared to the confusion of his own racing thoughts. What gesture would stop the Moors? He was unarmed! Strike with his bare fists? The authorities were quite evidently unaware of the danger in their midst. Troopers stood guard for the parade to pass. The populace cheered! The carriage rolled on.

Soon they were in sight of the same Park where he had knelt that bygone morning and shaved beside a pond. The same morning a mad young rider had almost trampled him to death! There, to the right, the majestic mound of walls and towers of Whitehall. There ahead, three gay, red and white striped tents, one large and two small, that had been raised in the shade of a thicket of trees. A wooden stockade, hung with bunting, surrounded the tents and Guardsmen were standing off the inquisitive crowds.

The Moor broke his silence for the first time. "The animal cages and the redskin are in the large, center tent. As soon as the royal family passes into the refreshment tent the cages will be thrown open. Our movements are timed to the second. All you need do is invite the royal family to take refuge in the van that will be stationed at the side entrance of the tent."

"And what if His Majesty refuses?" asked Challoner.

"He'll not refuse!" retorted the Moor. "It is his only chance to save his wife and children . . . not to mention his own royal person."

Hoping against hope, Challoner searched the crowds—

looking for someone whose training and station in life might cause him to answer a call for help. Admiralty agent? Guard royal? Perhaps yonder merchant in sober black? The well-dressed squire with eyeglass to his eye? The seedy clerk with wide-brimmed hat pulled down over his eyes? No! They merely watched the parade pass by.

The crowd's roar increased in volume with every prancing step of the bays. He set a last-ditch limit before he'd fall upon the Hadji with his bare fists. The blow would sign his own death warrant, for would not the last act of the Hadji's men be to take vengeance for the affront to the Holy Man? They were all heavily armed under their gala liveries. The coats of the driver and coachmen bulged with weapons. Yonder tree was the limit! He'd act as soon as they were abreast of it!

Suddenly, Challoner saw a rider break through the front ranks of the mob and charge at the carriage, head on. A pistol shot cracked. The coachman toppled sideways and was rolled under the wheels. The suddenness of the incident caused the crowds to panic. The horses took fright and, reins flapping loose, started to run. Challoner saw his chance!

Leaping to the box, he gathered up the reins, then, using his great hat as a frightener, he slapped the bays' backs, shouted, urged them down the Mall at racing clip. The Moor's footman tried to seize the reins. He sent him sprawling with a punch of his elbows.

Now the Hadji was tugging at his coattails. "Stop! Or by Allah I'll knife you!"

"I dare you! This team will kill you!" Challoner threw over his shoulder.

The bays had the bits in their teeth, they were pounding along, necks flattened, manes and tails flying. Would fear halt the proud King of Islam's hand?

No! Armed with a pistol, the Hadji leaped upon the box. The pistol went off. Challoner felt a sting through the right shoulder. The Moor tossed away the empty pistol and his dagger flashed in the sun. It would have found its mark had Challoner not let go of the reins and smashed his fist into his face. The blow set him tumbling to the ground —Challoner also lost his balance and fell. The two men rose and faced each other.

"Give up, Mohammed-ben-Dar!" shouted Challoner. "I am an agent of His Majesty, sent to bring you to this pass!"

The Moor's face twisted into a frightful mask of hate. "I never trusted you, Dog Infidel!" He made a sudden leap and the knife plunged straight at Challoner's heart.

But Challoner dodged the strike and his arms wrapped around the Moor in an iron hold. Savagely, relentlessly, he bore him to the ground, set his knee on the heaving chest, used his fists in blow after blow that turned the Moor's face to a bloody pulp. He was still hitting when two of the King's Men seized him, tore him away from his victim. He stared at them with empty eyes and collapsed in his own blood.

As it so often happens when great crowds are present at world-shaking events, no one really knew what had occurred. The final battle had taken place at the end of the Mall where only a few stragglers were passing by. The dead African servant of London's distinguished visitor was hoisted into a death cart. The wounded "Mr. Hunnicutt" was carried to the tent that had been erected in his honor.

The King, the Queen and their five children had just arrived in the royal coach. George was in a jovial mood. His Majesty's equerry, explaining what had happened, said, "The American's major-domo went mad! It was very likely the great crowds that frightened him. He attacked Your Majesty's Colonial subject and would have killed him save for the bravery of Mr. Hunnicutt."

"Mr. Hunnicutt? Was he wounded?"

"Yes, Your Majesty. He took a bullet in the shoulder. Your Majesty's physician is caring for him at this very moment."

The King seemed gratified, yet there was a note of disappointment in the royal voice as he said, "The wild American animals? Must Their Highnesses be deprived of the pleasure of viewing them?"

At this, the King's trusted First Sea Lord stepped into the royal tent. "Sire . . . the Admiralty had a hand in the arrangements today. It is my great pleasure to invite Your Majesties and Their Royal Highnesses to see the Zoo Mr. Hunnicutt is honored to present to Your Majesty in the name of North Carolina."

The King, the Queen, the Prince of Wales, the Duke of

York and the Duke of Clarence and the Duke of Kent and the Princesses Sophia and Charlotte filed into the animal tent. The band played. The royal entourage clapped approvingly.

Lord Frawley beckoned to Lord Wilmington through a side opening of the reception tent. "Freddie!"

"Yes, Greg?"

"We've laid hands on every last son-of-a-Moor. The *Atlanta* is under Navy custody. The escape ship has been seized where she lay at Tilbury."

"Where have the Moors been imprisoned?" said Wilmington.

"In a chamber beneath the Admiralty."

"As I hoped, Greg," muttered the First Sea Lord. "They must go to their deaths quietly. No one must know that a pack of Moorish pirates might have wiped out the royal family had it not been for the daring of one James Challoner."

"Do not forget the lady in stable lad's boots and cap who rode out against the Moor's carriage!" smiled Frawley. "For once, Lady Artis Grantley's dash and dare paid. One more thing, Freddie. I think it wise that Planter Hunnicutt should die of his wound. We'll give him to be buried at sea . . . according to his last will and testament."

"And . . . Mistress Hunnicutt?" said Wilmington.

"Poor lady!" sighed Lord Frawley. "It slipped my mind to tell you. She died at sea and was consigned to the waters of the Bay of Biscay."

The two lords shook hands.

"By the way, Greg," said Lord Wilmington in parting. "Send your chap around to the Admiralty as soon as he has recovered from his wound. There's a little matter of reinstatement that I wish to discuss."

"One moment, Freddie!" said the smiling Frawley. "You bet me a shilling to a china horse Challoner would never accomplish his mission. I'd like that shilling . . . now."

Wilmington dug into his purse with a wry grin, produced the shilling. "I never lost a bet in such good humor, Greg old friend."

"And I never won a shilling with more gloating!" Frawley answered.

18.

How the Adventure Ended or a Lady and a Pirate

IT HAPPENED, ONE AFTERNOON, THAT A CERTAIN BELOVED puppeteer changed his programme and presented a gala show entitled *The Beauty and the Beast*. Dramatis personae were a lovely princess and a great, hairy puppet animal called "Grizzly Bear." The show, staged in Hyde Park, attracted a great crowd of children. Their gay voices wafted into the high window of Grantley House where a handsome invalid was lying abed. Newspaper reports that "Planter Hunnicutt was sick unto death" had not been exaggerated. The bullet had done more than pierce Challoner's shoulder. The wound had festered. He had been in grave danger for several days. Now, roused by children's voices, he gazed speculatively at his surroundings.

This was no hospital lazaret—this was a fine room with rich furniture. The bed was soft. The nightshirt he was wearing was made of silk.

He tried to pull his thoughts into proper focus, remember. Ah yes! The carriage ride through the Mall. A shot! A wrestling match. A knife that almost found its mark. Suddenly a slim figure on a galloping horse rose before his mind's eye. He gasped out . . . "Kit!" It was she who had ridden down the bays . . . caused them to bolt!

"Artis!" he groaned.

"James!" murmured a soft voice.

He saw her coming through a haze. She was dressed in a simple gown of white with a yellow rose at her bosom.

"James darling!" she cried and sank down beside the bed.

Challoner groped for her hand with his good arm. "Artis! You made it to London!"

"Yes, my darling," she murmured, caressing his hand with her soft cheek. "Have you not observed that I always arrive where I wish to be?"

"You risked your life, braving the Moor head on!"

"I risked only what would have been worthless had you not lived."

Challoner gazed at her in astonishment and for the first time since the day they met, he was certain she was telling the truth. Her love for him was so great that she would have died for his sake. He turned his head, not to let her see the moisture that brimmed in his eyes.

And Artis, fearing she'd taxed her lover's strength too much, rose from her knees and kissed the hand that gripped her hand. "Darling . . . rest. I'll tell you the honor that has been bestowed upon you by the King when you feel stronger."

Her words brought Challoner upright in the bed. "What honor?"

"Darling!" gasped Artis. "Don't tire yourself."

"I'm not tired! Tell me, Artis! Tell me!" A hope fired Challoner—hope so great that it nearly choked him. "Has the King . . . ?"

"Yes!" Her red-gold curls danced as she nodded her head.

"You mean . . . I'm restored to the Rolls?"

"Better than that! You can hoist the blue on your own frigate, the *Paramour,* as soon as you have the strength to go aboard." Artis added a naval salute. "Rear Admiral, may I be the first to congratulate you on your promotion?"

"Thank God!" Challoner could say no more.

But the lady was not at the end of her news. "My darling, may I ask a boon of you?"

"Ask! All I have is yours!"

"Even . . . this hand in marriage?"

Challoner hesitated only an instant as a phantasmagoria swirled before his eyes. Ex-naval person, James Challoner. Ex-pirate, Captain Ironhand, now sought in marriage by Lady Grantley? Would a rear admiral's pay keep her in footwear?

"Artis. I am a poor man."

She snapped her little fingers. "Dear me! I forgot to tell

you what our gracious sovereign has bestowed upon you
. . . as His Majesty's own, personal gift!"

"I've been elevated to the rank of Rear Admiral. It is
enough," exclaimed Challoner.

But Artis shook her head. "No. You forget, dearest.
You saved the Crown as well as destroying England's foe,
the Hadji. King George has seen fit to make you a peer
of the realm with a crown grant of lands worth a hundred
thousand pounds. You are not a rich man according to
my standards . . . still, neither are you poor. Now, will
you give me your answer, Lord Challoner of Ironhand or
whatever your title will be?"

Challoner's brain whirled. It was too much! Yet, his
man's honest pride knew it was his just due. He had served
King and Country faithfully. He would have died to save
them.

A great light shone in his eyes as he drew Artis into
his one good arm. "The answer . . . dear Kit . . . is . . . yes!"